Praise for Lynne Connolly's *Venice*

"Venice is a fascinating book that kept me reading from the beginning until the end to see how the story would finish."
~ *Literary Nymphs Reviews*

"Venice is a very engaging romance. ...Connolly manages to keep a constant tension going about what is about to happen. The storyline is mostly unpredictable, from start to finish."
~ *Long and Short Romance Reviews*

Look for these titles by *Lynne Connolly*

Now Available:

Triple Countess Trilogy
Last Chance, My Love (Book 1)
A Chance to Dream (Book 2)
Met by Chance (Book 3)

Secrets Trilogy
Seductive Secrets (Book 1)
Alluring Secrets (Book 2)
Tantalizing Secrets (Book 3)

Richard and Rose Series
Yorkshire (Book 1)
Devonshire (Book 2)
Venice (Book 3)

Coming Soon:

Richard and Rose Series
Harley Street (Book 4)
Eyton (Book 5)
Darkwater (Book 6)

Venice

Lynne Connolly

A Samhain Publishing, Ltd. publication.

Samhain Publishing, Ltd.
577 Mulberry Street, Suite 1520
Macon, GA 31201
www.samhainpublishing.com

Venice
Copyright © 2010 by Lynne Connolly
Print ISBN: 978-1-60504-564-1
Digital ISBN: 978-1-60504-517-7

Editing by Angela James
Cover by Natalie Winters

First Samhain Publishing, Ltd. electronic publication: May 2009
First Samhain Publishing, Ltd. print publication: March 2010

Dedication

To the curators of the Victoria and Albert Museum—thank you for your help. As always, it was invaluable.

Chapter One

When the first light of dawn filtered through the curtains at the window, I gave up trying to sleep and dressed in a loose sacque, well out of date and faded with washing but comfortable. I sat in a stiff-backed chair by the window and watched my wedding day arrive.

The sun crept over the fields past our orchards, stretching its tentacles across the sky to herald the new day. This, to me, was a day like no other, but to most people in the world, today would be the same as yesterday, the same as tomorrow.

It marked the last day in my old room. I moved into it when I left the nursery and it witnessed my hopes fading and my dreams giving way to hard reality.

My brother, James, now the Earl of Hareton, had grandiose plans for this simple manor house, and this floor would form part of the new State Rooms.

Everyone had packed to leave this old house. James had rented a house nearby, as this one wouldn't be habitable for some time. I had lived here all my life and found leaving harder than I'd imagined.

A comfortable family home, Hareton Manor wasn't a special-looking house. Less than a hundred years old but unique to us, the Golightlys. I knew all the hiding places, which stairs creaked, and which doors didn't fit properly. I remembered all the items I'd dropped through the floorboards in the nursery, the thin ivory counters of a game I hated and some small coins, to bribe the fairies and elves I was certain lived under them.

Some rooms held my misery, like the day not so long ago when I realised I might remain on the shelf, a respectable spinster for the rest of my days. Only that room had seen my tears when I thought I would never leave this house, and now it would be destroyed, together with my misery.

Dawn is such a melancholy time.

I wished it were tomorrow, with everything over. No one, not even my betrothed, must see how much I dreaded the day. With spinsterhood came welcome anonymity. So many times I had watched attention slide over me and on to the next person. I had become used to the lack of regard, even welcomed it sometimes, but today I would be the centre of attention. Today was my day.

Anonymity had its blessings.

My wedding dress faced me in mute challenge. Arranged on a figure in the middle of the room, it awaited its owner—surely not me. Blue satin, silver embroidery and diamonds were surely meant for my lovely sister Lizzie, not me.

Here, in my last moments of self-indulgence I could admit that I was terrified, afraid I would let everybody down—afraid I wouldn't do what so many people expected of me. I had courage but it didn't extend to appearing as the centre of attention before so many people. I was moving out of my comfortable childhood milieu into a much larger world, one where I knew hardly anyone—my youthful nightmares come true.

When I shivered, I realised that late April or not, the morning held a chill, so I decided to find somewhere warmer.

Only one place qualified at this time of day. The kitchen. But when I set my foot down I heard an ominous crunch. My watch. The old watch I'd laid by my side had fallen and I'd trodden on it. I picked up the pieces, blinking away the tears. I would not cry on this day. But when I laid them on the nightstand it seemed like a reminder that my old life had gone forever, never to return.

After today this would not be my room, or my home. And I would have to buy a new watch.

I left my old bedroom and hurried down the back stairs to the kitchen.

The glowing fire in the grate and the hum of activity reminded me just how early a maid's day started. The maid-of-all-work, grubby and tousled, resplendent in her sacking apron and wooden clogs, started when I went in but the cook, Mrs. Tiree, smiled in welcome. "Good morning, Miss Rose. Come and sit by the fire, and I'll make you a dish of tea."

I sat on the comfortable wooden chair she pulled up invitingly for me. I could hardly see the chair for its colourful, unmatched cushions, and settling into it was like settling into a soft cocoon. I might never have been away.

I stretched my feet in front of the fire and enjoyed the company of the cook, who, in days long gone, had made me gingerbread men and comforted me when I ran away from my nurse and got into yet another scrape.

I accepted the proffered dish of tea gratefully, held it between both my hands and sipped the steaming liquid. It was kitchen tea, supposedly inferior to the sort we had upstairs but it tasted good and it flowed down my throat to warm my chilled insides.

Leaning back, I watched the maids preparing for the new day. Since the feast to celebrate the ceremony wouldn't be held here but at the neighbouring larger house of Peacock's, it was like any other day. Preparations for the family breakfast were well under way, even though it was barely six. Maids bustled about, beating eggs, slicing kidneys, and the kitchen filled with the aroma of baking bread. My sister-in-law, Martha, was one of the best housekeepers I knew, and she'd done her best to pass on her skills. I was a better study than my sister Lizzie, though that wasn't saying a great deal.

The cook talked to me while she worked on the great table by the fire, facing the room to keep an eye on the activity around her. "You'll be wanting an early breakfast this morning, miss. Lady Hareton's ordered it for eight, so you can set out for the Cathedral bright and early."

I smiled mechanically. "I don't think I'll be eating much, Mrs. Tiree."

She took my empty tea dish and put it on the table. "Don't you worry, Miss Rose. It'll soon be over." Her busy hands stilled in the mixing bowl. "Is that what's worrying you, Miss? What happens after?"

I shook my head. "No, Mrs. Tiree. I don't like to be the centre of attention, that's all."

"If you do what you're supposed to do, and hold your head up, nobody will notice."

That was probably the best advice anyone had given me. Through no fault of my own, I had missed the wedding rehearsal, and although I'd read the wedding service until I knew it by heart, so I knew when to stand, when to sit, and what to say, the thought sent tension tingling along my backbone. I could do nothing else now except send up a prayer of my own.

That time in the kitchen settled me and I could face the day with more equanimity. Mrs. Tiree had never done anything not eminently practical, never given advice that didn't have a firm root in day-to-day living. She could sense my fear since she knew me so well, and she didn't try to deny it as other people did. She was someone else I would miss.

My new maid came into the kitchen then, and peered at me before she recognised me and dropped a curtsey. My future husband had found her for me, a lady's maid and my bodyguard, hired to protect me from the dangers of my new world. I expected a superior dragon of a woman, and in a way, I was right. Adele Nichols could be formidable, but she surprised me with her forthright attitude. Perhaps she had seen more of life than the average lady's maid. I wouldn't be in the least surprised.

Nichols was slightly taller than me, and I was considered gangling by county society. She had a soft smile for such a hard-faced woman, and had first won my approval by dressing my unruly hair faster and better than anyone else I had ever met, without pulling too hard at my curls in the process.

My recent adventures had left me with a number of painful bruises, and Nichols had anointed them with a potion of her own devising that had eased the discomfort, and helped them to fade. However, I had reached the worse stage, when the black was just beginning to fade into greenish yellow. The red welts on my wrists were a worse problem, but I would cover them with lace ruffles, and no one would be any the wiser. Except my husband-to-be, and he'd already seen them.

"I'll have the fire lit upstairs, madam, and then you can come and sit in the warm," she said now.

"I'll have some more tea and then I'll come up."

Nichols inclined her head, collected her breakfast on a tray, and went out.

"She asked for something on a tray because she won't be able to come down for the regular kitchen breakfast," Mrs. Tiree informed me, her tones deliberately neutral.

"What do you think of her?" I wouldn't normally consider asking a servant that kind of question, having been brought up to avoid kitchen gossip, but Mrs. Tiree was different.

Mrs. Tiree put down her rolling pin and gave me her full attention. "To be truthful, Miss Rose, she'll do well by you. She's only been here two days, and she was with a marchioness before, but she's not shown any sort of superiority, the sort you'd expect from a London maid, and she keeps her own counsel. I don't think she's always been a lady's maid, though."

"I thought that too."

I didn't go back upstairs until I had eaten a bread roll, fresh from the oven, a treat I had always loved. Mrs. Tiree was concerned to see me eat. "Many brides don't eat until the wedding breakfast, and that's the reason they faint at the altar. They're asked to stand, and sit, and kneel, and the lack of food makes them unwell. I should think that's the last thing you'll want, Miss Rose."

I had to agree, and that made me determined to make a good breakfast. It was true brides frequently fainted at the altar rail, but this was usually explained by their sensibilities being overcome at the thought of the ordeal ahead, not by the lack of food that morning. It was typical of the cook to look for the practical solution, and it was also typical of her that she might very well be right.

I had to go upstairs. Time was getting on and the house was waking up.

My hour in the kitchen had done me more good than staying in bed fretting, and I felt much more myself by the time I returned to my room.

The silent room I had left was no more. Nichols controlled it now. My sister had arrived, sleepily sitting on the bed, still in her wrapper.

"Morning," said Lizzie, as she had when we were children and shared a bed.

"Morning," I answered her, smiling.

"Ruth has taken over our bedroom, as if she's the bride, so I thought I'd give her some space. Do you mind?"

"No, but won't you need more time?" Lizzie loved to take her time getting ready.

"I have my own preparations in hand. Never fear, I'll return and eject Ruth in a little while but I wanted to see how you are first. So are you ready for your big day?"

"No."

She laughed. "You should try to enjoy your wedding day. After all, it's the only one you're likely to have—it's not as if you're marrying an old man in his last decade."

Far from it.

I sat at my dressing table and let Nichols dress my hair. I was to have it powdered today, a process I disliked intensely, but there was no getting out of it, it had to be done. Nichols combed out all the unruly curls and smoothed pomade over them so the powder would stick. Then we went into the dressing room and I held the cloth over my face and tried not to cough from the fine powder flying in the air.

When we went back into the bedroom, Lizzie had gone, no doubt to get herself ready and eject Ruth from her place at the dressing table. Nichols drew out the chair for me. "Let your mind rest, madam, and I'll do what's necessary." She laced my stays tight, tied my garters, and put on my side hoops and petticoats in blessed silence. When she lifted the pocket to tie about my waist I stopped her, rummaging around on the dressing table and in the drawers until I found my old necessaire, the tiny container that held, amongst other things, a chipped mirror and a ruined pair of scissors. "It's a good luck talisman," I explained, and Nichols waited while I slipped it into my pocket—a familiar item to keep me company during the day.

The time came for the outer garments. The blue petticoat

was first, with its miraculous embroidery, and then the stomacher, relatively plain since it would hold a graduated row of diamond brooches. Nichols held the gown for me. It was a formal mantua, the pleats at the back shaping my body perfectly, made by the best mantua maker in Exeter, a miracle of heavy blue satin and silver embroidery. I stood still while Nichols hooked and pinned me in, and then pulled out the fine lace to fall in frothy waterfalls at my elbows and bosom.

I had not yet seen myself in the long mirror, but I looked now. Even without the jewellery, someone I hardly recognised stared back at me. Here stood an elegant society lady, one who knew instinctively how to stand and pose, one who was used to the fine things of life, who had never climbed trees and frolicked on beaches, who would never dream of ruining her complexion by going out in the sun without a parasol. We looked solemnly at each other, that lady and I, and curtseyed to each other, the wide skirts making expensive susurrations in the silence of the room.

Nichols examined me, scrutinising her work for flaws. Eventually she came forward, arranged the set of the skirt, and smiled. "You're every inch the great lady, ma'am." She came around to the front, adjusting a pin here, a frill of lace there. "Now I think you should go down to breakfast, and then we'll finish off with the diamonds. Please try to eat something, it's a long time before you'll sit down to eat again."

She meant well, but the worms gnawed at my innards again at the reminder.

I passed muster. Everyone, including fashion-aware Lizzie, said I would do very well. They watched me enter the room, and I stood while they took in my new glory. James made no comment. Martha decided I would do well enough in front of the large congregation in Exeter Cathedral.

I opted to eat my breakfast with a large white kitchen apron covering my finery, right up to my neck. Getting egg stains on my gown didn't bear thinking about, and I would much rather appear foolish here at home than in front of half of polite society later. My young nephews and niece were allowed downstairs to eat their last family meal with me and that, together with everyone in various stages of dress, led to an atmosphere of informality and near hilarity that I hadn't expected at all.

Martha wore her gown and petticoat, but not her jewellery. Lizzie was mostly dressed, but had left off her gown and worn a wrapper for the meal. None of the children were properly dressed, Martha wisely depending on the efficiency of the nursery maids to dress them later rather than risk their aim with their food.

James was in his shirtsleeves. His handsome face broke into a broad smile when the maid tied the apron around my neck. "You look like a very large baby."

It made me smile too, and the tense mood broken, I found I could make a tolerable breakfast. "I'm as nervous as a baby," I confessed.

"So am I." James was to give me away. This amounted to his first formal duty as Lord Hareton. We grinned at each other in sympathy.

"I can't remember ever seeing a nervous baby," Martha commented, ever practical. "Nervousness arrives later, after a child has been taunted or hurt. Just remember, my dear, it's your day and you should try to enjoy it. You may never get another one."

"Please God I don't," I said fervently.

"Amen to that," answered James and my younger brother Ian at the same time. With a grin, Ian leaned across the table and linked the little finger of his right hand with James's, an old gesture used by people in our district when they said the same thing at the same time. It was supposed to grant a wish. Our family link grew closer, and we siblings enjoyed this reminder of our childhood spent in this house.

The house might be gone, but my memories remained. What I underwent here made me the person I was, fit for whatever life would throw at me.

Breakfast over, we dispersed to have the final touches put to our appearance. James brought the diamonds to my room and Nichols put them on me. He'd put them in the safe in his study and set a trusted servant to guard them all night. To lose them at this stage was unthinkable.

When Nichols opened the box, my stomach lurched. A pirate's chest couldn't have offered better booty.

Nichols fastened the necklace of intertwined flowers and foliage around my throat, pinned the brooches to my stomacher, hooked the girandole earrings in place, and fastened the aigrette in my hair, a flower with a butterfly set *en tremblant* above it.

The woman in the mirror had become a very grand lady. Every time I moved I shimmered, every part of me glinted, silver embroidery and diamonds creating a dazzling vision. I watched the necklace respond to my breathing, glittering as I performed what was normally a disregarded function.

Nichols gave me my fan and opened the door for me to go downstairs. "During the ceremony I shall remain nearby for you, ma'am." My tension surged back and I took one more look at the woman in the mirror to give me courage, then turned away. I could hide behind that image.

Nichols must have seen my nervousness, for she stopped me at the door, and drew a small flask from her pocket. "I wouldn't recommend this as a rule, ma'am, but a small nip might help."

I took the flask and smelled good brandy inside, so I accepted it, took a small sip, and gave it back to her. "It's there when you need it, ma'am," she told me as she replaced it in her pocket. I smiled my gratitude and headed for the stairs. Nichols followed, holding my train out of the way. I would like Nichols very well, a remarkably resourceful woman.

The others waited for me in the hall. I savoured the communal gasp when they saw me caparisoned in the complete ensemble. Even my sister Lizzie was lost for words.

Martha, Lizzie and Ruth kissed me and left, until only James, Nichols, the butler, and I remained. I took a deep breath, and let it out again, and then I noticed James, his handsome face tight with tension. Nichols glanced at the butler and led him out of the front door, in the direction of the carriages.

"Come on then," I said briefly.

He didn't move. "Rose?"

I turned back to him. "Yes?"

He took my hands and looked me in the eyes. "You're sure about this?"

I decided to tell the truth rather than try to dissimulate to my brother. "I'm not at all sure, but I'm as good as married now, so let's get on with it, shall we?"

I turned to go and then turned back to him. "I'll tell you one thing, though." He lifted an eyebrow in enquiry. "I wish I were getting married in the village, with only our friends about us."

He smiled. "So do I, but you shouldn't have agreed to marry Lord Strang if that was what you wanted." The atmosphere lightened. "I still think Tom Skerrit would have suited you. Have you thought it through properly?"

I removed my hands from his grasp. "If I thought it through I'd run away now, but I have a feeling his lordship might follow me. He says he's determined to have me, you know."

James sighed. "I know. I hope you're doing the right thing."

I turned to the door. "So do I." I stopped, before I left the house and gave him a grin. "Could you imagine the gossip if I didn't turn up? They'd never forget it, and neither of us would ever live it down. Come on, we should be on our way." At least I'd made him smile.

It took a little time to dispose my gown and train so the least damage would be done to them on the journey, but we set off at last and were soon on the road to Exeter.

The other coaches waited for us, as we didn't want to risk robbery on the highway, a likely possibility, as everyone hereabouts knew what was happening and when. Not all our neighbours were honest.

We took a detour through Darkwater, our local village, where most of the populace stood in their front gardens. I smiled and waved my fan, and they waved back. I had known most of them since I was a child, later helped them birth their children, helped the ill and the injured. The dark shadow of free trading hadn't marked my relations with my neighbours until recently. The thought reminded me of the red rope burns from my recent imprisonment, lying under the pretty ruffles on my wrists. My mood clouded, but when we'd passed the village, I did my best to forget, and watched the gentle green of my native county pass us by.

James and I passed the greater part of our journey in silence, a friendly silence born of the absence of the need to talk, but before we reached Exeter I asked Nichols for her flask. She passed it to me and I took a sip, then passed it to James.

He accepted it with thanks and took a larger draught than I had. "I wish all ladies' maids would think of something like this."

Nichols produced a paper of lozenges to sweeten our breath, making James laugh. "I must remember to mention this to Martha. Do you think she could persuade Hargreaves to do the same for her?"

I shook my head. "I doubt it." Martha's maid had been with her since she was a girl, and she definitely wouldn't approve.

Despite the brandy, my nervousness increased with every mile.

This was the greatest wedding of the season in Exeter; indeed even in London it would have been remarkable. Much of the town was on its doorstep to see us. I did my best to smile, but panic had me in its grip and for two pins I would have flung open the door, leaped to the ground and run.

Soon we entered the Cathedral Close, crowded with people waiting to see the spectacle. We waited while the rest of the family alighted and went inside, Lizzie enjoying every moment.

Then it was our turn. Nichols got down first, then James, and he helped me to step down. I stood while the maid attended to me, straightening my gown and pulling my train into place, and then there was no escape. I was ready.

James and I stood together, waiting for the word from the Cathedral they were ready for us, both breathing deeply in an effort to recover some equilibrium. I looked at my brother, we smiled briefly at each other, then the sign came from the official in the porch, and we were off.

Music was playing on the great organ inside, and the congregation turned to watch us as we entered. This was the worst moment of all, to be watched by so many people, so many strangers, and assessed by them all. I knew many of them would find me wanting, as I had netted a man many of them had set their caps at and then despaired of; who had been on the town for many years without getting caught. The walk up the aisle seemed to take forever. The Cathedral was a large, imposing building and its aisle correspondingly proportionate. I saw the Skerrits as I passed their pew, and took comfort in their familiar faces, but James led me relentlessly on towards the glittering figure I could now see standing before the altar.

I could look at my lord as I approached him without meeting his gaze. Here, in his *milieu* he was supremely at home, as I was not. His appearance was almost unearthly. He had dressed in white velvet, embroidered in silver, sprinkled with brilliants, the finest Mechlin lace at his neck and wrists, the diamond he always wore to hold his neckcloth together winking in the gleaming folds. The perfectly dressed white figure seemed to me to be a field in winter, or the unearthly epitome of it, a figure from Nifleheim, the land of ice and snow that existed in the North before the gods came to bring order. Certainly nothing to do with me, that was for sure.

He didn't smile as I approached. He was watching me as was the rest of the cathedral's congregation, but as I came up to stand by him, he let his gaze meet mine briefly, and I saw the man within, just for a moment. Then we turned to face the bishop, who waited to begin.

Talking with other married women, I have found very few of them could remember the actual marriage service, but something had happened to me on that journey up the long aisle, a combination of brandy and panic. It was as if I was floating above the assembled company, watching the ceremony impersonally, as though it was nothing to do with me. I saw the elegant, brilliant congregation, the two glittering figures at its head, but I felt nothing until James took my hand.

I must have been giving my responses by rote, passing over that awful moment at the beginning when the bishop asked the people if they knew of any reason why we shouldn't be married. I had dreaded that, the silence that might be broken so fatefully, because although there was no reason, some might have done it out of malice. I must have made my response, because James took my hand and placed it into Lord Strang's, and I felt his touch for the first time that day. It brought me back into myself again, and when I lifted my gaze to his face to make my responses, I knew for sure that I was doing the right thing.

We made our promises to each other, not to anyone else. Everything else, the grand costumes, the congregation, fell away from us. We could be standing in the middle of a field and the ceremony would have been just as sacred to me. I understood why he wasn't smiling then—he meant it too, every word.

He took the ring and placed it on my finger without looking at it. His gaze never left my face, and I didn't look away to my hand, either. I kept my eyes on his, hearing his words as he made his promises, speaking my own as clearly as I could for him to hear.

We knelt, and then the bishop joined our hands, blessed us and declared us man and wife. Only then did I believe it. After the prayers and responses, we sat to listen to the sermon, and I could begin to understand what had just happened. I felt steady, as cool now as before I'd felt flustered and full of panic, but I didn't hear a word of what the Bishop said in his speech to the congregation.

We took communion, and at the end of the service, Lord Strang offered me the support of his arm. We walked to the vestry to sign the register, followed by Richard's twin brother, Gervase, and Lizzie, who were acting as our witnesses.

We signed the book, and then, as I stood again to return to the Cathedral, he took me in his arms and murmured, "My wife."

He kissed me long and lovingly, just as though we were completely alone. Richard wasn't given to public displays of affection, and in front of the bishop, his assistant and my sister and his brother, he gave me the kind of kiss we had only shared in private before. I should have felt embarrassed or strange in front of other people but I had longed to hold him since I first felt the touch of his hand. I only felt joy and relief it had happened, after all.

I was now Lady Strang, Viscountess Strang of Strang in Shropshire, but more than that—I was the wife of Richard Kerre.

Chapter Two

Richard held out his arm for me and we walked back down the aisle at a stately pace, smiling and bowing in response to the congregation, hardly looking at each other—hardly daring to.

Outside the cathedral, people waited for us to emerge, and when we appeared from the cool church into the light of day outside, they clapped and cheered. I spread my fan to cover my blushes, and Richard waved to them, but didn't stop, heading in a leisurely way for the end of the path and the carriage waiting for us there. "The important thing is to keep moving," he murmured to me as we stepped into the vehicle.

It set off immediately, rolling out of the Close and towards the edge of the town. We nodded and acknowledged the crowds, the shopkeepers standing outside their establishments, the people who always gather for a spectacle, but when the crowds thinned out he turned to me. He was smiling now. "Well, my dear heart?"

"Well?" I felt unaccountably shy.

"You can't go back," he said, just as if he read my mind.

I had no doubts now. "I don't want to. As soon as I saw you I knew I was doing exactly what I wanted to do. Up until then, I was so afraid..."

He lost the smile. "Of what, my love?"

"Leaving everything I know behind, saying goodbye, foolish things."

He caressed my palm with his thumb. "None of those concerns are foolish. You're bound to feel that. I know I could tell you we'll come back, which we will, but nothing will be the same again. I only hope you come to believe that you've exchanged what you had once for something better."

He watched me, looking supremely elegant despite the seeming carelessness of his pose, and I smiled. I saw through the grand clothes and precious jewels and lace to the man beneath. The man I loved. "I'm sure of that now." I grinned. "You outshone me. You're magnificent."

"Believe me, I could never do that. With the look on your face as we came out of the vestry, the sun would be hard put to outshine you."

I frowned, concerned I'd shown too much. He disliked that. "Did it show? I tried so hard to be the great lady, to hold it all in, I didn't want society to think I was nervous or so much in love I behaved improperly."

"It only showed to me. And perhaps to the few people in the vestry when I kissed you. But then, they saw my face as well."

He put his hand on mine and glanced out of the window behind me. We had reached open country. "Now at last I can say good morning the way I want to." He drew me into his arms and kissed me.

We were going to Peacock's for the wedding breakfast. This was the house that belonged to the Skerrits—an old house near the coast that had amongst its treasures a very large half-timbered medieval Great Hall. When Sir George offered the use of his home, we accepted with alacrity, not only because the house was perfect, but also because of its proximity to the coast. When the time came, Richard and I could leave with the minimum of fuss for his yacht where we planned to spend the next few weeks on our bride-trip. Now I could spend the last part of the day with my love at my side, the prospect of hours more celebration didn't appear quite so dreadful.

We had left the city, so by mutual consent we abandoned propriety. He leaned back at his ease and slipped his arm about me, so I could pillow my head on his shoulder. The velvet coat felt soft and comforting and I snuggled against it. "I didn't sleep a wink last night. I was up at dawn."

He moved his shoulder, settling me into its curve more

securely. "I slept well all night, but it took a bottle of wine to render me that way."

"I wish I'd thought of that."

He sighed. "Not if you had the headache I woke up with. Gervase suggested I drink another bottle this morning to put my head in the right order but I had no intention of appearing at the altar in that state. I ducked my head in cold water and waited, and it went soon enough." He laughed. "I've heard of, and seen, men at the altar hardly able to stand, but I don't think any of them went willingly." He turned his head to look at me, his eyes hot and needy, echoing the want echoing in my body. "I couldn't wait," he murmured, and tilted my chin to kiss me.

The journey to Peacock's would take at least an hour, a welcome respite in the all too public nature of the day, and I meant to enjoy it to the fullest, but despite my determination, I settled against his shoulder again and yawned. He put his hand over mine, and I fell asleep.

I awoke with a start as the carriage jolted over a pothole. I was flustered and confused. "Oh, I'm sorry!"

"What for?"

"Falling asleep. I didn't mean to, truly, and—"

He squeezed my hand. "It was the most peaceful hour I've spent in weeks. I held you, and watched you. I'll see you like that tomorrow, and the day after that, and as many days as you choose to allow me into your bed."

I smiled, mollified and then chuckled. "Still, I shouldn't have slept."

"Why not?"

"It's not very romantic, is it?"

He met my gaze. "On the contrary, I think it's extremely romantic, and in any case, you needed it. You've been under a lot of stress in recent weeks what with one thing and another, and I intend to see you get as much rest as possible in the weeks to come."

I suddenly sat up, fully awake and startled, and he seized my arm. "What's wrong?"

"My hair, I'm powdered...your beautiful coat!"

I laughed. He'd had the foresight to tuck his handkerchief under my head so we should arrive relatively unmarked. He smiled when he saw my relief and drew me back against him.

"Do you always think of everything?"

The corner of his mouth tilted in a wry smile. "Rarely. If I had, that man would never have come near you, and you wouldn't have these..." He took my hand, and eased back the ruffle on my wrist to reveal the red lines beneath. He touched the marks, with feather-light kisses I could hardly feel and restored the ruffle once more. "But he won't trouble you any more, or anyone else for that matter."

I shuddered at the reminder of what we had done, although we'd had little choice.

I deliberately put the thought from my mind and instead I put my arm around Richard's waist, luxuriating in his warmth. "Can we go now? Turn the coach around and go straight to the yacht?"

He laughed. "I've been thinking about that." He took my hand and threaded his fingers between mine. "How good an actress are you?"

I raised my brows. "I've not done much acting. It depends what you mean." Amateur theatricals never included me because I couldn't keep the masquerade up. I'd invariably giggle.

"You know we've given it out you've been ill over the past few days, and that's why you haven't received any visitors?"

"Yes."

He smiled. "When we've met everybody at this damned wedding breakfast, accepted their felicitations, eaten, do you think you could have a relapse?" I laughed in delight, understanding him immediately. "We could retire then, and slip away to the coast before most people have started on their second bottle. Unless you prefer to stay, of course, but then you risk the bedding ceremony." It was his turn to shudder.

I shook my head. "I don't want to stay, I'd much rather be alone with you. I think I can manage to faint."

"I thought you might." He kissed me, his tongue lingering warmly in my mouth as if he never wanted to leave.

All too soon, we found ourselves driven through the gateway of Peacock's, and we had to leave our temporary sanctuary and go inside.

Since we had left the cathedral first, and been quick about it, only servants were present as we went inside, including, to my surprise, Richard's valet Carier, who had also been at the wedding. He bowed low. "My lord, my lady."

I couldn't withhold my surprise at seeing him here before us. "How did you get here so quickly?"

He lifted his chin, the only sign of his pleasure at my response. "On horseback, my lady. I overtook you so I could see everything is in order here. I need not have feared." He indicated the Great Hall with a wave of one hand, and we followed the gesture.

Lady Skerrit had decorated the Great Hall with dozens of flowers. She must have stripped the hothouses of every house in the district, and the result took my breath away. Floral scents filled the hall, and the dark timbers were brilliant with colour.

I had had no idea she had planned this and the result filled me with delight. I moved forward to get a better view and gazed up at the ceiling, glancing back at Richard to see if he appreciated it too.

But he wasn't looking at the hall, and he wasn't smiling. He had seen something I had not, and the sight froze his face into its usual mask of polite indifference.

I went back to stand by his side, realising we could not be without company as I had supposed, and then I saw the people I had missed.

Mrs. Terry and her daughter, both in unrelieved black, stood by the door, waiting for us to acknowledge them.

Eustacia Terry had been the bane of my life, laughing at me when I sat by the wall at the various gatherings we attended, making my spinster role doubly difficult. An only child, her parents had very much indulged her but the brutality of her father's recent behaviour had forced me to think again. Hers must have been a very troubled household. I still couldn't like her, it was too late for that but I could understand more of what had made her what she was, and why she craved the attention of her peers.

Richard disliked Miss Terry as much as I did but for different reasons. She had accidentally eavesdropped on a quiet moment Richard and I had snatched at Exeter Assembly rooms, and heard things she had no right to hear. My beloved had a profound hatred of anyone entering his own intimate world to which he only allowed me and his twin brother access. He had lost his temper on that occasion and spoken to her with cruelty but at my plea, he'd left the rest of his planned revenge alone.

Because of that eavesdropping, the surviving Terrys knew Richard and I had a love match, not a joining of families, or a convenient linking of friendship, as the world at large assumed ours to be.

The ladies curtseyed, and we returned the courtesy, Richard's bow so elaborate it touched on mockery.

"My lord, Rose—Lady Strang, I mean of course." I knew Mrs. Terry's slip was deliberate. In subsequent conversations, I knew I would miraculously become "my dearest friend Lady Strang," and so I discovered another reason to be glad I was leaving.

"For obvious reasons we could not accept your kind invitation to the wedding—" had we invited them? I suppose Martha had done so, "—but we had to give you our congratulations, so we took the liberty of coming over early, in the hope of catching you before your other guests arrive."

Richard bowed, with the polite, humourless smile I never saw when he looked at me.

"It's very kind of you," I said, "especially considering your recent loss."

I watched them, certain I could see they had no idea of our part in Mr. Terry's recent "accident". Their faces remained grave for a short time, and then brightened considerably as they looked around the room.

Eustacia's face sobered once more. She took in the tables laid for the meal, the decorations, all the preparations for all the people she had always dreamed of meeting. Then she turned back to me, and absorbed the unusual grandeur of my appearance, her eyes widening when she came to my jewellery. "I must say, Rose, you make a very good viscountess."

I smiled at this, the very first compliment she'd ever paid me, and I savoured the sweetness. Richard took my hand to his lips. "I never doubted it."

That made me laugh, especially when I remembered the circumstances of our first meetings, with the dowdy clothes I wore, and then the sombre mourning. "How can you, sir. You know I wasn't at my best when we met. You must have been dreaming of someone else."

"Oh, I was dreaming, but I'll spare your blushes, my lady." He didn't spare them, but the sound of my new title on his lips sounded much better, almost right. Since the Terrys knew what we felt for each other, concealment would be pointless. I was glad to see he could open up, even this far.

I turned back to our sombrely dressed visitors. "I'll be coming back here from time to time, of course."

"Naturally you will wish to see your brother and his family," said Mrs. Terry smoothly, seemingly unmoved by my husband's demonstration of his affection. "But dear Lady Hareton has invited us to town this autumn, when we shall be out of mourning."

I felt the gentle pressure of Richard's hand on my own, and I knew as well as if he'd said it what he was thinking. "We can't promise to be present ourselves, ma'am, but if we are available we would be glad to see you."

"I'm not sure where we'll be in the autumn," Richard added, and I knew a secret thrill when he referred to us as a couple. I relished the sensation. "Though if you think you should like it, my lady, I think we should go. You have to be presented at Court, and that's as good a time as any."

My heart quaked at the thought of another ordeal. He watched me, and I knew he saw my expression of dismay although I tried to hide it, and laughed a little. "You'll sail through it. The most difficult part, I'm told, is walking backwards in a gown with a huge hoop and a train. My sister must have performed it satisfactorily, so perhaps we should ask her to teach you."

"I wouldn't like to put her to so much trouble," I protested.

"She'll love it. She's ten years younger than Gervase and me, and it would give her great pleasure to instruct instead of being instructed for a change."

I smiled, accepting his reassurance. After all, autumn was a long way away.

The Terrys took their leave, expressing their hope that they would see us in the autumn.

Carier came forward from the shadows and ushered us upstairs to a bedroom, where reposed two glasses of wine and our dressing cases. "If you would permit me to attend you, my lady, I think I can repair any ravages the journey may have wrought."

I accepted the seat at the dressing table and the resourceful valet attended to me, while Richard took his ease and watched as his man restored me to my appearance when I left the house that morning. He eradicated all the traces of my sleep in the carriage. Carier's fingers positively flew as he repaired the damage to my hair. "I'm sorry for the haste, my lady, but your guests will arrive at any moment."

"Shame," said Richard. I felt the same way he did. I would have enjoyed a respite. If not for the Terrys, we might have had longer.

Then Richard sat at the dressing table and I sipped my wine as Carier attended to his master, swiftly and skilfully restoring him to bandbox freshness.

It didn't take long, thanks to his skill, and although we would both have liked to linger in the quiet, comfortable room, we had to continue with the ceremony of the day.

We stood at the door of the Great Hall to greet the people who passed through it, and I had plenty of time to practise my new curtsey. The depth of the curtsey depended on my rank and the relative rank of the person I was curtseying to. Although Lizzie had made me practice the day before, I still found it hard to remember but everyone seemed satisfied, from the Duke of This to plain Mr. That. We greeted them as they arrived, because to wait until they had arranged themselves into their respective ranks was more than we could bear. No one took offence, so a mere half-hour after we stationed ourselves at the door, hearing the same sentiments repeated with varying degrees of sincerity, the Skerrits came through it.

All thoughts of courtesy dissolved when I saw my childhood friend and my fellow sufferer of the previous week, and I embraced him warmly, not caring what anyone thought, because Richard knew the right of it. I was glad to see Tom looking so well, back on his feet again after his severe beating. "Are you feeling quite well now, Tom?"

"Almost back to my old self." His jaunty reply didn't conceal the melancholy expression in his eyes. "And you look marvellous, every inch the great lady."

"Tom, I never knew you to flatter before!"

"Perhaps she'll believe it from you," Richard observed, "since I don't seem to be able to persuade her."

Lady Skerrit made a clucking sound. "Indeed, my dear, one would never know you spent half your childhood scrambling up trees." An exaggeration, but an understandable one, considering how often her staff had found Tom and me in her orchard. Richard gave me an unholy smile, and I suspected he would ask me to demonstrate my tree climbing ability one day.

The Skerrits passed on and I felt as though I'd said goodbye to another part of my life. I'd already asked them to visit us. Tom was almost a brother to me after our recent experiences. I knew I would never be able to cross the fields to their woods again as I had so many times over the years. That was where our nightmare had begun, and I knew I could never bear to go back.

The great hall filled to overflowing, hardly room for all our guests at the tables. At Richard's suggestion, every guest but the high sticklers had someone they hadn't met before to sit with, our local Devonshire society mingling with the London grandees.

True to her husband's ancestors, Lady Skerrit had a large table at the head of the hall, where we would sit and filled the rest of the space under that wonderful hammerbeam roof with two large dining tables on either side.

She had borrowed all the silver and dinner services in the

district, and the resulting display did us proud. Everything was polished to within an inch of its life, and the company now set it off to perfection.

Toasts were made, healths drunk, and I took care not to imbibe too much, mindful of my lack of sleep and the hours yet to go, but I drank deeply once.

When the toasts were drunk and the food was being brought in, Richard turned to me and raised his glass. "To your beautiful brown eyes. May I drown in them forever." It had become his usual toast to me, normally only said in private, but here, although quietly spoken, he made no attempt to hide it from our immediate neighbours.

I raised my glass in turn and toasted him, only substituting "blue" for "brown", but otherwise using the same words. He watched me drain my glass, and signed for it to be refilled but kept his attention on me, in a pledge only partly expressed by the toast.

He made sure I ate and a short time after, took my hand. "Are you feeling quite the thing, my dear?"

I almost laughed, which wasn't the effect he wanted. Instead I put my hand over my mouth and then to my forehead. He rose and helped me to my feet, giving me his arm to lean on, and we left the room.

Although the formalities of the occasion were now relaxed, most of the company watched us leave. I couldn't hear any comments as I passed the tables, but I could guess at some of the speculations.

He took me straight outside, to the carriage we arrived in and helped me in. "I've left notes to thank our hosts, and to explain to our families," he explained, as with a jerk the vehicle began to move. "The people who matter to us most know what I planned, and they will say you've had a relapse from your illness of last week, so I'm taking you away to rest." He leaned back, smiling at me, society attitude gone.

I laughed. "Do you think of everything?"

A gleam of amusement lit his eyes. "I try. Carier and Nichols will join us on the yacht, if they're not there already. Our luggage was stowed aboard yesterday."

"And I haven't even seen it yet," I reminded him, still smiling.

"No, but I have hopes you'll find it to your liking."

"What if I don't?"

He moved with a whisper of heavy silk, and took me in his arms. "We'll have to see, won't we? I have so much to show you—so much..."

Just before his mouth reached mine I heard a loud report, and then another, and a searing pain lanced the side of my head, just above my ear.

Chapter Three

Richard threw me to the floor of the coach and fell on top of me, yelling "Spring 'em! Go back to the house!" to the coachman. The man needed no urging, and instead of leaving the grounds of Peacock's he wheeled the carriage around and headed for the safety of the courtyard we had just left.

Richard lifted his head. "Oh God."

"What is it? What's happened?" The pain and the suddenness of the event confused me.

"Sh—shh." He put his hand to the side of my head and it came away bloody. "Lie still," he urged, and placed his hands either side of my head to keep it still. A flash of pain shot through me when the cobbles of the courtyard jolted the carriage.

As soon as we halted, Richard flung open the door, kicking the steps out of the way. He returned to carry me back into the house. He wasted no time in the open, but used the nearest entrance, the back one.

The servants milling about inside looked about, confused at his precipitate entrance. One resourceful footman took in the situation quicker than the others and called, "This way, my lord!" and led the way to the back stairs. He took us up two flights, along a corridor and into a bedroom, where Richard laid me on the bed and leaned over to examine my injury. I stared back at him, trying desperately to keep calm, concentrating on his face. If I were badly injured, I wanted my last sight to be him.

"Send for the Haretons, my valet and her ladyship's maid,

but tell no one else," he snapped. "Don't let word of this get out. If anyone asks, her ladyship stumbled and she has decided to rest before we travel."

"Yes, my lord." I heard the door close behind the footman.

"Richard—"

He hushed me again, and put his hand to my injury. I felt him gently smooth back the hair above my ear, so he could see the area more clearly. He studied it with absent concentration, holding his breath. "A flesh wound." His breath sighed out. "Thank God, thank God."

He left me and went to the washstand, finding a cloth and wringing it out. "Cold water only, my love." He returned to the bed and applied the cloth, holding it in place for me.

Too stunned to take the impact of what had just happened, I appreciated the silence. Eventually I managed, "What happened?"

"We were shot at. I heard two reports, very close together, but definitely two. Can you remember how many you heard?"

"Definitely two," I said, remembering now.

"Then it was no accident, no opportunistic effort. Someone lay in wait for us."

"Oh, Richard!"

He gave me a soft kiss, then drew back to look at me. We regarded each other for a few moments in silence. "Dear God, what I nearly lost," he whispered.

I tried to smile to reassure him but I found I couldn't, so I lifted my arm and drew him closer and we held each other. His body trembled in response to mine.

When the door opened, he didn't pull away, and I didn't release my hold immediately but when he did sit up, we saw Gervase had accompanied James and Martha.

Richard gave a wry smile. "I might have known. Did you guess something was wrong?"

"I felt your shock," Gervase told him.

This time I found the strength to smile. "It's not too bad." I put my hand over Richard's where he held the cloth, and pulled it away so they could see.

Martha's face turned white. "What happened?"

"Someone shot at us," I said.

Martha gripped her hands together. "Poachers, perhaps?"

"Should we send someone after them?" James's face was white too. My head could not be a pretty sight by now, bloody and messy where the powder and grease had been partially washed away.

Richard's expression was grim. "Not an accident. Someone wanted to ruin our wedding day."

"Who would want to do such a thing?" Martha took the cloth from Richard and went to wring it out in the bowl, coming back with that one and a fresh one to sit on the other side of the bed. She shoved her fine lace ruffles out of the way while she worked to clean my face, holding the other against the wound.

Richard watched her carefully. "Any number of people. My guess is Julia Drury."

"The lady who ran off with our curate?" James said.

"The very same." Richard followed my gaze and looked down at his arm where my head had lain. Blood stained his beautiful white coat. Impatiently, he stripped off the gorgeous garment, threw it across a chair, and came to sit down on the bed next to me once more. I tried not to wince as Martha cleaned the wound, though now my original fear had dissipated a little I began to feel the soreness more. I reached for his hand, which he took and held firmly.

"You don't mean the Drurys have come all the way to Devon to take pot shots at us?"

"Hardly." He lifted my hand to his lips. "But they could have paid someone to do it."

"Is this what I can expect from married life?" I said, trying for levity.

"Not if I have anything to do with it." He frowned. "I've had the Drurys watched since they came back from their bride-trip."

Gervase spoke from where he lounged against the heavy washstand. "I will make sure they're watched while you're away."

There was a thoughtful silence before the door crashed open and Tom Skerrit burst in. He paled when he saw me on the bed and Martha carefully dabbing at my wound, but listened while James told him what had happened, and then sank heavily into the nearest chair. His horrified stare never left my face.

"May I sit up? I feel much better now."

Richard lifted me while Martha put the pillows behind me, then he leaned me against them, watching me to make sure I was comfortable, so I smiled for him.

He kissed my forehead. "My poor sweetheart! You've been through so much recently and now I fear there may be more to come." He kept his arm around my shoulders.

I stared at him, new fear rising. "What do you mean?"

He kept all his attention on me as though we were the only people in the room. "I don't think we can risk the yacht now."

"Do you think they might have got to that, too?" Gervase demanded.

Richard shrugged. "I think it highly likely. I'll have it searched by people I can trust without question before we use it again and that would take too long for what I have in mind now." He lifted his head and looked around. "Our new plans must go no further than this room."

Murmurs of agreement followed and Richard nodded his thanks. "We will still go away, but more circumspectly. The yacht was no secret, moored at the coast for the last two weeks. Anyone could have got to it in that time."

Frowning, he leaned against the bed head. I closed my eyes and rested my head on his shoulder, taking comfort from him. Martha made the only sound as she crossed the room to wring out the cloths and then returned to bathe my wound.

Richard took a deep breath and opened his eyes. "Very well, this is what we'll do." He tucked his free arm behind his head. "We'll confuse anyone pursuing us by spreading rumours and with your help, we'll make them all seem likely. We'll put it about that Rose is seriously injured and she's at the house." He shot a quicksilver glance at James for permission, and James nodded. He bared his teeth in a feral smile. "If we start the word in the servants' hall, it'll be all around the district by morning. We'll put someone in a carriage and send her to the house we've hired as if she were Rose. She will slowly recover, of course, and then you can send us both away, perhaps to my house in Oxfordshire, where we will not receive visitors for some time. If you say Rose is disfigured, that may go some way towards satisfying the Drurys, if it was indeed they who ordered this. We can spread other stories, too, about this incident, because I want a smokescreen. Be as inventive as you wish. Say she's seriously injured, that we've gone straight to the yacht, that I've taken her to my parents' home in Derbyshire, and that we've gone to London to seek the advice of a good surgeon. Anything you wish."

He paused while they nodded or murmured agreement. "For the knowledge of the people in this room only, here's what we're really going to do. I'll send the yacht on its way as another decoy, but Rose and I will travel on the public packet and then by road." He sat up, sliding his arm from behind my shoulders and he took my hands in his, turning me to face him. "I'm sorry, my love, but I fear we must travel separately."

I couldn't believe he'd said that. "No! Not now, we can't!"

He smiled ruefully. "I said I was taking no chances with you and I meant it. If they're watching the ports, they'll be watching for couples. We have no way of knowing if this was one chance attempt or a concerted attack, in which case they will try to hunt us down and the rumours we set won't hold them for long. You may travel from Topsham, being the closest to Peacock's, and I'll travel from further up the coast."

This news sent me into more shock than the shooting. I bit my lower lip, forcing the tears back. The last thing he needed now was a feeble woman. He gripped my hands as if he'd never let go. I wished that were true.

"We'll travel under assumed names, of course. Carier usually has some papers."

This last made James and Tom exclaim in astonishment.

Richard left them to draw their own conclusions. "I'll travel alone—I can move much faster that way. I'll scout the route and make sure everything is as it should be."

"Should you mind if I came with you?" Gervase said.

Richard lifted a quizzical eyebrow at his twin. "And advertise our presence so loudly that they'll be waiting for us? I think not, brother."

Gervase scowled, but Richard was right. Everyone knew he was one of identical twins, and for them to travel together would be virtual suicide. "Truly, I'll be better alone. But I could use an agent here to communicate with Thompson's and send word when it's safe for us to return. Not that I can promise to return immediately, of course." Such was my confusion it took me some moments before I got his meaning. It was our bride-trip, after all.

Martha and James alone of the people in the room didn't know what Richard meant by Thompson's, but he didn't enlighten them.

Thompson's was a registry office for domestic staff that Richard had helped his manservant to finance. Carier's army pension, Richard's investment and the mysterious Mrs. Thompson had made it into the best agency for upper staff in London. Also a spy network and it provided the means for a private army. Now he would use the network to try to find out who had tried to kill us.

"Carier and Nichols will travel with Rose, ostensibly as her personal servants, but also as her bodyguards. I will not have her in any more danger. She may pose as a lady travelling to join her husband abroad, or even a widow." He shook his head. "No, not a widow." That relieved me because I didn't wish to become a widow, even in pretence so soon after my wedding day. His tone gentled when he addressed me. "Do you remember when I asked you to come away with me if my parents tried to push me into marrying Julia? We would marry quietly and go abroad, I said."

I blushed, remembering the time only too well. "Venice."

"I meant it." He'd said he wanted to make love to me there, with the windows open to the light. "That would be the best place. The apartment is small, but comfortable. I've only ever used it for myself, as a bolthole. I had an identity for us both drawn up at the time, and if Carier has done his job, he should still have the requisite papers."

I stared at him, astonished. "You weren't leaving anything to chance, were you?"

"Not once you said yes, my love." His gravity disarmed me. "I shall be a wine merchant, and you may be a wine merchant's wife, travelling to join him abroad. Should you object to that?"

"Not if I'm still *your* wife," I replied shyly.

He gave me a tender smile. "Oh, I have you now, and I intend to keep you." He kept my gaze for a moment, as if we were the only people in that room and then he grinned, his mood changing in a flash. "I do hope Carier and Nichols had the foresight to unload some of our luggage. I can hardly travel in white velvet."

After settling me on the pillows behind us, he rose and crossed the room to the window, not standing before it but to one side. "It seems quiet enough now."

Tom spoke. "I sent servants outside to see if they could find any lurkers, but I fear whoever it was is long gone."

"You're probably right," Gervase said. "Whoever fired the shot wouldn't linger. Richard, give me a note of hand and I'll ride for London. In fact, I'll set out in a coach dressed in something of yours. Set the rumours going."

Richard turned back from his contemplation of the scene outside. "I would appreciate that. I should be gone as soon as it can be arranged, so if you don't mind, I'd like a little time alone with my wife."

He had made it perfectly clear that I was his now, by word, deed and intent. Nobody gainsaid him. I had half expected James to protest, to offer to take care of me for a while, because he'd had his doubts of Richard from the first, but he said nothing of the kind now.

The others left the room. Martha embraced me, frowning in a worried way, but she only murmured for me to take care before she left.

Richard closed the door behind them. I sat up and swung my feet over the side of the bed, heading for the mirror to see what damage my appearance had suffered.

The diamond hair ornament was gone, shot away from its position above my ear. It probably lay in pieces on the floor of the coach. Martha had taken off the heavy girandole earrings I'd worn, but now she'd washed the blood away, I could see that the wound was negligible. I touched the site gingerly. I looked piebald where the white powder had been washed away to reveal the brown hair beneath. Yet again, my appearance was ruined and while I was not vain, I would dearly have loved to show to advantage before Richard for once. My husband.

I turned around, feeling suddenly shy, but he strode across the room, took me in his arms, and kissed me as if we had all night.

He drew away. "I'm sorry sweetheart but I think we may have to wait a little longer for our wedding night." He kissed me again. I responded, trying to show him how much I needed him, but he set me away gently.

"Venice was my first choice for us, and now it will happen that way. But it won't spoil anything—I promise you."

Despair clutched my stomach, threatening to eject the small amount I'd managed to eat at the wedding breakfast. "I don't mind where we are, I've always told you that. But can we not travel together? Do we *have* to part?"

He frowned. "I'm afraid we must. I've done this journey before, and I can travel swiftly, but I want the road clear and I want you guarded. I believe whoever wishes us harm is conning the ports closely. They'll be watching the yacht, that's for certain, and probably the main ports as well."

"Don't you think you're exaggerating the danger? Couldn't it have been one stray shot?"

He took me in his arms again as if he couldn't stop himself. "Someone was aiming at us. One shot might possibly have been an accident, but two—no. That argues a plan, and they won't give up with one failure." He held me tighter until my stay-bones creaked under the strain, but I didn't protest. I wanted closer to him than this, skin to skin. "Rose, sweetheart, wife, I want you with me for a very long time. I won't jeopardise that for an impatience we can overcome. We have no way of knowing who is after us and why, and I won't put you in any more danger."

"Who do you think it is?"

"If I knew for sure, I could rest easier. I've made enemies over the years, and it could be anyone. But I think it more likely to be either the Drurys, or the Cawntons." The Drurys, Julia and Steven, our erstwhile partners whom we'd jilted to be together. Or the large and organised gang of smugglers who owned this part of the coast. "I'd rest easier if I knew it was the Drurys, because the Cawntons have deeper pockets and more resources." He sighed. "If we can find out who is behind this, we may be able to move swiftly and bring them to justice."

"Like Norrice Terry?"

I hated that I'd said that, but I needed to know. Richard shook his head. "No, emphatically not. Although if they'd hurt you any more—" His angry stare went to my wound and he lifted one hand, only to feather it with a touch I couldn't feel and then return it to my waist. "No, not that. But if we can find out who it was, then I'll join you abroad and we'll travel together." His gaze softened. "Will you promise me something?"

"Anything." I wanted to alleviate the anxiety he'd revealed now we were alone.

At least I made him smile. "Then promise me that for the next few weeks you won't go anywhere without Carier or Nichols. Nichols will sleep in your room and Carier will arrange the bodyguards for the road and watch over you at night. I know it will irritate you, I know you love to be on your own, but for the time being, it's too dangerous. Promise me."

I promised. "Then I'll have you to look after me at night." I put one hand to his cheek.

"So you will." He caught my hand and kissed the palm, sending shivers of desire through me.

I couldn't weaken now—the last thing he needed was to watch me, lachrymose, waving him away tragically. I was his wife and nothing could alter that now—except one niggling doubt, and maybe a way of persuading him to share the bliss we felt together. "Don't we have to consummate the marriage before it's fully in force? I read something once about Henry VIII, about how he divorced one of his wives for non-consummation."

He grinned. "Anne of Cleves. He disliked her on sight. He

was looking for an excuse to be rid of her respectably. Of course, if you should want rid of me, you could always apply for an annulment..." He lifted an eyebrow.

"Oh no, if you want an annulment, you'll have to do it yourself, because I'm so happy to have you, I'll trail around over half Europe after you."

"Then you are truly my wife, and I'll make good the other part in Venice."

"Promise?"

"I swear it." His breath shivered over my face before he kissed me so hard I could barely breathe. I wanted him so much I didn't know how I could bear even a day apart.

He drew away and lifted his hand to remove the diamond pin he always wore at his neckcloth. He handed it to me. "Keep this safe for me?"

I forced a smile and closed my hand over it, feeling the warmth it had collected from his body.

I remembered something recent events had put from my mind, and drew out a small, silk-wrapped parcel from my pocket. "I have something for you. I meant to give it to you in the carriage." I watched him unwrap it.

I'd had a miniature of myself done in Exeter the previous February, when we had spent some time apart. Martha assured me Richard would like to have it, but I felt foolish, giving someone my own likeness as though he should thank me for it. That was why I'd never given it to him before, but if he ever wanted such a thing, I supposed it would be now.

He studied it in silence, and then looked up and gave me his perfect smile. His eyes were brighter than usual and his voice wavered when he spoke. "What a lovely thought. It will improve my mood when I'm on the road. Thank you, my love. I'll keep it safe." It was the nearest he came to breaking. I held my smile too, to honour him.

The sound of horses arriving outside drew us to the window and we saw Carier and Nichols get out of a small, unremarkable carriage. The basket behind it did contain some luggage and I recognised one of my bags. They wasted no time, but hurried into the house.

Richard took me in his arms one last time. "I fear that's our cue to part. I must leave as soon as I can. I may find a passage across to France tonight, and gain a head start on you." I couldn't stop my stricken look then, and he held me tightly. "You know everything I want to say," he murmured next to my ear—the uninjured one. "I've loved you from the moment I first saw you, and I love you still. I have no doubt I'll love you until the day I die."

"Oh, don't say that!" I pulled back to look at him.

He was smiling. "What? I love you?"

"No, that you'll die."

He caressed my cheek. "I'm not planning on it for a few years yet. I'll take the greatest care, I swear it. Even if we travel the entire distance separately it won't be much more than three weeks before we see each other again. That, in exchange for years to come, should be worth waiting for."

I tried to smile. "I love you. All this is bearable because I'm married to you, and I know you'll wait for me."

"Not for too long, I hope," he murmured, trailing tiny kisses across my jaw.

He took my mouth once more, then he crossed the room and left, without looking back.

Chapter Four

Nichols entered the room as soon as Richard left.

She frowned thoughtfully, studying my condition. "If your ladyship can bear it, I would like to wash the powder out of your hair and then dress it over the wound. If we can make it less noticeable it will help us to pass unremarked."

I underwent the procedure after Nichols had helped me take off my finery. "The rest of your ladyship's luggage is on the quayside at Topsham. It will be sent separately to Venice, by a different route. I have transferred all we will need into smaller boxes." I found her efficiency in this crisis deeply impressive.

Just as I left the dressing room after having my hair rinsed, I heard the sound of a single horse, clattering across the courtyard below. I knew who it was and I tried not to listen as the sound died away, but I knew the minute he went out of earshot.

Carier came up to tell me his master had left. I would not break, would not cry. "I know, I heard. When do we leave?"

"As soon as your ladyship is ready. The reception will break up shortly and I hope the guests' departures will help to mask ours, even though most of them will leave from the front of the house and we will not." He stood behind me where I sat at the dressing table, so I could see him in the mirror. "I have papers for you under the name of Mrs. Locke, travelling to join your merchant husband in Venice. We will avoid telling people our destination if we can. His lordship will travel under the name of Philips, although he will use the name Locke when he arrives at Venice, since his papers say Mr. Philips is unmarried. It will serve to confuse any pursuers further. I will check he is not followed, and I will try to do so without impeding our progress. His lordship is anxious we reach our destination without unnecessary delay."

I suppressed my smile, sure security wasn't the only reason Richard urged speed. "So am I. Did you examine the yacht?"

Nichols draped a lock of damp hair across my brow and removed the pins from her mouth to secure it in place. "We had no time my lady, although Carier left orders for it to be done. We received the message that you had been hurt, and we set off at once."

"Before we left Topsham, I took the liberty of obtaining passage to Cherbourg on a packet leaving tomorrow morning. I also booked a room at a respectable, though not fashionable inn. I trust that will be in order?"

"It sounds perfectly sensible," I replied.

Carier bowed and left the room so I could change.

I couldn't hold back any longer, so I let myself cry. Nichols handed me clean handkerchiefs as I needed them but said nothing. She kept busy about her work, as a good maid should, but her harsh features softened. I felt better for her unspoken sympathy. This was not the wedding night I had anticipated. But I was alive and married, so I had a lot to be thankful for. I dried my eyes for the last time and prepared to leave.

Tom waited for me in the lobby downstairs, by the back door. He held out his arms and I embraced him, feeling comfort in his friendly hug. "I thought we passed all that last week," he commented, referring to our recent adventure together.

"We are. This is only a precaution. I think the most dangerous part is this part—getting away from here where they might be watching."

"Do you think it's the Cawntons? Getting revenge?"

"It could be any number of people."

Tom studied my face. I kept my expression deliberately calm, as if I was used to being shot at. "I have footmen watching, Rose. If your carriage is followed, they'll catch them."

"Was Richard followed?"

Tom bit his lip. "No. Strang has given me your direction in

Venice, and if we hear anything, we'll get in touch." That was a sure measure of Richard's trust in Tom. "Don't worry." He tapped his forehead. "It's in here, not on any sheet of paper."

For two pins I would have burst into self-pitying tears again, but instead I forced a smile and took Tom's hand. "We'll come back and see you as soon as we get back home. You know it'll never be the same again."

He shook his head. "I know. And now you know something I never should have told you." He gave me a crooked smile.

"Oh, Tom!" I knew what he meant. In our captivity together, he'd told me he should have proposed marriage to me before I had ever met Richard. I might have been happy, but the feeling for Richard had been all engrossing, complete and thorough, so Tom's confession had engendered nothing more than guilt and sorrow. "I hoped that was something you only thought you felt. That when you were free you would realise it was only brotherly love after all."

"No," he said. "But I'm happy for you, Rose, happy to see you so fulfilled. Only—I don't think you'll see many peaceful times, not with Lord Strang. He seems to me a driven man."

I smiled ruefully. "You don't know the half of it, Tom. But he loves me, and I'm hoping I can help him to achieve a kind of peace."

Tom nodded. "I overheard some comments today that might amuse you. They didn't think you were his style, you must be a great heiress to have captured him. I even heard that you were carrying his child. None of them wanted to face the real reason."

The comments made me smile. "Could you tell?" Richard hated parading his private feelings in public, hated people knowing his true feelings and I had done my best to conceal my love for him, for his sake. One day he might feel more comfortable sharing that knowledge with others but for now I wanted to give him the room he needed to come to terms with his new state.

"I don't think so," Tom said. "And his mother's putting it about that it is a dynastic arrangement. His sister was to have married the fifth Earl of Hareton but called it off, so instead, the sister of the current earl is marrying him."

"That's very clever, I shall tell him." Carier waited for me outside, the only sign of his impatience his foot tapping on the ground. "I have to go, Tom."

Tom looked doubtfully at Carier and Nichols. "Will you be safe with them?"

"Perfectly. They're not just servants, you know, they're my bodyguards. Carier is his valet, so you might say Richard's made a great sacrifice."

That made my friend laugh, so I hugged him and left him laughing. The stairs of the carriage were folded up and we left, Carier on horseback in front of us, Nichols in the coach with me.

Topsham was past Exeter, so it took us a couple of hours and more to reach it, and when we did, we went straight to an inn near the quay. I was shown to a comfortable room upstairs with a private parlour. There was always the danger someone might recognise me so close to home, so Nichols warned me to keep myself close. "I beg your pardon, my lady, but I have to call you ma'am from now on."

"I'm more used to it," I confessed. "I was 'ma'am' until this morning, so I should be fine with that."

Nichols managed a smile. "Should you like to take some dinner now, ma'am?"

"I suppose so." Although I hadn't eaten much at the wedding breakfast, I still wasn't hungry. "Where's Carier?"

"Making sure everything is as it should be, ma'am. That no one followed us, and no one has booked a passage on the boat we're to take in the morning *after* we bought our tickets."

"Is there an alternative plan?"

"There are other routes, ma'am, other identities but we shouldn't need to use them. From now on I will refer to your husband as Mr. Locke, in public and in private."

I felt like a piece of valuable baggage, to be preserved at all costs, but not consulted. "Do I have any say at all in any of this?"

"Mr. Locke said you would ask sooner or later and he asked me to give you this." Out of her pocket, she took an unsealed note. I took the note and sat down on the hard chair by the window and read it.

"My dearest life,

I know all this protection will irk you, and I know you will ask. All I can say is this was arranged in too much of a hurry and you must forgive us if we seem a little high handed. Carier and Nichols have my full trust. Please do as they say, they have only your interests at heart. Travel safely my heart. You have all my love.

Yours, R."

I closed the note and held it tightly. He must have taken time to write it just before he left.

Nichols's pragmatic tones broke into my melancholy. "You must destroy it, ma'am,"

I clutched the paper closer. "Why? He hasn't signed it."

"It has his intentions in it, and it's in his own handwriting. I'm sorry, ma'am," she added, as she saw my face.

I gave her the note. "You do it, Nichols. I haven't the heart to." I watched as she tore the note into shreds, put the pieces in a dish, took a light from the fire and ignited them, all very methodical, very calm. She was right. It would be a foolish chance to take at this stage. I assumed my luggage now held nothing personal, not even the new monogrammed toilet set Martha had given me as part of her wedding gift.

"He sent you something, ma'am." Nichols went over to my dressing case, the old one I'd always used, without any fancy lettering, and lifted out the first layer, and the second. Then she pulled out something from underneath and gave the objects to me.

I weighed the knife in my hand, one of the wicked little Italian stilettos Richard was in the habit of carrying. He threw them with great accuracy, a skill he said he'd learned on the Grand Tour. I couldn't do this, but still the knife might be useful. It was slim, flexible and razor sharp, resting in a plain leather scabbard that I could easily slip into my pocket.

The other item was a pair of small pistols in a box. "Can you shoot, ma'am?"

I gave her a look of derision. "I'm a country girl, Nichols. Of course I can shoot." Better than she thought, I'd wager.

Beautifully chased and blued, with a box of ammunition and one of powder, yet with no trigger I could see. I held a pistol up and saw a small groove where the trigger should have been.

"It's a new design," Nichols informed me. "The trigger pops down when you cock the hammer."

I made sure the weapon wasn't loaded before I pulled the hammer back. Sure enough the trigger appeared below from a spring mechanism. It was like a magic trick.

"It stops it going off in your pocket, or when you withdraw it, ma'am," Nichols explained. I saw the reasoning, and I could see how it would make carrying it around that much easier.

I released the hammer and watched the trigger slide back inside the slim, metal tube. "I shall sleep better with one of these under my pillow. Are you armed, Nichols?"

For answer my maid put a hand into her pocket and withdrew a pistol from it; larger than mine, but just as useful. She pulled up her skirt and showed me the dagger hidden beneath it and then showed me a device I had never seen before, which looked like a series of finger rings joined together.

"What does that do?" I asked, diverted by the intriguing object.

The maid slipped the device on her right hand, and made a fist. "Now if I hit someone it will make much more damage. You can get a good effect if you hold something hard in your hand, as well, such as a handful of stones, or one large one."

I listened, appalled and fascinated in equal measure. "Good God, Nichols, where did you learn those tricks?"

"On the street, ma'am." She put her lethal rings away. "I wasn't always a lady's maid." I might have known. Richard had a highly eclectic circle of friends and influence. I imagined Nichols came from the more colourful side.

I ate as much of my dinner as I could when it was brought to me, and read a book until it was time for me to retire—or rather, tried to read.

Nichols slept on a truckle bed in my room and I didn't give way to my tears until I heard her deep, regular breathing.

The next morning at about six we went aboard the packet,

an unremarkable vessel, much like many I had seen over the years, but never boarded until today. We sailed down the estuary towards Exmouth. Carier and Nichols insisted I remained below decks, out of sight while they investigated the other passengers. My cabin did have a porthole and as we left, I looked back, saying a mental goodbye to everything I had known up to now. I felt no excitement as I should have in the circumstances, no elation. It should have been so different, this morning. I saw a vessel unlike the others, smoother, sleeker, and guessed that must be the yacht. I should be aboard, sleeping the morning away in my husband's arms.

A plume of smoke went up from the ship, and a tongue of bright orange flame, piercing the peaceful blue of the sky. After a second, the dull sound of a percussive note filtered through the porthole and heedless of my guardians' warnings, I ran out of the cabin and up on deck.

Passengers and crew crowded to one side of the packet, affording a perfect view of the yacht, now fiercely alight, fire shooting out of the portholes and licking at the sails, until now neatly furled against the masts. I stared, numb with shock until I felt Nichol's hand on mine and I realised I was clutching the handrail too tightly.

A respectable looking matron, her eyes aglow with excitement, gave me a small nod. I nodded back and decided to pretend ignorance, the better to discover more. "What on earth is that?"

"An explosion, ma'am. About five minutes ago, maybe ten, it was. Just went up like it was full of gunpowder."

Tension clawed at my throat. "An explosion? Was there anyone aboard?"

She gave me a curious stare. "Did you hear about the society wedding in Exeter yesterday?"

"I heard something, yes." I exchanged a brief glance with Nichols.

"Well the groom, Lord Strange—"

"Strang," I corrected her automatically.

"Yes, Strang, that's it. He was taking his bride on a cruise. They might be on that ship. Poor things," she added, more as a sop to conscience than with any real concern, I thought.

"So they were aboard?"

"I don't know for sure. Certainly someone arrived on the quayside late last night and took ship, and from the coach they arrived in they weren't servants. The new Lady Strang was taken ill at the wedding breakfast. Nerves, I'd say—" She winked at me. "I'd lay a pound to a penny that was them last night."

If I hadn't taken such a firm hold of the rail I would have fallen. It would have been us if matters had fallen differently, or if Richard hadn't decided to take precautions. The world eddied around me. I felt Nichols's hand on my elbow, anxiously trying to steady me. "How terrible," I managed, my voice sounding strangely normal.

The lady seemed to notice nothing unusual in my reaction. She leaned towards me in a confiding manner. "I went into Exeter yesterday and I got a glimpse of them when they came out of the Cathedral."

"Oh yes?"

"Beautiful they were, both of them. I've rarely seen the like. They were married here because she's a local girl, you see. Can't place her myself and I've been following local society all my life but I know about her family. Her brother's just become an earl, and by all accounts, it's gone to his head something dreadful. He's planning all kinds of things to his house. I know because my brother's been asked to help. He has a building business, and he's forever up there these days, working on plans and the like." I knew how small Exeter society was, and how wise Carier was to check the passenger list before and after we came aboard. "It's a large family, so I daresay they need the room. We were all surprised when they came home, as they'd gone up North when they inherited. Still, I always say Devonshire's the best country in the world, you can't beat it for beauty, and I've always thought it must get cold up North." I murmured some kind of agreement and let her run on, like a stream of never ending gossip, but it gave me the respite I needed to gain control of myself once more.

"We've got half London society here, but they won't stay long, I don't suppose. They don't know quality when they see it, these people. Are you a local girl, dear?"

"From the other side, near Bideford," I managed. Nichols's hand was still firmly at my elbow, supporting me.

"I met someone from Bideford once," the lady mused. "Nice woman, but I can't remember her name."

"How do you hear all these things?" I asked her.

"Oh, I take an interest in the gentry." She gave a careless wave of her hand. "I've got prints of almost all of them at home. Strange I haven't got one of the new Lady Strang, though; I had a look yesterday. I found one of her sister—beautiful girl by all accounts." She would have one of Lizzie. "Poor lady! Most likely dead, her and her new husband."

That was enough for me. I let Nichols lead me back down to my cabin. Carier, who had been watching the exchange from a distance, followed us. Nichols found some wine and I invited them to take a drink for themselves and sit, which they did.

"I will send a communication ahead to Mr. Locke when we dock at Cherbourg," said Carier. "He must be told as soon as possible. I would ride for him myself, but I'm under strict orders not to leave you under any circumstances, ma'am."

I nodded. "What if I ordered you to go?"

"With all due respect, ma'am, his orders must come first with me." I wasn't surprised; Richard was very thorough in his planning. "There's no doubt, ma'am, we're in this for the long haul. That was a follow-up to last night's attempt. When they heard that had failed, they would have made plans to board the yacht."

"Wouldn't it take time to load gunpowder on to it?"

Carier grimaced. "Not necessarily, ma'am. A few travelling trunks and the thing is done. We offloaded your luggage as quietly as possible, but with all the coming and going ashore, they could have put something aboard before we tightened the guard around the yacht." He sipped his wine and put it aside. "If it's the smugglers, it could have been meant as a warning, as well, something spectacular to prove they're kings of the coast. That seems likely to me, but we must leave the investigation to others ashore. In that case, they could have loaded the gunpowder with the regular supplies."

"Can you find someone quickly in Cherbourg?" I was as

anxious as he that Richard should be informed.

"There should be a Thompson's man available. I'll send the message in code," he said.

I took a sip of the tart wine and understood why Carier had rejected it, but I needed the fortification. "That will have to do, then. I hope no one was killed on the yacht."

"We have no way of knowing that, ma'am."

I wasn't too concerned by this fiery confirmation, only by the narrow escape I'd had. That was what had made me feel momentarily faint on deck, not the thought that someone hated us enough to try to kill us. Richard had made many enemies in the past. To kill him as he attained his greatest happiness was the best kind of revenge. I began to see that Richard's reticence in public on the matter of his feelings for me was protection for me, as well as his natural inclination.

Nichols gave me a ring, an old wedding ring, scratched from use, which must serve me until Venice. Mrs. Locke had been married for five years and would not have a brand new wedding ring such as the one I wore. Taking off my ring came as another wrench, because Richard had put it there, but I saw the necessity and put it on the gold chain to join my ruby betrothal ring, hidden below the neck of my gown.

We reached Cherbourg safely, and another anonymous, clean, comfortable inn. I kept my own counsel, my melancholy deepening with every night I spent with only Nichols for company.

For the next five days, I remained sunk in gloom. We travelled post chaise, changing horses frequently to ensure speed. I kept thinking about what should have been and every time we reached an inn I had a faint hope I would find a message there, but there was never anything. Carier didn't ask about Richard, as this might have drawn attention to him, and he could find nothing out from the people he got into casual conversation with. Sometimes I caught Nichols watching me with a particularly sympathetic expression in her grey eyes, but she said nothing. There was nothing she could do.

Chapter Five

Carier began to pick up messages from Richard, but after the one I had received in Topsham they were all verbal, left with trusted messengers at inns along the way, encrypted so Carier had to translate them for me. We knew he had passed that way, when, and that he was well. These messages helped me immeasurably—to know he was safe was all I asked. He was pulling away from us, getting faster where we maintained a constant speed, although we wasted no time either. At first, I watched nothing, took interest in nothing, but I could not spend my whole time journeying and not taking note of my surroundings and my experiences. Nothing a seasoned traveller would consider notable, but to my eyes and ears, noteworthy indeed.

It was getting warmer as May became more advanced, and we travelled further south. The scenery became more interesting as spring blossoms began to bloom and the terrain less flat. I grew interested in what lay over the next rise, what the next small town would look like. The buildings we passed were more unusual to my English eyes, painted white or a pastel color. Carier procured a map for me, and I could follow where we were and how far we had come.

By the time we reached Chalon-sur-Saône, we had been on the road for two weeks. I was heartened to see very soon we would arrive in Italy, with Venice that much nearer. Carier assured us that if the weather stayed fine we'd be in Venice in less than a fortnight; the thought made me excited and impatient. Now I really *was* travelling towards something. Did ever a newlywed woman travel so far on her bride-trip without her husband?

We were two days on the diligence before disembarking in Lyons, which seemed to be a very pleasant city. We didn't stay there above a night, setting out for Nice.

Now came the most difficult part of our journey. From Nice, we were to travel to Piedmont on the Tend Pass, across the Alps, a journey taken by many intrepid passengers before us. I thought the sea passage would be preferable, but Carier explained the sea journey wouldn't be any quicker than the mountain pass. "We can acquire a chair for you, ma'am," Carier said, "but that would add two days to our journey. If you would consent to use a mule as transport we could cross in three days, God willing."

"Is it dangerous?"

He shook his head. "Not if we ride carefully, ma'am. I've taken the precaution of bespeaking the best guide in Nice. He will take us all the way to Piedmont, and ensure we come to no harm."

I agreed it seemed like the best way. We were deep into May now and past the worst of the weather, but Nichols was careful to find some warm cloaks for the journey.

I found I could ride a mule as well as I could ride a horse, which was tolerably well.

The first day passed without incident, and I found the scenery fascinating. I wished I could paint as well as my sister Ruth, to capture the purity of our surroundings. I had the time to take a few sketches for her. Although the inn we stayed at that first night was not the best we had encountered on the road, I fell into bed early, hoping we could set out as early as possible the next day.

It dawned fine but noticeably colder, and I was glad of the cloak Nichols wrapped around me. Our guide was a rough looking man of few words, and those I didn't understand, being spoken in a patois I was wholly unfamiliar with, but he seemed to know his way.

One moment I was looking at the beautiful view from one side of the pass, and the next I was coming around, the hard road under my back, feeling decidedly sick, pillowed on Nichols's lap. When I put my hand to my throbbing head I touched a bump as big as a hen's egg, or so it seemed to me. I didn't remember falling, but she told me my mount had stumbled and thrown me.

I sat up. Nichols held me steady while I vomited and then took a cloth from her pocket and cleaned my face. She used snow to wet another cloth. The cold cloth refreshed me and helped to bring me around properly. I lay still for a while, regaining my equilibrium. I realised with relief that my sturdy steed was unhurt and we could continue our journey once I'd recovered.

"What happened?"

"The mule stumbled and threw you, ma'am," Nichols said. "Lie quietly for a while. You should rest, and then the guide will take you up." If it meant we could make progress, then I was all for it.

I shivered, and Carier stripped off his coat to put over me, afterwards walking to where our luggage lay by the side of the road to find another travelling cloak. Our guide had taken the opportunity to take the worst of the loads from our animals and set them to grazing.

"How long was I unconscious?" I whispered. I was developing one of the worst headaches I had ever known. Anything above a whisper hurt.

"Not long, ma'am," my maid replied. "Maybe ten minutes."

I sighed. Another delay before we reached Venice. Then, to the evident apprehension of my attendants we saw several figures coming towards us along the road, including two sedan chairs carried by four sturdy men. The chairs were slightly ahead of the attendant mules, which were laden with heavy luggage. As they neared our sorry little party a lady popped her head out of the window of the second vehicle.

"Oh dear!" the lady cried. "It is poor Mrs. Locke!"

I had no idea who they were, but luckily Nichols did. "We met them two nights ago when we had to eat with all the other guests at the inn. They did their best to ingratiate themselves with everyone and their name is Ravens." I nodded. I still didn't remember, but perhaps the accident had knocked it out of my head.

Both she and her husband got out of their chairs and came over to me. Both well-upholstered individuals, made bulkier by the warm clothing they wore. Mrs. Ravens, her bosom jutting before her like a shelf, bent down to me and I felt a momentary fear that I might be smothered.

"Poor Mrs. Locke, what a shame!" I shivered when her cool hand touched my forehead and she drew it back. She smelled strongly of lavender and lily-of-the-valley, neither of them favourites of mine, although I believe lavender is supposed to help with headaches. Mine had gone beyond headache and into head-splitting territory.

Carier briefly told them what had happened.

"The poor lady must take your chair, sir!" exclaimed Mrs. Ravens to her husband, a suggestion to which he readily agreed. Carier frowned. We had little choice, it seemed. I couldn't abide the mule again, not until my pain subsided, but we couldn't stay here and no hostelry lay within easy reach.

"If you would lend me your mule," Mr. Ravens suggested, "we will do very well. You must not ride in your condition, madam, the chair is infinitely preferable to that."

Carier was not eager to take up the offer, but Nichols interrupted his polite refusal. "Madam is shivering, Mr. Williams, and I fear she will take a chill or worse if she stays here much longer." "Mr. Williams", as Carier was known on this trip, was forced to agree. My appearance must have been severe for him to consider it, or maybe he realised it was this or nothing.

Carier and Mr. Ravens helped me into the chair, and Nichols made sure to tuck me in a travelling cloak and blanket, with a hot brick at my feet. I felt much better, and deeply thankful to my hosts, who showed such touching concern for my welfare. Carier would ensure they or their attendants meant me no harm, and would no doubt free us from their company as soon as he could. But I needed this passage over the mountains, or we might be on the mountaintop come nightfall. Even in May this wasn't a pleasant prospect.

Nichols and Carier remounted their mules watching me anxiously, Carier still obviously ill at ease. I was much more comfortable in the chair, and although our progress would be slower, at least we were still moving. In fact, I was so comfortable, I fell asleep, not waking until much later in the day.

When I sat up, I found my headache had subsided to bearable. The next staging post wasn't far off, and as I had supposed, Carier had acquired a vehicle for our use the next day. Our altitude was quite high now, and it wasn't as warm as it had been, but we were well equipped with blankets and the like.

The Ravens invited me to share their dinner, and I accepted, only taking the precaution of asking my maid should be present, "in case I fell ill again"; a fatuous excuse, but it did the trick. I remembered Richard's strictures that I should never be without either Carier or Nichols with me and I considered it a reasonable precaution to take. Carier disappeared to discover what he could about our hosts.

So Nichols was present during dinner, stationed behind my chair as I let the Ravens drink and become more garrulous. I ate and drank only moderately.

Both the Ravens declared their delight to see me so much better. "If there is no chair available, please don't hesitate to make use of ours for as long as you require."

I smiled and thanked them for their kind assistance, although I already knew there would be a chair available for our use once Carier had seen to it. I didn't know how much this journey was costing, but I guessed a lot had been expended in making it as smooth and fast as possible. Carier took care of the day-to-day accounts and we always paid in cash, without resorting to the local banks, although Richard held accounts in several of them. Carier must have a considerable sum stowed somewhere about his person, but I didn't think anyone would be successful in relieving him of it.

"Your maid tells us you too are going to Venice," said Mrs. Ravens. "We would very much like to see you once we reach that fair city."

"That is very kind," I murmured, wondering what had got

into Nichols to reveal even that much.

While the Ravens were wonderfully kind, I found their presence a trifle overwhelming. I guessed them to be a little older than Richard and I but their showy dress and air of ostentation did them no favours in my eyes. Mrs. Ravens' flowery phrases bid fair to bring back my headache.

"Of course, my dear Mrs. Locke, you must have guessed some of our secret," said Mr. Ravens. He twirled the rich red wine around his glass thoughtfully. I felt Nichols's hand leave the back of my chair, and knew she was putting her hand in her pocket, as indeed I was. I felt the reassuring butt of my pistol, curled my hand around it and found the hammer with my thumb.

"I know I can confide in you," Ravens continued, glancing across the table at me. "Did you not notice our clothes in Chalon, how much more superior they were than a mere Mr. and Mrs. Ravens could afford? It was a pardonable extravagance." He smiled conspiratorially at his wife. "We are tired of travelling incognito. The truth is," and he leaned over the table towards me, his voice dropping. "We are really Lord and Lady Strang. Perhaps you've heard of us?"

I gripped the butt of my pistol convulsively, feeling the stillness behind me as Nichols took in what Ravens had just said. Mrs. Ravens smiled fondly. Try as I might, I could see no resemblance to me in her face, though it was evident her husband had seen Richard, or a print of him, because he had tried for ostentation in dress, although the quality and natural elegance were notable by their absence. He was still speaking, smiling. "I see you've heard something. You see, dear ma'am, there was an accident to our yacht, and we have been forced to take to the road, but the road being what it is, we thought it safer to travel incognito."

I made a tremendous effort and put a polite smile in place. He was telling me about the wedding, and the yacht, as though I hadn't been there and seen it. I felt as though I floated in a dream. The slight feeling of unreality engendered by my accident earlier in the day didn't help, but I had Nichols there to corroborate what I was hearing.

Mr. Ravens didn't look very much like my husband. He was older, for a start, and his face was heavier, pale and lined, but he wore the elaborate clothes and style of wig Richard affected and he struck elegant poses in a blurred mirror image. Where Richard's body seemed to fall naturally into elegance, here this man was making an effort. His face was also made up, much as Richard's had been when I first met him. If they had attended the wedding, even as members of the public, why did they not recognise me? But they didn't—or they were pretending not to.

Mrs. Ravens was not at all like me, but there had been much less opportunity for them to see me. I had been in mourning when I had first become engaged to Richard, and then ill, so my public appearances had been much more restricted. By the time society had realised it should be interested in me, I wasn't generally available for its scrutiny.

Mrs. Ravens was smaller and plumper than me, and I knew I didn't simper like that, nor wear so many patches on my face. I wasn't sure I liked anyone impersonating me, but I think it would have been worse if she had looked more like me.

I had to find out what I could. "So you decided to go to Venice—my lord?"

Mr. Ravens clasped his hands together in a most un-Richard like gesture. "Such a beautiful city. We were always going to go there eventually. Such a shame the yacht let us down!" *Wasn't it just.* He continued. "We hired a fine palazzo. Hopefully the time will give us an opportunity to engage in some business ventures there."

"You're in business?" I said.

His hands now went out in an expansive way. "I dabble only. I understand your husband is in business?"

"He's a wine merchant, my lord," I replied. "Not in your league, I'm sure."

He smiled graciously. "Maybe not."

I saw the light, or at any rate, a glimmer. This could be the beginning of a trick, a fraud. Not our pursuers, or more likely not. They hadn't recognised me, and surely the assassins would know what I looked like? I hadn't seen a scrap of recognition and if Carier and Nichols had seen anything at all, we would be heading back the way we came, preparing to take the sea route to Venice. So I decided to fish for more clues. "I thought Lady Strang had suffered an injury. The news was all around the ship on the day we left for the continent."

He took his lady's hand tenderly. "A slight injury, no more. As you can see, she is back to her lovely self." The lady simpered again, and I had a sudden urge to hit her. If she was impersonating me, the least she could do was to get it right.

I released my hold on my pistol and smiled sweetly. "Some wine?" Nichols moved from behind me to pour it. One handed.

They seemed to want to play down the assassination attempts, and this was only explained to me later, when Nichols, Carier and I were locked in the safety of my bedroom.

Carier frowned, but since this was close to his habitual expression it was hard to know what he was feeling. "I spent the evening intoxicating their servants. They seem to believe the rumour that the shooting was an accident, some stray bullets from a poacher, and the explosion was an accident, a fire on board, so they have read about it rather than knowing anything firsthand. I've put enquiries in train and I think it best if we were out of here as soon as daylight dawns.

"If you're up to it, madam?" he added, in belated remembrance of my injury.

I assured him I was. I too was anxious to get away from these impostors. "It's like being in a bad dream. One where everything is confused and nothing is what it should be."

We were up with the sun the next day, and left quietly for the pass over the Alps. I left a carefully worded note of thanks for the Raven-Strangs but omitted to mention our address in Venice. If the road had been safe, I thought Carier might have suggested we travel all night, but we had to wait until the guide could see which was road and which was Alp.

I had a terrible day. Worries and speculations about the fraudulent Strangs kept me from looking out too much as we passed dizzying drops and snow-encrusted peaks. "Some people come here on purpose to see these peaks, ma'am," Nichols commented, leaning down from her mount to make sure I was all right.

"I would travel extra mileage to get away from them, if we weren't in such a hurry," I replied, clutching the armrest as though it could save me if I needed it to. I was not impressed by the spectacular scenery. I have never been particularly fond of heights.

Carier had changed our reservations at some of the inns on the road ahead as an extra precaution. "These people tend to choose someone as their targets. They call them conies or marks. Then they play on them until they have what they want, usually money."

"Then you think they're tricksters?"

He nodded. "All my investigations seem to point that way, ma'am."

"Just as well they don't know what we have, then," I murmured. All through the journey Nichols had carried my jewellery in a large bag under her skirts, in case I needed to become Lady Strang again. But I wore only simple jewellery, had my hair dressed in severe styles and wore modest, plain clothes as the wine-merchant's wife.

I had created a character for Mrs. Locke on this journey, one totally unlike me, partly to help the deception, but also to create some amusement for myself. She was an independent lady, used to travelling long distances, though she would usually be with her husband. She was very practical, and liked to oversee her staff personally, much as my sister Martha did. She was childless, but it didn't matter much to the Lockes, as they were not of the landed classes, so didn't have to think dynastically, and my Mrs. Locke wasn't the maternal type. She could speak some languages fluently, and was used to the customs of many countries. On the whole, I thought I should like to be Mrs. Locke, I was sure her life would be intensely interesting. I thought she would keep a journal, and since I have kept one all my life, that wasn't difficult to keep up. I just had to keep any personal references out of it.

After another day coming down the other side of the mountain range, something I do not want to dwell on too much, we reached Piedmont, and I was thankful to be able to ride in a coach again.

The bump on my head had localised to a tender spot, only hurting if touched, I was anxious to get on as quickly as I could. My bruises had all gone now, and the graze on my head left by the bullet had healed completely.

Leaving Turin, we reached Milan in two days. I liked Milan, a busy city with many fine buildings, and a breathtaking cathedral. I wondered what it would be like to be married there, in the sun of Italy, instead of the splendours of Exeter. I made the coachman drive round it twice before we left so I could study it, though I didn't stop to go inside. I wanted to get to Venice.

Due to Carier's vigilance, we didn't see the fake Strangs again, although he was now having them watched. "When we reach Venice," he told me, "I'll have a Thompson's man or two put in their household, so we can find out what they're up to."

I agreed it would be a sensible move. "But I don't want our identity compromised."

"Indeed, ma'am."

It took another three days to reach Venice. It was dark when we arrived, but I insisted we push on, instead of putting up for the night somewhere. I couldn't bear being so close, but not yet there.

I grew increasingly agitated as we drew closer to the city, excited by the prospect of reunion with the man now my husband, my anxieties crowding in on me, taking advantage of my exhausted state.

Richard had known so many women, none of his affairs lasting very long, so I didn't know how long his passion for me would last. Since I knew more about him than I did when I met him, I found more to worry me. His affairs typically followed a flash-flood pattern, reaching high tide quickly and ebbing away just as fast, leaving devastation in their wake.

My love for Richard would last as long as I did, but the fears he had worked so hard to dispel still emerged when I was tired or dispirited. Yes, he'd married me, but I'd been a spinster, most unlike his usual flirts, but that only meant he was ready to beget legitimate heirs for the estate. I tried to dispel my worries. He didn't deserve them, and the concern came from me rather than from him.

We'd committed to each other within our first few weeks of meeting. No warning, no courting, nothing. I'd known of his reputation, but not the pattern it followed and by then, I could do nothing to draw back and think about what I was doing. In any case, I'd fallen for him just as deeply. But if I'd known him better, made his acquaintance, I wouldn't have felt so unsure of myself and where I fitted into his life.

We approached Venice from the land, not over the Lagoon, but I wouldn't have seen much of the city, even had I been looking, as night had long fallen by the time we arrived. At one point, we were transferred into a boat, but by then, I was past caring. It could have been a barge on the Exe for all the notice I took of it.

We were taken to a building on the Grand Canal, and disembarked at a wharf. Carier took us inside and up a flight of steps to the door of the apartment where, if he was not out somewhere, Richard was waiting. We had been apart for a month, but it felt like eternity.

Chapter Six

In the small entrance hall, with a wide-eyed footman bowing, Carier opened a door in front of us and showed me in. I took a deep breath and, holding my head high, went inside.

I found myself in a pleasant drawing room, furnished in fine taste, with large windows that must open to a view over the Grand Canal outside, but the shutters were drawn against the night. The main impression was one of quiet elegance, but I only looked in one direction after one quick glance to take in my surroundings.

He was dressed more simply than I was used to, and he had obviously been taking his ease. A bottle of wine, a half-full glass and a book flung down at an open page reposed on a small table by the side of his chair.

Nobody said anything; the stillness seemed palpable as I stood there, suddenly shy, unable to read the expression in his cerulean eyes.

He got to his feet, smiling, and opened his arms to me. Heedless of anything else, I ran forward and felt them close tightly about me. I rested my head on his shoulder and held him while he held me, feeling his presence like a balm, forgetting the rigours of the journey and the adventures we had been through. I felt him move and realised he must be rubbing his cheek against my hair, over and over as if he wanted to memorise the sensation.

After a time Carier cleared his throat. Richard released me but kept one arm about my waist as he took me to a sofa and sat down with me.

"How did it go?" he asked quietly. "Do fetch yourselves a drink and sit, tell me your news. And bring one for my lady, if you please."

Carier went out of the room and came back with two fresh bottles of wine and some glasses, which he distributed. I was happy to sit on the sofa, Richard's hand warm in mine, sipping my wine while I listened to Carier tell his master what had happened on our journey.

He listened carefully, smiled when Carier said they had hired a clavichord for me at one stage in the journey, but didn't interrupt him as he told the story of the Ravens, and then the accident. He exclaimed, concerned when Carier told him I had been knocked unconscious, but I assured him I was perfectly well now, and the bump had almost gone. Then his face darkened as Carier told him about the Ravens' startling change in identity, and he leaned forward, frowning. "We can't allow this. It might draw unwanted attention here."

Carier put his half-empty glass on a table. "I fear that might be too late, my lord. From what I understand, these people have announced their presence on every stage of their journey." Richard's hand tightened around mine. "You mean I've brought Rose all this way trying to ensure her safety only to drag trouble behind us?" He was not pleased.

"We have two choices here, my lord—to move on, or to use the situation to our advantage."

I had considered that, too. "We might be able to draw this assassin out if we let the Ravens get on with whatever they have planned." I'd had enough of travelling. "We can still continue the Locke story, but watch and wait. We won't be safe anywhere if we don't find out who did this."

Richard was still frowning. "I can't say I like it. My first instinct is to take you away, and leave it to Carier to deal with."

He looked enquiringly at Carier, who nodded. "It would be a sensible precaution, my lord. Will you allow me to suggest a strategy? If you can stay close to the apartment for a few days I will put some of our people in the palazzo they've hired and then we'll know more."

Richard nodded, but was still reluctant. "I don't want any

interruptions, any dangers. But you're right, it might be wise to give it a day or two. We're safe enough here."

Nichols and Carier stood then, preparing to leave. "I owe you both more than usual," Richard said, acknowledging the care they had taken of me on his behalf. "I'll leave this matter up to you for the next few days, if you please, but I'd like to be kept up to date should anything important occur."

Carier and Nichols bowed and quietly left the room. Only then did my husband turn to give me his full attention. My initial tumult had subsided and I could return his smile with one of my own, only a little tremulous. I was nervous. Despite what we meant to each other, it seemed to me that we'd spent an eternity apart. I felt like a stranger again, waiting for his response.

He must have seen my anxiety because his first kiss was very gentle, very courteous, but he slid his arm around my shoulders and I tentatively put my arms around his waist, under his coat. "A little delayed," he murmured, "but none the less desired."

"I missed you so much," I confessed, almost whispering in my nervousness.

He smiled and stole another soft kiss. "That's over now. I made up my mind on this journey I would never willingly let you out of my sight for that long again. Does that dismay you?"

"No."

"Are you hungry, shall I order you something to eat?" Despite his obvious need of me, he still considered my welfare.

Despite my sudden shyness, I couldn't bear any more delays, so I smiled and shook my head.

"Are you tired, my love?"

I couldn't meet his eyes, looking down instead. Heat rushed to my cheeks. "No, I'm not tired, but I would like to go to bed."

He laughed softly and stood, took my hands and drew me to my feet. Then he picked up our empty wine glasses and the bottle we had not yet drunk, and I followed him out of the room and along a corridor, at the end of which he paused. I opened the door, since his hands were full, and we went in.

He deposited the bottle and glasses on a small table by the

unlit fire, then came back to where I stood and closed the door gently behind us. He was so close I could feel the heat radiating from his body, though he didn't touch me. "You heard Carier. He thinks it wise if we remain in the apartment for a few days. Between ourselves," he added, looking at me with a warmth that, perversely, made me shiver, "I had no intention of going anywhere for a while. It would have been a grave blow if we had been forced to move on, but I don't think I could have given up this time with you any longer."

"Carier wanted to put up for the night just outside Venice," I confessed, "but I made him press on. Even if it was midnight, I would have insisted."

He smiled, and in a quick movement gathered me up and pushed his hand into my hair. A shower of pins tumbled down my back. This time his kiss held nothing gentle about it, releasing his passion and need. I returned it, my shyness evaporating chimerically as my desire for him rose in a heated rush. Our mouths opened, tongues met and I knew what I was hungry for. It wasn't food.

I felt his fingers unhooking the front of my gown, as he had done for me twice before, but this time there was no need for any concealment, or anything furtive. I helped him, but when I tried to unbutton his waistcoat he put a restraining hand over mine and drew back so our lips separated. "Let me. I've been thinking of little else for the past few weeks, and I know how I want it to be."

I let him. He undressed me carefully, each garment falling to the floor unheeded by either of us. He touched each part of me newly revealed by the loss of each piece, occasionally brushing kisses across my bare skin, reducing me to incoherent gasps and moans until finally I was stark naked. He was still fully clothed. I had never dreamed of such a situation before, and I found it immensely exciting, something I was unable to hide. The remnants of my shyness only added to my state of arousal and from my heightened breathing and my flushed skin I knew he must be aware of it.

"I want to look at you," he whispered, his lips next to mine and I nodded, beyond words now. He stepped back while I stood unashamed, and let him look.

He took his time, scanning me from head to foot and everywhere in between. It felt like bathing in blue. His voice was thick with hunger when he spoke. "You're as lovely as I remember and twice as desirable."

Taking my hand he led me to the bed, but didn't sit with me. He went over to the table and picked up the bottle and glasses, glancing to where I sat, still waiting, and hardly able to breathe. He poured out two glasses, gave one to me and put the other on the table by the bed.

Then he undressed himself, much faster than he'd stripped me. His gaze rarely left me as his clothes fell on top of mine. He increased my need for him with every garment, until eventually, obviously as aroused as me, he picked up his glass and sat on the bed, still careful not to touch me. "To marriage," he said formally and chimed his glass with mine.

"To marriage," I echoed, my voice unsteady. We drank.

He took both glasses and leaned over to put them down but instead of returning to his previous sitting position, he laid his arm over my shoulders and drew me down to the soft, cool, satin-covered bed. Our first kiss then was a pledge, an unspoken promise, but after that he kissed me with more passion, and I responded eagerly, tasting him, tasting his need for me.

"We have all the time we need now and I can love you as you deserve, at last. How can anyone have thought of you as anything but beautiful?" He lay next to me, one arm holding me close, the other moving over my body in a series of caresses, increasing my desire for him with each smooth stroke until I thought I might dissolve with need. His last caress ended at my breast. He dipped his head and took the nipple into his mouth, turning his tongue around the hard peak.

I caught my breath on the sensitivity he unlocked in me. "Oh, Richard, Richard—" I managed while his hand, still smoothing my skin, but lower, slipped between my legs and gently caressed the tender bud there.

I touched his shoulder and upper arm, felt the thin line of the scar he bore, reminding me what that wound had meant to us both. His hard shaft pressed against my leg, and I pushed against him, hearing his whispered, "Rose my love, you taste wonderful." He kissed my breast and worked his way down to my stomach, making it quiver in tune with my anticipation. It felt so taut and sensitive now, I didn't think I could bear it much longer.

I tried to draw him up, but he resisted, exerting gentle force against me. "Wait—wait. I want to learn your body, know it as well as I know my own. Starting tonight." He kissed me right down to my feet, and then up again, pausing just long enough at the seat of passion to make me moan my need for him, then back up to my mouth, so his body lay over mine. I didn't know it was possible to want someone so much and survive.

He entered me carefully, slowly. We watched each other, knowing this was the first act of married love. I pushed my body up to meet him, to hear his, "Careful, careful my sweet, my precious. I want to make you feel truly, completely loved before I find my peak. If you do that much harder, I don't think I can promise that."

He smiled down at me and I smiled back, my arms wrapped about his back, my legs cradling his. His pause was of necessity, as we hadn't made love for a month, and I'd only ever done it three times in my life, and eager though I was, his body didn't fit so easily into mine.

He took the time to speak to me and move one hand down my body once more, in a long, aching caress. "You're everything I need, all women, all loves. You excite me, make me want you so much I can hardly bear it, but I need to care for you too. Need it."

"I feel that." I lifted my hand to his head, smoothed it down his shoulder bone and lean muscle, and flexed to support his weight. "I wanted you before I knew what it meant. I wanted you to touch me, to feel my skin against yours. It's everything I dreamed of. And more."

He smiled at that and bent his head to kiss me, beginning to move inside me, each stroke taking him deeper, bringing with it the dimly remembered heat that had kept me yearning through all the lonely nights since I last knew this. I knew only he would feel like this. He kissed my neck when I made a wordless sound of love, found the pulse at the base, increasing the ecstasy building deep inside me. "Oh yes," he murmured, his breath hot on my skin.

My head went back when I cried out. He kissed my throat and then my mouth once more, pushing his tongue inside, exploring as he was exploring below. I made a sound deep in my throat, and when he lifted his head I took a deep breath and unable to hold back any longer, arched my back and cried out, "Oh! Oh! Richard—oh, Richard!" past pretty speeches, almost inarticulate.

"Yes! Don't hold back. I'll take care of you, Rose. My sweet wife, my dearest love!" I lost myself, trusting him to take me wherever he wanted to.

It must have taken all his skill and powers of self-restraint to keep me at that height. We'd made love before, but it was nothing like this, this protracted joy, seemingly unending. He knew by some sixth sense when to push hard, when to hold me close.

I'll never know how he held back for so long, but eventually he let himself go, joining me in the heights of love as he called out my name and pushed, unheeding, inside me. I felt the throb and the warmth as he gave me all he had. His head sank onto my shoulder and his ragged breathing heated my skin.

He lay back on to the bed beside me, and we held each other in peace for an uncountable time.

"I love you." I could think of nothing else worth saying at that moment.

"I love you." He kissed my lips and lifted his hand to touch my cheek. I caught it in mine and kissed the palm.

He smiled. "So you won't object to staying in the apartment for a day or two?"

"Does anywhere else exist?"

"Not now."

We lay in blissful silence for a while and then he turned his head to look at me, caressing my body with his gaze. "It's been a long, lonely road, but I've come home at last."

I laughed from sheer happiness, and watched his loving smile in return. This was what I had dreamed of for weeks. I reached my hand across to touch his chest. "Married a month and only made love once since then."

He laughed too. "Give me a few minutes, my angel, and we may be able to put that right." He paused. "Do you think marriage will suit you?"

"It will probably make me sleek and self satisfied," I was still purring inside from his attentions. "But will it suit you?" I was only half joking. It was the fear it wouldn't that marred my happiness.

He saw it. He was certainly aware of my anxiety because I had mentioned it before, despite my determination to keep such things to myself. "You are the culmination of everything that went before. The zenith of womanhood, the peak of desire for me. Why should I risk all this for a second's gratification somewhere else? Why should I want to give this up?" He touched me intimately once, gently.

I shook my head. "I don't know. And you're entitled to me, whatever else you do. But I've known nobody other than you like this, and I think my lack of experience may be my stumbling block. I don't know," I repeated, and then looked away, feeling foolish. He'd broken down all the defences I had built over the years. I couldn't hide anything from him and my fear was as much at finding myself so raw and open to someone else as it was an issue of trust. "I'm afraid if I let you down, I'll never get over it. You have such a hold over me I wouldn't be able to do anything if you should—it would kill me if..."

He took my hand to his lips. "You shouldn't tell me that. You'll give me such an inflated idea of myself I might get too complacent. Then I'll get fat and contented."

He stopped when I laughed derisively. "Fat, you? More likely I'll grow fat, in a few months, maybe."

His head turned sharply, and he stared at me, studying my body with a new alertness. "You've quickened?"

I shook my head. "No."

"It's what my father prays for daily." He touched my stomach with the flat of his hand. "I, on the other hand, would prefer to keep you for myself a little longer, but in this case we must leave matters to Providence." He kissed me again and some time passed before he said anything else. "I can't imagine a situation where I wouldn't want to be near you."

"What if I'm one of those women who seem to quicken every year? I mean to do my duty by the family if I can, but I'm not sure I want thirteen or fourteen children."

He shuddered in an exaggerated way. "What a terrible thought! We'll just have to cope with it if it happens, and pray we aren't too fertile."

"Are there ways we can prevent it?" I had heard of such things, but nobody spoke to a maiden lady about such matters. Well I was a maiden lady no more and I would definitely ensure I learned more about the conditions that would affect my body and how I could better control them. I had every intention of providing my lord's father with the heir he craved and Richard with the children he wanted to have with me, but I would not wear myself out bearing them.

"We'll see about that if it happens. Meantime," he breathed, his lips against mine, "we have this, and each other, and all the time in the world."

I did my best to reciprocate by exploring his body, trying to find out what he liked me to do for him. I had a spot at the base of my throat which, when he kissed it, sent shivers of desire through me. He'd found it early in our relationship and used it shamelessly. I didn't think I had found a corresponding place in him until I put my fingers on the base of his spine and drew my nails up his back. I felt him shudder and pause in what he was doing. I did it again, more firmly, and laughed when I felt him quiver again.

"If you do that too much," he said, "I won't be responsible for anything I do next."

I cried out his name in delight, as he entered me once more, not as gently as last time, more sure of my response. I lifted my legs and wound them around his waist, determined he should stay where he was and gasped when his penetration deepened. I tightened my hold on him, then heard a particular chuckle deep in his throat—the one he made only when he made love to me. He gave a corresponding gasp, echoing the sounds I was making, combining us in ecstasy.

This time it wasn't gentle. His hands on my body were firm and hard. He pushed me to greater heights and joined me there. I forgot who he was, who I was, where we were.

It went on forever, but not long enough. All too soon I felt him climax, shudder and then slump in the moment of surrender, but he didn't leave me immediately. He opened his eyes, took his weight on his hands. I unwound my legs and put my feet back on the bed. He didn't smile, but stared down at me wordlessly, all his exquisite elegance swept away in this torrent of lovemaking. I met his astonished blue gaze with wonder, and we stayed like that for a long time, not speaking, only our breathing making our bodies move. Then he did move and to my astonishment I felt him grow again, fill me once more.

He laughed and I felt the vibrations deliciously in my own body. Joined together, one person. "A miracle, my love, of which we should give thanks and take full advantage." He lifted me so we sat breast to breast, my legs behind him, his under me.

I laid my head on his shoulder and felt the closeness, marvelling at the new thrills coursing through my body, as he loved me again. He kissed my throat. I put my hand up and touched his bright fair hair, feeling the close-cropped silken waves under my hand. I ran my hand down his back, felt his response and then felt mine, as the waves of rapture coursed through me again, and I cried out in joy. I let my body fall back into his arms, and he bent his head to kiss my breasts, taking the nipple into his mouth, brushing it with his teeth and then releasing it again repeatedly, intensifying the sensation.

No longer capable of anything but passion, I let it take me as it would. I gasped I loved him, he was everything, he could go on forever.

Time left us. "Oh Rose! Rose, my love, my love!" We held each other for a while, feeling our hearts beating precisely in time, then he kissed me tenderly and lowered me to the bed.

He went and poured two glasses of wine. He drank his first glass quickly and refilled it, looking ruefully at the mess we had made of the bed, and made me laugh shakily as I too looked about.

I sat up, and tried to straighten the covers, pulling them over us when he joined me again. He put his arm around my shoulders and gave me my glass. "You're an astonishing lover. I discovered something of it when we made love last time. Do you remember what I said?"

"You wanted to explore it—me further." I sipped my wine. I was quite thirsty.

"I still do," he said gently. He looked down at me with a smile but then something made him frown. He took my left hand in his. "I know why you used this ring on the road, but I would far rather you used the ring I gave you from now on—where is it?"

"On the floor, with my clothes. I wore both the rings on a chain around my neck all the time."

He nodded and put his empty glass down before swinging his legs out of the bed and going to search the tumbled heap of clothing on the floor. "By the way," he said casually as he went, "your dressing room is through that door, if you need anything."

That was thoughtful of him. I put down my glass, crossed the room and went through the door he had indicated to a pretty dressing room, where I found the necessary. To my surprise, I wasn't too sore, probably a result of how much I'd needed him, and his skill as a lover. Not that I'd had any intention of telling him even if I was.

After I washed my hands, I picked up a brush and tried to put some kind of order into my hair, but it was useless. It had always been unruly, and even now only Nichols could tame it into shining compliance. I put the brush down again and studied my reflection in the mirror by the light of the single candle I had taken with me. I could see nothing different in the shadowy figure that stared back at me, although I felt everything about me had changed in the last—how long had it been? I had no idea. Hour or so, presumably.

I went back into the bedroom, put down the candlestick and crossed the room to where he waited for me in the bed. He threw back the covers to let me in and then pulled them back over us both. The action seemed thrillingly intimate.

He had found the rings. He removed the old one from my finger and replaced it with my own, topping it with the ruby betrothal ring. "Much better," he said with satisfaction. "I think we can risk the wedding ring when we go out, if not the other. I don't think Mrs. Locke would own such a piece."

"No, she would not. I amused myself while I travelled by

making up quite a character for her. I'm not sure what Lady Strang will be like, though."

"The toast of society," he said without hesitation. "If you should like it. I can help, but you have some qualities of your own that should ensure it."

I laughed at him. I'd never had any illusions about my appeal. "I spent years ignored at Exeter. I don't think London will be any different. The only difference is, I don't care now."

He threaded his fingers between mine. "I don't think the people at Exeter had enough taste to appreciate you. You'll be a great success in London after you're presented."

I meant it when I said I didn't care any more, discovering with surprise that another burden had left me. I yawned unexpectedly, and he laughed and laid me down on the cool, reordered sheets. "I think we'd better get some sleep now, sweetheart."

He got out of bed and extinguished all the candles. I watched him drowsily as he moved with effortless grace around the room. He wasn't consciously aware of his movements but he remained essentially elegant. I was filled with contentment, now I knew we could sleep together without subterfuge.

Richard rejoined me, and gently kissed me. I settled against his chest, his arm around me and sank into a dreamless sleep, knowing I too had come home.

Chapter Seven

I woke and stretched my arms above my head, aware through my closed eyes of the light, but I didn't remember for the moment where I was until I heard Richard's amused voice beside me. "Dear heavens, it's a cat, I've married a cat." I opened my eyes to meet his, so blue I could have dived into them.

"Good morning," I bade him, turning into his warmth.

"Good morning, my sweet love. Are you hungry?"

"For you." I kissed his chest, the nearest part of him I could reach.

He laughed, but lifted my face to his and kissed me properly. "If you can bear to wait a little while, I've ordered breakfast. They'll bring it to us here."

Startled, I began to draw the covers away and get up, but he restrained me by curving his arm around my waist. "Not ashamed, surely, my wife?"

"Never." I leaned against him once more.

"Nichols has already been in, while you were still asleep. She's taken the cast offs away, and she'll see something is brought through to us to eat."

"She's probably used to clearing things away like that."

"She told you then?"

"Bodyguards as sharp as Nichols don't grow up in domestic service."

He laughed. "You're right. I didn't want to tell you in case you objected, but she was the only one I could get at such short notice who could look after you the way I needed."

"Tell me."

"Yes." He gazed at me. "I don't want you hurt. Nothing is more important than that. Nichols came to us looking for work. She had begun as a maid in a big household, but the old story happened when the husband seduced her and the wife threw her out without a character. She was working at a high-class London brothel when she visited us."

"Nichols?" I hadn't imagined my tall, gaunt maid would attract much custom.

He grinned. "It takes all kinds. But no, she was still working as a maid. She prepared the rooms and helped with the more recalcitrant customers, proving so good at the work that she did more protecting than maiding. If that's a word. But she tired of the work, and came to Thompson's with a forged character. Too much of that happened before we set up the agency, but Carier saw something in her and we had her investigated. I had to poach her from a marchioness, but when I asked her personally, she came to work for you. If that offends you, I will replace her, but I would rather not do so until we clear up this mess."

"Why should it offend me? She's the best maid I've ever had. Why, she can even make sense of my hair." I tried to run my fingers through the tangled mass but gave up. He laughed and pushed his hand into the bulk, pulling me up to kiss him.

When the door opened, he was trying to disentangle himself. He made me laugh, but I was helpless against him while he unwound his hand. "Well now I can really say you've tangled me in your coils," he said as he removed the final finger and I could turn to see who had come in.

It was indeed Nichols and she pushed in a table on wheels, filled with pots, plates and dishes. She set out two chairs and only left for my dressing room when she'd arranged everything to her satisfaction. She came back bearing a magnificent dressing gown I had never seen before, but obviously meant for me. It was ivory satin, embroidered with flowers, in a foreign style I was unfamiliar with. I got out of bed and let her help me put it on. Not by a twitch of her face did she betray this scene might not be familiar to her, or that this was not the way I started every day. With a shock like a ribbon of cold water down my spine, I realised this might be the way I started the day from now on.

"Good morning again, Nichols," said Richard, his voice full of mischief.

"Good morning, my lord." She gave him a glance and dropped a brief curtsey.

He threw the covers back and got out of bed. "Do you think we could have the shutters open?" Nichols went over to the windows without comment.

I found it difficult to reconcile myself to my husband's total disregard of servants' sensibilities. Like many of his kind, he seemed to be able to treat them like furniture, unlike my sort, the gentry, who were forced to live in much closer proximity to them. Our houses were much smaller. He wasn't even aware of his attitude, having been brought up to it, but I didn't think I would ever be so unselfconscious in front of servants.

He padded across the bedroom and went into what I assumed must be his dressing room, emerging in a few moments in the extravagant confection I had first seen at Hareton Abbey; a dark blue robe covered in tiny Chinese figures going about their very busy lives.

Nichols poured a cup of chocolate for me, one of coffee for him, and left the room after he said, "Thank you, we'll serve ourselves."

To my surprise, I found I was hungry. "Do you know what time it is?"

"About ten," he replied.

I stared at him, amazed. "I had no idea I slept that long,"

He raised his cup to his lips. "The results of the journey, anxiety, or something else, maybe."

I smiled. "We were awake late."

He laughed, watching me. "Very late. I have an idea there might be more late nights to come, but since we can go nowhere for a few days, it matters little."

I buttered a roll, trying not to think of it while I ate. I found the thought too stimulating to be compatible with making a good meal. "Were you awake long before me?"

"About an hour," he said. "I woke up, and the first thing I saw was you, so I watched you for a while."

I smiled. "You didn't wake me?"

"Why should I? You looked so peaceful, so beautiful, I would have watched you for a lot longer had Nichols not come in."

I laughed then, and nearly dropped my cup. "With my hair like this! And I'll wager I wasn't completely silent. My love, you *must* be besotted."

"I must. Totally besotted." He turned the word into a verbal caress. A thrill coursed through me, following the route previously taken by the imaginary ribbon of cold water.

I pursued my advantage. "This gown is lovely, but it's not mine. Do you think someone might have left it here?" I put my empty cup down and helped myself to bacon and eggs.

He shook his head mournfully. "My reputation precedes me. No, my sweet, I bought it for you. I remembered the serviceable gown I saw you in before and went looking for something more appropriate for you. Besides, don't you remember? I told you I've never brought anyone else here. This apartment was my sanctuary, my place of peace—I came here when I couldn't stand ordinary life any more. Only Gervase knows my exact direction in Venice, and he knows better than to ask for Lord Strang when he comes."

This touched me, more so than his thoughtfulness in the matter of the dressing gown. "So I'm the first woman you've ever brought here?"

"To this apartment, yes." He leaned forward and helped himself to more coffee. "Many men do come to Venice with their mistresses, but it is rather late in the season and I'm hoping that when we finally venture outside we don't meet anybody we know. Once Carier gives the all-clear, of course."

"It's highly unlikely I'll meet anyone. Could you imagine Tom Skerrit and his mistress here?"

That made him laugh again, and I laughed with him at the thought of home-loving Tom setting up a paramour, and then bringing her to Venice. "Where *did* you take your mistresses?" I asked, all innocence.

He raised his eyebrows, smiling. "You know a well-brought-up young lady like you shouldn't ask about those matters."

"But *I* was your mistress until we married," I pointed out.

"Despite my better judgement." He lifted one of the covers. "I had apartments in Paris and here, as well as Rome, but I've sold them all."

I stared. He glanced up at me. "*What* a poor opinion you have of me, my love. I have no need of such places any more, and I wouldn't insult you by taking you there. If we need such establishments, we'll use the Southwood possessions, or buy new. Which reminds me, on our way home we should probably visit Versailles and make you known to the French court, so we will need to make arrangements for that. Should you like that?"

I was shocked at the thought of me, a country gentleman's daughter, being presented at one of the most glittering courts of Europe. "I don't know. If you think I should, then I will, but I have to admit the thought of it makes me nervous."

"I'll be with you," he said softly.

It was very generous of him to think like that. Nervousness and shyness were not often tolerated in the society in which he, and now I must move, being more frequently thought of as a sign of poor breeding.

I smiled gratefully and, finding I had eaten enough, went through to my dressing room to tidy up. He caught my hand as I passed him, and kissed the fingertips. Even that small touch made something inside me melt.

I found Nichols unpacking, so I asked her to brush my hair. I sat back in the chair in front of the mirror, and closed my eyes, totally at ease for the first time in weeks. First, the unpleasant experience of my abduction, then the tension engendered by the wedding, then the long tedious journey here had all conspired to undermine any serenity I might have possessed. But it all seemed so far away now, as I sat in the little room in the Venetian sunshine feeling my tangled mass of curls being turned into a shining sheet by firm and expert hands. I felt sleek and loved, like the cat Richard had compared me to.

I wouldn't let her pin my hair up, or put a cap on top of it, but went back into the bedroom, where the trolley had now gone. Richard sat at his ease, waiting for me. He got up, took my hands and drew me close to kiss me and then he released me to run his hand through my hair, which he could now achieve successfully. "Such a temptation."

"Me?"

"You."

I slid my hands under his robe and I felt him fold his arms around me, holding me tight. I put my head up for his kiss, and knew I wouldn't be going much further than the bedroom that day.

Much later, I lay on my stomach on the bed. My husband was stroking my back from the shoulders down, slowly repeating the movements, filling me with a contented, dreamy drowsiness. I was able to look around and take in my surroundings properly.

The spacious bedroom was charming, simply but beautifully furnished in light colours with touches of gold. The bed was draped with embroidered white and blue satin, the drapes pulled well back to let in the light. To spare our blushes there were gauzy curtains at the windows that let in the bright May sunshine but ensured we weren't overlooked. We were at least one storey up and probably more, the tops of buildings visible below the bright blue sky. The stone fireplace in the chamber appeared older than the rest of the furnishings but it was unlit, the day being warm.

"What is this place?"

He didn't stop his caresses. "It's an old palazzo that's seen better days. From the outside it's unremarkable enough, but the view is lovely—" He broke off and I turned my head to see him looking at me, smiling. It was clear he didn't mean the view over the Grand Canal. "It was owned by some grandee who came to a sticky end a hundred years ago after a meteoric rise and a great fall, the kind Italians seem to specialise in."

"The only Italian I'm really familiar with is Machiavelli. Ian and I read *The Prince* together one rainy summer years ago." I let my mind slip back to that time when I was still hopeful, still eager to appear at the local assemblies, sure someone would want me. My quiet, scholarly brother introduced me to things other than fashion. I had reason to be grateful to him as I'd now married a man with an agile, intelligent mind.

"A name to conjure with," he said now. "Machiavelli worked for Cesare Borgia, who was the pattern for many a petty prince of the time. A Pope's son, no less."

I turned over so I could look at him properly. "You're joking! How can a Pope have a son?"

"The same way anybody else has one, my sweet." He smiled at my naïveté. "Roderic Borgia was the first Pope to acknowledge them as his children, though many had paraded their nieces and nephews in front of the Papal court before him."

"I suppose Ian thought I was too delicate to be given such information," I said, smiling. "His sense of chivalry must be greater than I thought. I shall have to rely on you to tell me the scandals attached to the classics, won't I?"

He gave a short laugh. "You should ask Gervase. He knows far more than I do. He used study and research as his crutch when his lover left him languishing in Rome."

"Poor Gervase." I thought of Richard's brother, how he'd been forced to give up the man he loved for the sake of society and convention. I understood so much more since I'd fallen so hard for Richard. Unlike ours, Gervase's love story had no happy ending.

Richard shrugged. "He seems to have done well enough since."

I wasn't shocked at his seeming callousness. I knew much of the story, and guessed some of the rest. Gervase had run off with his male lover, a respectable married man, thus outraging society's morals and its territorial imperatives in one go. The lover had been persuaded to return after six months, but Gervase had spent the next eleven years abroad, eventually returning from India so wealthy that people would forgive him anything.

Richard had been forced to face the consequences at home, and only Gervase and I really knew how much that experience had damaged him. He had faced it, become cold and uncaring, a strong citadel, until I had stormed the ramparts I wasn't even aware of, seeing only him and my need of him, not knowing enough of his history then to know what I had done.

"Have you heard from Gervase about the shooting—and the explosion?" I asked Richard now, this being the first time I had thought of it since yesterday.

He shook his head. "Nothing. He'll let us know the moment Thompson's turns anything up, but either he's not been successful yet or the information is still on the road."

"I saw the explosion—or at least the aftermath." His hands stopped their rhythmical caresses and he stared seriously at me. "I was on the packet that left that morning. The yacht exploded, Richard, it didn't catch fire and it was no accident. Only then did I appreciate the precautions you were making us take, and only then I was glad of it."

He stared at me, his eyes bleak, then touched my cheek. "It must have shocked you." I nodded. "I saw nothing. I went the other way, took passage that night, so I was in France by the time it happened."

"You haven't told me about your journey," I reminded him.

"There's nothing to tell, really. I've taken it before, although the sea passage was different, but I was soon on the usual road again. I travelled mainly on horseback, and I took public transport when I tired or when I took to the water. I kept travelling as much as I could to get here first, and make sure everything was in order. I made enquiries with people I could trust, left messages and made sure you weren't followed."

"How did you do that?"

"I had people watching as you passed. They would have killed anyone suspicious if they felt the need. I was taking no chances with you, my sweet life."

I was startled at his ruthlessness on my behalf. I realised at that point he was quite capable of killing the Ravens if they became dangerous to us. I knew I meant as much to him as he did to me, and I wondered if I would kill for him. Reluctantly, I realised I might very well do so.

"I would have been safer staying in Devonshire and

marrying Tom Skerrit after he confessed his passion for me, wouldn't I?"

He lifted his brows and I realised I had inadvertently let out Tom's secret. I was at once sorry for it. "I didn't mean to tell you about Tom. You won't tell him you know, will you?"

He touched my shoulder in a gentle caress. "I knew already. I saw the way he looked at you sometimes, when he thought no one was watching. When did he tell you? Was it when you were captured?"

I nodded. "Yes. I thought it was just the appalling mess we found ourselves in, but it's not so. He said he realised he loved me when I went to Yorkshire, and he missed me more than he thought he would."

Richard stared at my midriff, lost in thought. "I see. So I'm fortunate he didn't realise before?"

I took his hand. "A marriage with Tom would have been suitable, far more than one to Steven Drury. Before I met you, I'd have been happy to accept him, for friendship's sake, but when I saw you I knew what I wanted. Or at least, when I saw you after the accident, when you were hurt and you needed help. Before that, you seemed remote, someone almost inhuman."

He gazed at me, through me as if he wasn't seeing me, his expression unfathomable. "I wanted it that way. I cut myself off from the world but the first time I saw you everything changed. I had reconciled myself to a life without love but with as much power as I could draw to myself. Julia was part of that, you know."

"How so?"

"I knew she could never touch me emotionally. I didn't know she had any kind of feelings for me, other than triumph. I never wanted this, you know; you've disrupted my life completely." He looked at my face and seemed to come back to me. The glow returned to his eyes.

I smiled at him, glad I'd disrupted such a sad life, glad I'd had the courage to accept his word, to let him see how much I wanted him. He had so much to offer it would have been a tragedy to put all that aside.

I put my hand up. He caught it and carried it to his lips, his gaze never leaving mine. "I still don't understand what it was about me. No, don't pay me any extravagant compliments, but look at it from the outside. I was a daughter of the gentry, overlooked by my peers, no style, in deepest black after the first week I met you. I never understood why you should look at me. Lizzie is far more beautiful than me, and Julia Cartwright too, everything a fashionable lady should be. I'll never stop thanking God that you chose me, but I'll never understand why." It was the truth, and a measure of my trust in him that I chose to tell him the secrets my pride had kept close for so many years.

He kept hold of my hand and gave me truth for truth. "I flirted with marriage for years. I chose the most dazzling debutantes, encouraging them and then abandoning them. They called me dangerous, but I was looking for something I didn't understand. The first time I saw you, I knew. Do you remember?"

I remembered his cold, blue stare, the incredulous glance from Gervase as he recognised what his brother had just felt. "I thought you were looking at Lizzie."

"I never noticed her. Most unlike me," he said smiling. "It was always you, and I knew if I didn't have you I was doomed. I suddenly understood what I would be missing in a loveless life."

"So you're not here with Julia, but with me."

He sat completely still, all his attention on my face. "I would *never* have brought Julia here." He grinned and his mood lightened. "She would have made me sell it and buy something more appropriate to her station."

"I like it."

"You've only seen the drawing room and the bedroom," he said smiling.

"That's all I need to see." I reached my hands up and pulled him down to kiss me and love me again.

I was becoming more adventurous in my loving, feeling more secure. I knew he was a connoisseur of the art, but he was letting me find my own way and become more confident in what I did. Comfortably lying on a bed in the afternoon with a man, both of us naked would have been beyond my understanding a year ago. Being able to initiate the act of love would have been completely foreign to me, but with Richard, it felt so natural.

He seemed to enjoy my enthusiasm, my desire to explore, and this time he took my hand, showed me what to do to please him, and I accepted it gladly—touched him and felt his shaft harden beneath my hand.

He kissed me. "Do you remember when you showed me your poor bruised body, I promised to kiss every bruise away? Well I couldn't do it then, but I think I can remember where most of the marks were."

I swear he kissed every inch of me, lingering at my breasts, and coming to a halt at the most intimate part of my body. His close examination left me with no blushes, but moaning with the need for his touch. He made me wait before he touched, explored, kissed, with a lavishness I had never known before. He sent me to heights I would never have imagined existed before I knew him until there was only one thing I wanted. I squirmed under him restlessly, but he wouldn't let me go, holding my hips firmly so he could plunder me and drive me insane with wanting him.

He murmured, "Sweet as honey," and then he came inside me.

With one powerful twist of his body, he turned us so I was on top. Pushing against the bed, I sat up, delighting in the control he had just given me and the sight of his beautiful body under me. He waited for me with a smile curving his mouth. When I moved, I heard him catch his breath in a responsive "Ah!" I laughed, joy and bliss combined.

It was my turn to give pleasure, but I received as much as I gave. I rode him, as he'd shown me, but my riding skills were improving all the time and I added a few variations he didn't expect until I had him groaning my name. He tried to turn under me, but I didn't want to surrender my control, so I planted my knees firmly on either side of his body, and carried on. I urged us both on, felt his hands on my breasts, on my waist, losing their careful elegance in favour of fumbling urgency.

He drew up his knees so I could lean back against them,

and then pulled me by my hips hard on to him. I cried out in exultation. Then I found I couldn't think any more, so I let him take over. He sat up to take me in his arms and drove us both on to satisfaction.

We sank on to the bed, wet with sweat, exhausted by passion, and lay there for a long time, twined around each other.

"My God, my God," he whispered, laughing a little. "Have you been taking lessons?"

"It just seemed right."

He kissed my shoulder. "Oh, it was right. If I hadn't taken your virginity myself, I would swear you were born to it."

I don't think he would have said that if he'd been cogent. I sat up starkly. "Whore's tricks?"

He sighed. "Better than that. You're a very fast study, my love." He opened his eyes and looked at me with an expression that made me catch my breath, serious and open. I knew then that he'd never opened his soul like that to anyone before. "Never judge yourself by the narrow standards of others. What we do together here is our business, nobody else's. Never, never doubt what we have just done is anything but love. Never let yourself be restricted by thoughts of what society would have you do, what it would accept or condemn. Please promise me that."

"Yes, I promise," I whispered.

"I love you," he went on, cerulean eyes intent on mine. "I would love you if you hated making love. That you don't is a joy almost beyond bearing." He pulled me back into his embrace and I went gladly, so we lay quiet for a while, enjoying the glow that comes after love.

"Do you know how special you are?" Richard murmured.

"Only to you."

"Isn't that enough?"

I turned my head so I could see his face "More than enough my love. In truth I don't know what's happening to me, but I have to let it go on, to see what comes next."

"Probably me. I couldn't have waited for you all these weeks, had I known any of this." He drew me close and kissed me. "Thank you."

"You're welcome," I said primly. I propped myself up on one elbow. "Do you think I would make a good whore?"

"I beg your pardon?" He was truly astonished, his brown eyebrows arching almost to where his hair tumbled over his forehead in golden disorder.

"Well, I wondered recently what a hundred-pound-a-night whore would have to do to earn it. It can hardly be what we've just done, that was too wonderful to be bought, so what do they do?"

He laughed, loud and long. "Such a mixture! Innocence and wantonness!" He drew me back down. "Hundred-pound whores are efficient, beautiful at least in their bodies, and clean. And fashionable. If a man can say that he's had, say, Kitty Fisher, it gives him certain kudos amongst his contemporaries. What we just did doesn't compare in any way."

"You won't tell anyone I said that?"

He smoothed the hair back off my cheek in a gentle, proprietorial gesture. "Who would I tell? This is our marriage bed, as secret as the confessional. This can't be for anyone else."

"I know. I suppose I'm just a—well, overwhelmed is the nearest I can get to it."

He laughed and kissed me. "I have to admit it. So am I."

Chapter Eight

I didn't see any more of the apartment for another day, nor did I wish to. I would willingly have stayed there with him for much longer, but time passed and the world would eventually catch up with us.

The next day Richard took me on a tour around the apartment. It took up one story of the old palazzo, the first floor, the one that would once have held the state apartments. Other people occupied the rest of the building. We shared the kitchens with the other occupants, and our floor contained our personal servant's quarters and our rooms. There was the drawing room I had already seen, a dining room, another bedroom, a smaller reception room, and then he opened the door on to a room, which, he said, was for me.

I clapped my hands together in childlike delight when I saw the lovely harpsichord set by the window. I could look outside as I played, but the instrument was set so the sunshine wouldn't dazzle me. It was a pretty thing, inlaid with musical instruments depicted in marquetry, joined together with bows and knots of ribbon in green olivewood. He'd had it tuned the way I preferred, in the new style, and he watched as I lifted the lid, sat down and ran my hands over the keys.

He sat on a small sofa where he could watch me, and I played a little piece, one I knew well, to see how it played. The tone was lovely, fine and pure.

I found some sheet music and I played for him. I didn't play for anyone except myself as a rule, but Richard loved music and so I played for my husband, for my love. I don't know how long I played because I always lost time when I concentrated like that, and Richard didn't interrupt me at all, content to sit back and listen. I must have played for some time because when I stopped the sun had moved across the sky and hunger gnawed at my stomach.

I put down the lid of the harpsichord, sat back, and for the first time, I looked out of the window. I caught my breath in wonder.

I hadn't realised how beautiful Venice could be. The old buildings on the other side of the Canal glowed in tones of honey and terracotta, highlighted with flashes of white stone, dark marks at the base where the water lapped at high tide. The pure gold of the sun bathed it all in a glow the like of which I had never seen before.

I lost myself until I felt my husband's hands on my shoulders. I put up my hand to cover one of his. The blue-grey water of the Canal glinted with white when the gondolas passed, never calm, always mobile. "I didn't know it was this lovely."

He said nothing, but watched the scene in front of us with me. Then he took my hand and drew me to my feet. "Come."

I hadn't noticed the window of this room was full length, or that it opened on to a balcony outside. I was self-conscious in just the dressing gown, but it was a substantial garment, and I pulled it closer around me as he took me outside.

The broad balcony outside ran the length of the building, and as he opened the window, Richard let all the sounds of Venice in. The shouts of the boatmen, the sound of the everlasting water, all came up to greet us when we went outside, but no one noticed us, of little importance in that stunning scene. I leaned on the wall at the front of our balcony and watched the activity below.

"It used to be a lot livelier than this," Richard commented, "but Venice has lost a lot of its trade in recent years to Trieste and Leghorn."

I watched a gondolier negotiate the Canal. "I've never seen anything quite like this,"

"There is nothing else quite like this. The people here are

different to most other Italians, their patois is different, and nowhere else I know of has this feeling in the air."

"I love it. Why can't we live here, stay here forever, forget everything else?" I turned to him, smiling, and he watched me through eyes narrowed against the sun, the expression on his face, in his eyes, full of love and contentment.

"The way you put it, it almost sounds possible."

"Why not?" I knew as well as he did we had to go back sometime, but the conceit seemed to amuse him. "What if we *had* been killed, or pretended that we were—permanently? I never wanted to be a viscountess, I just wanted you. I have a feeling life as Mrs. Locke would be exactly what I wanted."

I could see the smile lurking in his eyes. "A wine merchant, who travels around the countryside, and locates the best vintages? Perhaps, my love. But it would leave Gervase rather exposed, wouldn't it?"

"Perhaps he should take a turn." I smiled at the thought. "He would make a very good earl, in the course of time, and if he made the effort, I'll wager he could even manage to make an heir."

Richard frowned. "I fear it's too late for that."

"You know he proposed to me once?" I said impulsively.

"*What!*" I had all his attention now, the lovely scene in front of us forgotten. "Gervase? Why should he do that?"

"It was while you were still contracted to marry Miss Cartwright. He thought if he married me, you could fulfil your obligations, and still have me. You had said you wouldn't consummate the marriage with her, even if she forced you to the contract, so if I produced a child by you, it would still be the heir your father wants. Don't be angry with him. He said he owed you a lot, and perhaps he could help."

"Dear God!" Richard exclaimed, nearly speechless for once. He leaned on the wall with his elbows, chin in his hands, brooding. I watched the Canal for a while, to give him a chance to assimilate what I had just told him. Eventually he looked at me again. "You know I would never have allowed it?"

"I know it now."

"I've always wanted you for my wife, so I could share my life with you, not just my bed," he said, not touching me, but leaning on the balcony, as I was doing. "Even if your bed was available to me, it wouldn't have been all I wanted. A little bit of scandal would have been a small price to pay to have you to myself. I only wanted to spare you the opprobrium of society. Did you ever take his proposal seriously?"

"He offered it to me as an alternative, in case it became impossible for us to marry," I said. "He didn't want to see you lose me, you see."

He turned then, and looked at me. "I had plans for us to elope. You knew that, but you didn't know how far I went with the plan before it became irrelevant. I used it to get us here, to Venice. I never told you that, did I?"

"I would have gone with you, if you'd only offered me a *carte blanche*." I took his hand. "It was kind of Gervase, but I don't think I would have gone through with it, though I wanted you so much that I might have done it just to be close to you."

His intimate smile warmed me somewhere deep inside. "Too late now I fear. You're mine now, signed and sealed."

"So I am." He drew me into his arms and tenderly kissed me, heedless of anyone who might be looking.

"I wouldn't have made Julia a very good husband," he said then, his arm comfortably about my shoulders. "I hope Steven Drury suits her better."

I was surprised. "You don't wish her any ill?"

"No. I wronged her after all, by trying to break the contract between us. However if the Drurys are behind the attempt on your life, yes, I wish her ill. I saw Drury at his worst, I'm guessing, when I'd taken you from him, but his behaviour then does not give me a good impression of him. Tell me, in a more temperate mood, in your opinion, could Drury have agreed to this?"

I considered it, frowning until he kissed it away for me. "I think so. He hated me enough at the end. He wanted me for the small dowry I had at the time and the social standing, not for anything of me. At first, I was the most desperate and the most eligible of the young ladies available but when James inherited the title, that made him more determined to have me. I thought he might have been happy with Julia, a member of society and much richer than I will ever be, but now I'm not so sure. Perhaps together they're worse than they would be apart." I was idly watching one of the boatmen, while he struggled to free his pole from the edge of the Canal, where it had stuck fast. Somehow, it seemed far more real than the thought of Steven and Julia plotting together.

"It's what I've been afraid of," Richard admitted. "That together they might be more dangerous than apart. I placed Thompson's men in their household, I had them put there when they returned from their elopement, but I don't know what they did while they were away."

They could have planned our assassination then and made the arrangements. No, I still couldn't believe it. I still thought the Cawntons were behind the attack.

The gondolier finally freed himself and poled away, intent on his business. The Drurys seemed so far away now. "Couldn't someone else have done it?"

"Any number of people might try, but to do it like that, on our wedding day, looks to me like revenge of the most personal kind. I'm sure the Cawntons weren't so very distraught about the way matters turned out for them. They lost one big haul, but regained control of their organisation when Norrice Terry died. We parted on as good terms as you can in such circumstances but there might have been someone in their organisation who supported Norrice Terry enough to look for revenge for his death."

"Not his wife and daughter?"

"Not if he abused them like he abused you. No one, save the most perverted, would want that." His sombre expression made me sorry we had ever broached the subject.

"But I'm here, and well, and happy," I reminded him.

He lifted his head from his contemplation of the Canal and looked at me, and his expression lightened, became something else. "So you are," he agreed, and took me indoors again.

The following day Carier returned to the apartment with news. Nichols had served us during the last few days, and

Richard had contrived to shave himself, although he complained it took him twice as long as it took Carier to do it. We'd still not dressed properly, luxuriating in the freedom from society's rules, the lack of visitors, and our pleasure in each other. But Richard had insisted on a proper dinner that day. He claimed he needed the nourishment, and that I would wear him out, so it was served to us in the dining room for the first time, although I doubted we would have time to dress properly.

Nichols brought word to us in the middle of the afternoon, where we sat by the window in our bedroom with a pot of coffee, supremely at our ease. She told us Carier had returned with news, and waited for us in the drawing room, so we went straightaway.

Carier studied us curiously when we went in, but his expressions were always hard to read. I hadn't even known if he approved of me until Richard told me he did. We sat together on the sofa I first used when I'd arrived.

"Carier?" Richard prompted him.

He cleared his throat. "I've discovered something, my lord. I thought I'd tell you as soon as I heard it."

Richard nodded. "About the false Strangs or the disturbances at home?"

"The false Strangs, my lord. We've heard nothing from England yet." He drew out a sheet of paper from his pocket and consulted it. "It was easy to place some of our people in his household. They seem determined to make a splash, and they're recruiting everywhere. When they called themselves Ravens, it seems to have been the truth. I had the good fortune to find someone who recognised them from a previous time, and who could give me some very useful information—with a little persuasion." I wondered if the persuasion was pleasant or the opposite, and decided I would rather not know. Carier continued. "They use the name Ravens frequently, and for all we know it is their true name. They're card sharpers, my lord."

Richard grimaced in distaste. "That's all? Common card sharpers?"

"Yes, my lord, although they prefer to operate on the grand scale."

"But I don't play cards above the social level, everybody knows that. Why choose my—our name?" He glanced at me apologetically and we exchanged a smile.

"They know you're away on your bride-trip, my lord, and you could be anywhere, since you seem to have given society the slip." Carier gave just the hint of a smile. "They're careful to avoid anyone who knows you—"

Richard leaned forward, interrupting him. "Who is in Venice who knows us, Carier?"

"Freddy, my lord, and one or two others who know you slightly, but I've been unable to locate anyone else," the valet replied.

Richard pulled a face. "Oh Lord, I think we'd better try to see Freddy and apprise him of the situation, just in case he goes to visit the false Strangs."

"Just so, my lord. No one here knows her ladyship," he continued smoothly.

I smiled wryly. "I'm not surprised, but the Ravens don't seem to know me either."

"I would be inclined to agree, my lady," Carier said. "The gentleman tries for a passable imitation of your lordship, but the lady seems to have very little to go on. She is a brunette, and she rarely powders, but those seem to be the only connections she has with your ladyship."

"So they've seen me, but not my wife," Richard mused. Warmth curled through me when he used the word wife. "Well that wouldn't be difficult. Where are they living?"

Carier turned his well-used piece of paper over. "In the Palazzo Barbarossa, further down the Canal towards the Lagoon, my lord. They are making a splash, spending money lavishly."

"Is it theirs? Or have they run up bills for me to pay?" asked Richard then.

"I have dealt with that aspect, my lord," replied the manservant smoothly. "They are finding credit hard to come by when they try to use your name."

"I'm glad to hear it. When I spend money, I like to get the benefit of it." Richard leaned back, relieved of that care.

Carier bowed. "I have made extensive enquiries and I'm almost completely sure they had nothing to do with the attacks on your lives in England." I sighed in relief, and I felt Richard take my hand and press it. "They were elsewhere when the attempts took place and they haven't enough money, or indeed the desire to do such a thing."

Richard's expression lightened. "So they're simple tricksters?"

"I have every reason to believe so, my lord," said his valet.

Richard looked up. "In that case," he said, his eyes glittering with mischief, "I should very much like to meet these people. Should you like to visit them, my love?"

I could see no harm in it. "I would like you to meet them. If I hadn't been so anxious on the road, I might have found some amusement in it."

"Do you think it would amuse me?"

"Undoubtedly."

Richard never relied on his consequence for the sake of it, and I thought he would enjoy meeting "himself," and perhaps derive some fun from it. After all, we could call a halt at any time, merely by announcing our identities.

Richard glanced at me, and then at Carier. "And I want the Ravens watched closely. The assassin may yet arrive."

"Doesn't he know us by sight?"

Richard shrugged, the blue dressing gown catching the light of the sunlight streaming through the window. "I don't know. What do you think, Carier?"

Carier spoke slowly. "The assassin may not know you by sight, my lord, in fact I am beginning to doubt that he does. Killing a man and wife on their wedding day doesn't imply personal knowledge. Nor does planting gunpowder on their yacht. Here, you are Mr. and Mrs. Locke and I believe you are safe while that remains the case."

Richard looked at me, his eyes clouded with concern. "I don't want my wife put at any risk. What do you think?"

"I think, my lord, we should ensure her ladyship is always accompanied by Nichols. She is the best available, and there wouldn't be much risk if she gave the matter her full attention."

Richard frowned at his valet. "She is good, I know that."

I was tired of being talked about. "Don't I have a say?"

Richard smiled in agreement. "Of course you should."

"I'd like to stay, for now," I said. "I'd like to see more of Venice, and I'd like to see these impostors with you. If there's any risk, then naturally I'll leave, but not alone. Where you are, there I am."

He took my hand and kissed it lightly. "Oh yes. I won't let you go on your own. Not again."

"If I may suggest, my lord."

Richard waved a negligent hand. "Suggest away."

"If you could take her ladyship on a small outing tomorrow, dressed as the Lockes, I could contrive to follow you and have you followed so we might observe anyone who took an interest in you."

Richard stroked his chin. "It's a thought." He glanced at me. "We could leave Rose here—"

"No." I scotched that before it went any further. "I think Carier's right and if the assassin is here, he doesn't know us by sight outside our usual milieu. The Ravens certainly did not. There's no harm in discovering it for sure."

Richard nodded and turned to Carier. "Very well. Make the arrangements, if you please. We can achieve little today. We'll walk down and send in our cards tomorrow, but for now, keep up the vigilance, and try to find Freddy."

"Yes, my lord." Carier bowed and left.

Richard turned to me, and his tone lowered to an intimate purr. "We have an hour before dinner and I haven't made love to you for at least four hours. Could you bear it before you dress?"

"Oh yes," I breathed. He put his hands under my arms and drew me close.

The next morning I woke and it felt right, natural. Real. Richard was still asleep, so I moved closer, laid my cheek on his back and slid my arm around his waist. I must have woken him however, because he turned slowly, and put his arms around me. His eyes were still closed, but he was smiling. "Good morning, sweet wife."

"Good morning, dearest husband." I snuggled into his warmth.

The next time I looked up at his face his eyes were open. "I wonder," he said slowly, in his rich, low voice, "if I'll ever get used to this."

"I'm not sure I want to." I tilted my head for his kiss. "After these last few days, I'm more used to being naked with you than I am clothed."

He chuckled. "I'm very glad to hear it."

I reached down and touched his morning erection. I loved that he woke hard, although he explained it happened to many men, even when alone. I had a lot to learn, but I knew this particular hardness was mine. He laughed and swung me on to my back. "Hussy! What *have* I done? Perhaps I should have insisted on the traditional wedding night!"

I walked my fingers over his chest. "Which would be...?"

"The bride is fully robed in her new, voluminous night rail and cap. Her friends put her into the marital bed and leave her there. She sits and waits tremulously for her new husband." He closed his eyes and fluttered his eyelashes in imitation of the tremulous bride, but he ignored my laugh. "The groom enters with his friends, who have had a great deal of fun disrobing him and arraying him in his nightwear. They're all drunk, because it's the only way the groom can get his courage to come to the sticking point. After all, he hardly knows the girl."

He stopped and kissed me. "I needed sustenance. To continue. They pull back the sheets, exposing her shivering with fright. They put him in, to the accompaniment of ribald joke usually only considered appropriate for the dining room after the ladies have retired, but are now considered perfectly all right for the poor, quivering virgin. Then they leave them. She is terrified, he is drunk, and they must make the best they can of it." He paused, and looked down at me. "In the old days they would wait until the couple had actually consummated the marriage, claiming it was necessary to witness it to prevent annulments. All good sport, I've no doubt."

"I would pretend," I said, after I had thought about it.

"But you're a virgin. You know how the animals copulate, but you don't know what humans look like. You probably know what they sound like." I smiled, thinking back to the house I was brought up in. A small manor house where sounds carried in the night. "But you don't quite know what to do, and your new husband is so drunk he can't help you. A fine start to a marriage; no wonder so many fail."

"Do you think ours will fail?"

"Not if I have anything to do with it."

"But no one saw us consummate our marriage!" I said, pretending shock.

"Do you think anyone, seeing us over the last few days could doubt it?" His voice became a caress as he bent his head to kiss me again.

"No," I breathed, when I could.

"No?" He lifted his head to look down at me.

"No, no one could doubt it."

"Oh." He bent his head to me again.

"Richard?"

"Hmmm...?"

"Aren't we supposed to get up today?"

"Eventually."

"Can you do that again?"

"This?"

"Oh yes!"

As a result we were later rising than we had planned, and we breakfasted in our bedroom again. When I went through to my dressing room, I felt almost strange, getting into my day clothes after so long without them. Nichols said little, but went efficiently about her business of turning me into Mrs. Locke.

I watched her in the mirror. She dressed my hair into a tight knot, then fastened a serviceable cap over it, and laced me into a simple blue gown of good, but not best, silk. No elaborate embroidery for Mrs. Locke, a simple row of silk bows covered her stomacher, the robings of the gown edged with braid. Even her stockings were plain. I thought I might like Mrs. Locke, had she existed, but another part of me admitted I liked the finery Lady Strang was now expected to wear.

When I went into the drawing room, I had to wait for Richard to arrive, and when he did, a harassed-looking Carier followed close behind him. "My lord, you can't wear that lace. Mr. Locke would never have lace that fine."

"But I have to have *something*," my husband protested, "You seem to think Mr. Locke has no pride at all in his appearance."

"Some people do not, my lord," Carier protested.

"He must have some idiosyncrasy."

I pulled something out of my pocket, something I had forgotten over the last few days. "What about this?" I held out the diamond pin he had given me in England.

Richard laughed and took it from me with a smile of thanks, but he didn't put it on. "Now even I know that's too fine," he said, handing it over to Carier instead. "No, I'll keep the lace. Perhaps Mr. Locke, keen to impress a lord, might put on his finest lace, but he wouldn't stretch to a solitaire of this size."

"No indeed, my lord." Carier left the room to take the pin away.

"Well?" my husband demanded. He opened his arms and let me look at him.

I was forced to laugh. I had never seen him so plainly dressed. He wore a tawny coloured cloth coat with plain buttons, his waistcoat, instead of the finely embroidered creations he usually wore, an ordinary one, trimmed with only the lightest of braids. The lace at his wrists and neck, while good, wasn't the finest, and his neckcloth was of plain white linen.

But what made me laugh most was the wig he wore. He usually sported a powdered, tied back wig, with a queue, or a silk bag and solitaire, the thin black ribbon that comes round to tie at the front of the neck over the stock. Instead of these fashionable items he wore a plain bob wig, a short wig that finished at the shoulders, lightly frizzed, the sort men of business and elderly gentlemen tended to prefer.

"Why, you look almost ordinary."

He smiled to see my amusement, not at all put out. "Didn't I tell you once, that fine clothes can make a difference? Do you believe me now?"

I couldn't allow him to be ordinary. "No. There's still something about you that marks you out as special. The way you think must show through, too." I regarded him thoughtfully. He was a remarkable man for sure and there was still something of intelligence and grace about him, despite the disguise. I was sure my partiality for him did not overweigh my consideration. I gave up for the time being and crossed the room to put my hand on his arm.

"One more thing before we go," he said. "Outside this apartment we're sir and madam."

"I can remember that. Probably better than you. I've been ma'am all my adult life. It's 'my lady' I still find difficult."

"I suppose so." He laid his free hand over mine. "But that is what you are now."

"A small sacrifice."

He opened the door for me and we went out of the apartment for the first time since I had arrived in Venice.

I hardly remembered what lay outside, such was the nature of my agitation when I arrived. A staircase went down two floors to the main entrance, where a boatman with his gondola waited outside. Richard informed me we had our own gondola, as most people here did, much as at home we would have our own carriage but since he preferred to live here privately, it wasn't adorned with coats of arms or monograms. The boatman didn't row the gondola, he poled it, and after Nichols and Carier climbed aboard behind us and we settled, the man poled it away from our building and set off down the Grand Canal towards the Lagoon.

Fascinated, I watched Venice pass. The buildings that faced the Canal were mostly grand and palatial, and although made out of similar material, so different in style to each other as to be like foreigners. Modern buildings nestled next to others that were obviously hundreds of years old, all with that dark, high-water mark. Richard informed me some of the buildings, especially the ones closest to the Lagoon could be awash at certain times of the year. The owners would live upstairs or further inland. It was so different to anything I had known before. While Richard took his ease, watching me and the passing scenery, I leaned forward to see as much detail as I could.

I turned to him eagerly. "When you met me I'd just been on the longest journey of my life, from Devonshire to Yorkshire. Now I'd like to see more of the world."

He took my hand. "Then we shall. But there's nothing else remotely like Venice anywhere I know of."

"I've heard Amsterdam has the canals."

"It has a different feel," he said. "Have you noticed the light here?"

I looked about. "It's golden, but I thought was because I was here and in love. Everything would be golden."

He smiled. "It probably would, but even when not in love, the light is still there. I've spent time here in abject despair, and the light has helped to console me." I felt a pang for him. He'd let no one see that before me. His nature and his pride had kept him from it.

We began to pull in now, threading our way through other gondolas towards a large building on the other side of the Canal to our own. Our gondolier exchanged words with others on the Canal, but although they sounded interesting, my schoolroom Italian wasn't up to a translation. Still, I listened, and tried to differentiate some of the words and commit them to memory, because they might come in useful sometime. I glanced at my husband and saw him watching me, a lazy smile on his face. I could feel myself blushing, and as we came in to the mooring, he murmured, "Hoyden," so only I could hear.

We sent our cards up, or rather the Locke's cards, and waited in the gondola. Very soon, a liveried manservant came down to us. Richard's mouth set in a hard line when he recognised the blue and white livery his family used. Although the masquerade had amused him in theory, the practice might infuriate him.

He said nothing when the man indicated we should follow him. We climbed out of our gondola and Nichols followed us up the stairs. Carier stayed behind, presumably to find out what he could from below stairs.

The man led us through a very fine hall, and up a flight of stairs. The walls were painted all over with mythological figures, almost life-size. Then we passed into a grand salon, where my acquaintances of the road were waiting for us, alone.

We bowed, making our courtesies suitably obsequious, and they bowed back. I introduced Richard, but it was only during the introductions I realised we hadn't thought up a suitable first name for him, and I tried hard to remember the name on the false papers we had, but failed. My name, I recalled, was supposed to be Ruth.

"My husband, Mr. er—Roderick Locke," I said. Richard shot me a darkling glance from beneath his brows, but bowed and took Mrs. Ravens' hand, deliberately clumsy. It was then I knew I was going to enjoy this.

Richard straightened and took a good look at his namesake. Seen together, there was no possibility anyone who knew my husband would recognise him in this man, even at a considerable distance. The impostor was shorter and thicker in build than my husband. Older, too. His smile reached no further than his mouth, and his eyes were more grey than blue, his complexion unhealthily pale rather than naturally so.

His wife was a composite of what a fashionable lady should be. I thought I could probably give her five years, but she had remembered to leave her brown hair unpowdered, the way I preferred. If Richard caught me with such a haughty expression he would have teased me mercilessly, especially if it had been in the presence of people such as we were supposed to be.

They indicated we might sit. "I have much to thank you for," Richard said. "I understand you came to my wife's rescue recently?"

They smiled graciously. "Please think nothing of it," Mr. Ravens said. "We had met a day or two before and been charmed by your wife."

"I think I mentioned, I found a clavichord," I explained, but of course he remembered. I had snatched a few moments' practice and the Ravens caught me leaving the room.

Richard's eyes danced with mischief. "My wife's family is a very musical one. Some of them have even played professionally."

"Oh, really?" Mrs. Ravens exclaimed. "Have they played at court?"

Richard smiled wickedly. "Oh yes. In fact her uncle has served in the court at Prussia." I gasped at the huge lie.

"Indeed? I understand the king insists on the finest, so that must mean he is indeed distinguished," said Mr. Ravens. I listened in astonishment to my beloved's embellishments to my family life, but I said nothing. "Would I have heard of him?"

I thought fast. "I don't know. Frederick Barber?"

"No, I'm sorry, I can't say I've come across him." I wasn't surprised, since I had just made him up.

Richard leaned back in the elaborately gilded chair. "Have you been to the court in Prussia?"

"Oh yes," said Mr. Raven airily.

"Is it very grand?" I asked, deliberately naïve.

"Did you never visit your uncle there?" Mr. Ravens asked in surprise.

"Oh no." I decided Mrs. Locke would be confiding and gossipy. I loved gossip, along with most other people, even those who never admit it, but I preferred to listen in the usual course of events. "My father would never allow it. I was brought up very respectably and quietly. Mr. Locke always says he will take me there, but he never has, have you, my dear?"

I met his eyes with a look of roguishness which I am sure would have driven him away at sight had I ever tried it on him for real. As it was, I could see the amusement gain hold over the outrage he had at first felt, and his smile became far more natural, to me at least. "We are not at fashion's disposal."

I could see Mr. Locke develop before my eyes. If his wife were garrulous, he would be pompous and deeply aware of his station in life. They would make a fine pair. He sat up, pulled his waistcoat straight and fixed the impostors with an expression of deep sincerity. "I have a business to take care of and much as I would like to gallivant about the courts of Europe, I am afraid our commitments do not allow it."

"Indeed, duties are paramount." Mr. Ravens nodded gravely. "Tell me, sir, are your commitments so very onerous? Never having engaged in trade myself, I'm completely ignorant of such things."

That could be a test, to see if we really knew about the business. I prayed Richard did. "I prefer to oversee most aspects of it for myself," Richard said now. "It could be easier, it is true, but then the business would not be as profitable as it is now and my wife would have fewer luxuries to console her."

He was setting them up, turning their enquiry into a hook of his own. After all, they were card sharpers looking for likely subjects. As we watched, Ravens withdrew a silver snuffbox from his pocket, flipped it open and offered it to Richard.

Richard accepted a pinch, but without his usual display of elegance, although he took his normal infinitesimal amount. We watched, fascinated, as our host dipped his finger and thumb in, shook it, got his lace entangled in his littlest finger, tried to make the gesture elegant anyway, and failed. It was as good as a pantomime, but I did feel guilty taking such pleasure from his discomfiture. This particular gesture was one my husband was famous for, the elegant taking of snuff. It was considered akin to the graceful use of a fan by a woman. Youths studied his attitude, the angle at which he held his thumb and forefinger.

The man took his snuff and we tried to look on admiringly without laughing, while a footman brought in some refreshments. He took one look at us, and the tray on which was set a decanter and glasses wavered before he regained control. I guessed he might be one of the Thompson's men Carier had been busy putting in place.

Richard didn't look at him, but Mrs. Ravens looked up and tutted in irritation. She apologised for the man's clumsiness as he bowed and left the room, and then returned almost immediately with another tray on which was set tea and cups. Then they brought another tray with little biscuits and the like. They were taking good care of us.

I wondered that they should bring wine so early in the day, but Mr. Ravens made this clear when he asked Richard for his opinion of it.

Richard took a glass of the wine and sniffed it appreciatively. I didn't know how much he knew about wine. He made a great play of looking at the wine in the glass, "for clarity," and then he tasted a tiny amount and rolled it about his mouth. "Very pleasant. A local wine, if I'm not mistaken."

"Indeed, sir." Mr. Ravens knocked back his own glassful with much less ceremony, and poured himself another. Richard refused a refill, and I was content with tea. "Do you deal in much Italian wine, Mr. Locke?"

"There's a market for such things but in general, my main business is in French wine."

"You deal with the superior part of society then?" asked our host.

"They do drink the most fine wine," Richard admitted. "It is the more profitable side of the business."

Mr. Ravens smiled and lifted his finger. "Do you not find the duty on wines to England an impediment? I have heard as much as two-thirds of the tea and wine drunk in England could be smuggled goods."

Richard looked serious, perhaps remembering something he would rather forget. "I don't just trade in England. I distribute French wine all over Europe."

Mr. Ravens nodded sagely. "Sometimes I wish I wasn't prohibited by birth from engaging in trade."

That was utter nonsense. If the English aristocracy didn't have members engaged in trade there would be far more titled beggars in the streets. Richard seized on the statement with delight. "But I had heard your brother, Mr. Gervase Kerre, had made his fortune in India."

"You are well informed, sir," Mr. Ravens admitted, not forthcoming, perhaps to give himself time to think.

"It's good for business, my lord." Richard leant back and waited for the reply about Gervase.

"India is one thing," Mr. Ravens said. "But I cannot think my parents would approve of *my* engaging in trade."

I couldn't imagine what had given him that idea. In France, the aristocracy was indeed prohibited from taking part in trade, but in England, one of the ways it kept its power was to spread its interests, akin to the way they did business here in Italy. Thompson's probably amounted to trade in Mr. Ravens' eyes, although its effective influence spread much further than commerce.

I saw the gleam in Richard's eye, indicative of his growing enjoyment of the situation. "The duties of the heir to the Earldom of Southwood must be particularly onerous?"

"Indeed, sir," said Mr. Ravens in a very stately manner. "This sojourn in Venice is, as I am sure you are aware, in the nature of a bride-trip."

"I had heard," said my husband gravely. "You must allow us to give you every felicitation."

Mr. Ravens inclined his head graciously, as did his wife. Then, as though she had just thought of it, she clapped her hands in an expression of delight. "We are going to the Opera tomorrow night. Do you go?"

"We had not planned it," I said cautiously.

"You must allow us to persuade you to join us!" she cried. "Should that not be delightful, my dear?" Girlish glee did not sit well on her ample shoulders. She must in her late twenties at least, probably more. I was twenty-five and I'd left girlish glee behind years ago.

Her husband looked at her as though he had not thought of the idea before, although I had no doubt this was a previously worked-out ploy, designed to catch us or any other victim further in their nets. Richard had given them enough information to show them we were worth catching, and now they would proceed to do it.

Richard looked doubtful. "I'm not sure we can impose on you to that extent, my lord. It was very kind of you to see us this morning but we are not accustomed to moving in such exalted circles."

I glanced at him. Toadying of the worst kind, but Mr. Ravens lapped it up. He waved a gracious hand. "Please think nothing of it. It would give my wife great pleasure to see you again."

She smiled encouragingly. "We would enjoy the pleasure of

your company. Just go to the Opera, give your names, ask for Lord Strang's box and you will be shown there."

"You're very gracious, my lord." I spread my fan to hide my blushes—and my smiles.

The footman returned with a card on a tray. We watched as Ravens read the card and blenched, but retained it, and said to the footman, "You must inform Freddy we are otherwise engaged, but we would be delighted to receive him another day."

Richard immediately stood, so I did the same. "I cannot allow you to turn away such a distinguished visitor on our account. We must take our leave of you, my lord, my lady."

Ignoring their protests he bowed, and waited only until I had risen from my own curtsey, before he swept me away, promising to attend the Opera the next night. We went out of the room so quickly that the footman nearly missed his cue to open the door for us.

The footman followed us out to show us to the door. "Are you from Thompson's?" Richard asked him tersely, when we were out of earshot of the main salon.

"Yes, my lord."

"And you know me?"

"Yes, my lord."

"Three things," Richard snapped. "We're letting this affair run its course for now. Remember I am Mr. Locke and address me accordingly, if you please. And don't let Freddy in here for the time being. Refer him to Carier." The man concurred, bowing, and we went down to the hall.

Chapter Nine

As we crossed the marble vastness, a door opened and we almost collided with the figure that erupted out of one of the rooms. "Richard! I thought you were busy." He stepped back. "And *what* are you doing in that fright of a wig?"

Richard didn't laugh, although if we weren't still in disguise I thought he might have done so. "Come with us, please, Freddy. I promise we'll explain when we're in a place of safety."

Freddy looked somewhat surprised but followed us. We climbed into the same gondola we had arrived in, and travelled back up the Grand Canal in near silence, once Richard had put his finger to his lips and gestured to the gondolier. I took my husband's hand, and watched the passing scenery, now bathed in bright sunshine. I should have to consider my complexion and find a broader hat next time we ventured out.

When we reached the palazzo we went upstairs with a somewhat bemused Freddy and let ourselves in to the apartment, where a footman lingered in the hall. Richard ordered some refreshment and we went into the drawing rooms.

Freddy looked about. "This is more your style, Richard. Elegance without pretension. I thought that palazzo was somewhat grandiose for your taste."

"It is," Richard replied shortly. "That Lord Strang is not this one."

Freddy's heavy brows shot up. "Eh?"

"He's an impostor," Richard explained tersely. "It's his misfortune I chose Venice as well. By all accounts we should have been on the yacht enjoying an extended cruise or I should be in Devonshire, nursing my sick wife."

The footman brought some tea and I poured some for everyone, after the gentlemen refused anything stronger. I watched Freddy's expressions as Richard explained the facts, starting from the time when we left the wedding breakfast.

I had met Freddy for the first time at Exeter Assembly rooms, after my engagement to Richard had been formally announced. I liked him very much. His complexion was as dark as Richard's was fair, and he possessed a pair of lazy brown eyes that seemed to take a great deal of amusement from life. He was one of Richard's set, the men who had been on the town for some time but remained miraculously single. He dressed as well as my husband customarily did but with less attention to detail, the effect being of expensive carelessness.

He was now under increasing pressure from his father to find a bride, particularly since Richard had announced his betrothal. His surviving parent reasoned that if Richard, who had been notorious for his amorous escapades, could find a bride, then it was time his son did too. In fact, that was one reason he had come here, as he explained to us when Richard demanded to know what he was doing in Venice.

"Fact is, my father hasn't stopped since your betrothal was announced and I thought I might kill him if he said 'marriage' one more time. So I made good my escape and came here. He might well have followed me to Paris," he continued reflectively, sipping his tea, "but he won't come to Venice. Says it's too vulgar for his taste."

He let Richard laugh and nodded to me. "My father doesn't like a place without a court in it. And he doesn't count the Doge."

That made me smile. "But you've put us in quite a spot here, Freddy." Richard put his tea dish on the table at his side. "Everybody knows you and I are well-acquainted. How many people know you're here?"

Freddy looked furtive. "Not many."

Richard looked at him thoughtfully. "Freddy, are you here on your own?"

I burst into laughter when I saw Freddy's face then and his

indignant, "Really Strang! I don't think that's a proper question to ask, in the circumstances!"

Richard looked at me where I sat, still laughing and smiled. "I know my wife has led a sheltered life up till now but even she would guess what you were doing here sooner or later."

I found a handkerchief and wiped my eyes. "It's not only that. It was the whole experience this morning. To see you calling that man 'my lord' and his graciousness and then he said his sort didn't engage in commerce!"

"He said what?" Freddy said, temporarily diverted. "Half the upper five hundred are supported in one way or another by some sort of commerce! What does he think we are—French?"

That only set me off again and when I looked at Richard, I laughed more. He looked at me questioningly. "It's the wig!" I managed then, trying to control myself.

Freddy joined in and admitted a similar impulse to laugh had consumed him when he had first seen Richard in the wig, hurrying down the stairs at the Barbarossa. "Are you going to wear it all the time you're Mr. Locke?"

"Only if I'm not met with deadly seriousness," said the only serious person in the room.

Richard left the room, returning within five minutes in one of his usual wigs, which did much to restore him to his usual self. He was in a good temper, though and by that time, Freddy and I had managed to control our mirth and return to being respectable members of society, although in Freddy's case, not quite respectable enough.

"Who have you brought with you, Freddy?" he asked, determined on revenge.

Freddy grimaced. "Really, Strang, not the question with ladies present!"

I looked as innocent as I could manage. "Would you like me to leave the room, sir?"

"Not at all," Richard said. "Since he has seen fit to admit it, the least he can do is to tell us who it is." He looked enquiringly at his friend, the picture of polite concern.

Freddy turned slightly pink, but had to give in. "Charlotte Outridge."

"Dear Lord!" Richard said. I longed to ask him if he had known the person in the past, but I thought it might be going too far. "That must be costing you a pretty penny!" He must have read my thoughts, because he looked me in the eyes and said, "No."

He turned to Freddy then. "I'm sorry, Freddy. It was something we were—talking over this morning. I won't ask you any more questions, I promise."

Freddy looked from one to the other of us curiously, but said nothing.

I poured more tea, regaining my serenity. "The thing is," said Richard thoughtfully, as he accepted his refill with a smile. "What are we to do now?"

I took my seat. "What are our choices?"

"We can have the man arrested," Richard said.

I wasn't so sure I liked that idea. "They did rescue me on the road. I owe them something for that."

"Very well, we'll put that aside for the time being. We could tell them who we are and let them go. That would be the sensible option." He paused and watched us, then continued. "But where would be the fun in that?"

"You shouldn't look for fun in it," Freddy demurred, but then spoiled his effect by smiling. "But they have rather put themselves in your path, haven't they?"

Richard grinned back at him. "I would call it an invitation." His face lost the smile. "But I do want to keep them under observation. If the people who tried to kill us on our wedding day turn up, I don't want them here. I want them there. These people are useful decoys."

"Rather hard, Strang."

He shrugged. "They're being watched. I'm doing my best to see they come to no harm. But it's more important Rose is safe. If there's even a whisper of danger to her, I'm taking her away." Freddy looked at us again.

Richard put his tea-dish down and sat very still, something I associated with his more unusual thoughts and ideas. "I rather thought that we could plan something between us that would keep them busy. I've a fair idea what their game is."

"I had begun to wonder," I admitted.

"And what *did* you think, my dear?" He turned to me, steepling his long fingers and flexing them together.

I had, indeed, been thinking. "They don't need such a grand setting to set up a card-sharping exercise. But I believe they enjoy their masquerade and I think they're planning something bigger. They must know what a risk they're taking by doing this so the rewards have to be worth it. They might be playing with us and several other people for all we know. I think they'll come up with a business venture."

Richard threw his head back and laughed, a short bark of laughter. "Ha, I knew I'd chosen well when I married you! Oh yes, a business venture. We have to be dazzled by them, don't we, so they will suggest a brilliant money-making scheme that can't fail."

Freddy saw, only a few moments behind us. "Then they disappear with the money. How did you know they were card sharps, by the way?"

"I asked people," Richard said simply. "Freddy, can you come to dinner?"

"Yes, of course. I have to send word to—to—"

"Miss Outridge," I finished for him.

He flushed. "Yes. But it would be an honour to spend more time in your company, ma'am."

"Half past two for three?" I suggested.

"That would be delightful, my lady," he replied.

Richard smiled. "We can draw up some kind of plan then. And please, Freddy, don't tell anyone we're here."

"Who would I tell?"

When he had gone, Richard turned to me, smiling. "Hungry?"

I shook my head. "Not particularly. Are you?"

He smiled, stood and held out his hand to me. "Not for food."

I took his hand and let him pull me to my feet. "Have we time? Isn't there something else we should be doing?"

"Nothing more important than this." He drew me into his arms.

We went into the bedroom and frightened a maid who wasn't expecting us at this time of day. She scuttled out of the room, but I had no eyes for anything but Richard and he didn't look at anyone but me.

We were everything to each other now and in the course of a few days I had come to love the intimacy. It had even become necessary to me. Not the lovemaking alone, but having him close, feeling his warmth, hearing his voice. I had loved him before, when our experiences of intimacy were necessarily brief and clandestine, but now, when we could linger and enjoy the experience, I loved him more than ever. He was unfailingly considerate, courteous even and as I told him when we were once more naked and lying together side by side, more than I had ever expected, even from him.

"I'm curious to know what you did expect," he said.

I smiled. "I know I'm fortunate. Most women look on this as a duty, a responsibility."

"Are you sure?" he said gently. "My experience has been just the opposite."

I sighed and lay back, unable to resolve the conflict. "Perhaps marriage does something to people."

"Only to the wrong people. That is, people who are wrong together. Not us."

He put his hands on my waist and ran them up to cup my breasts and thumb the nipples until they were stiff and then laughed softly at my sigh of delight as he did so. "No, not us," I agreed, as I opened my mouth and my body to him, an invitation he accepted with as much pleasure as I gave.

When I went into the dressing room and called for Nichols, I found my luggage had finally arrived and I could wear something more cheerful than Mrs. Locke's drab garments. I found a yellow figured silk gown and petticoat, embroidered and flounced, fine lace for my elbows and neck and filigree gold jewellery. Nichols dressed my hair to perfection until it gleamed, leaving a curl to drop forward on to my shoulder. Not for the first time, I wondered at her genius in turning my unruly mop of curls into such an elegant creation.

When I went into the drawing room, I found Richard's luggage had also arrived, as had Freddy. They were both dressed in the height of fashion, in such style as would make Mr. Ravens' mouth water. I was pleased to see Richard was once again wearing the diamond solitaire at his throat.

They smiled and bowed and Richard came forward to take my hands. "*Much* better."

As we looked at each other, the memory of our siesta came back to both of us. We glowed with it and it was then Freddy made his discovery. "By God, it's a love match!"

Richard turned his head then to look at Freddy. "Yes, of course. Who wouldn't love her?" His simple tribute meant so much to me, much more than any fulsome compliment would have done. He led me to a sofa where we sat together, his hand lightly over mine.

Freddy studied us. "I knew you liked each other, but—" He shook his head.

Richard shrugged. "The day I met Rose I knew I wanted her for my wife and I've never regretted my decision since. Yes, Freddy, it's a love match."

Freddy laughed. "Society doesn't think so. Your mother, Richard, has put it about that this is a dynastic arrangement. Since your sister failed to come up to scratch with the last Lord Hareton, you did your duty with the sister of the present one."

Richard stood, went over to the sideboard and poured some glasses of wine from a freshly filled decanter. He brought them over for us. "I'd heard something of the sort. Very clever of her," he said indifferently, handing his lordship his glass. I was sorry for his careless attitude to his parents, but I felt I didn't know enough about them yet to be able to help in any way. Certainly his parents seemed cold towards him but that might have been as much his fault as theirs. He had repudiated them along with the rest of society when they'd sent Gervase abroad, but they may have had little choice. I knew little of that time, only of the misery it caused the twins.

He sat down again. "So Society thinks I have contracted an

arranged marriage?"

Freddy smiled at us. "For now, yes it does, but if any of its members sees what I've just seen, the scales will drop from its collective eyes. Do you want anyone to know?"

Richard stretched his arm along the back of the sofa. "Thank you for asking, Freddy. I think we might let matters take their course." He turned his attention to me. "Should you welcome society knowing of our feelings for each other, my love?"

I didn't need to think. "I don't care who knows. At least it might help to keep your old lovers from the door."

Richard gave a crack of laughter, at my frankness and at Freddy's evident surprise. "My wife doesn't believe in equivocation."

At that moment a footman came in to announce dinner was ready so we went in, informally since Freddy couldn't provide a partner. Over the course of the meal I found him extremely good company. He was in many ways the antithesis of my husband; relaxed where Richard was alert, careless in appearance where Richard preferred meticulous elegance, dark where he was fair, but they were the product of the same kind of upbringing, always in the public eye. This kind of informality, an ordinary occurrence to me, was rare and precious to them. I knew my husband well now, but I didn't know Freddy, or if his pose was real or assumed. He seemed genuine to me.

This was a new experience, to be alone with two gentlemen, even in the presence of servants, but this aspect of the dinner didn't occur to me until later. It was one of the privileges allowed a respectable married woman in our world, more freedom in society.

I enjoyed that meal and the company but I must have drunk more wine than I should, for towards the end I felt quite giddy. I was pleased to leave them for a short time afterwards. I had tea served to me in the drawing room.

When they rejoined me, they didn't immediately sit. Richard held out his hand to me and with a smile I stood up and laid my hand in his. He gave me a wicked smile. "I've been telling Freddy how well you play and how evilly you dance. We thought, if you didn't object, we could go into the music room and persuade him to pick out some minuets. I'll see what I can do to help you to dance without watching your feet or counting."

I sighed in relief. I wasn't in any state to demonstrate any kind of prowess on the harpsichord. My fingers might get lost, but I would willingly try to improve my dancing skills.

Richard had been amused by the way I had to watch my feet during the Grand Minuet we danced at our wedding. I'd had very little practice outside the schoolroom, especially at the formal dances at the beginning of an evening. To make matters worse, when my younger sister Lizzie had been learning the steps, she'd recruited me to take the part of the gentleman, which made my confusion even worse. I was sadly aware of my lack of prowess and I'd determined to practise when I had the chance. I didn't wish to let my elegant husband down.

Freddy sat at the harpsichord and began on the flourish at the start of the dance. Richard sketched an elaborate bow. "Mind your steps, my love."

I stumbled, but he wouldn't let me stop and he commanded I kept my attention on his face. "This is a courtship dance, a dance of flirtation, sweetheart. Seduce me." That made me worse. I could see this amused him by his smile. A tease. These days everything turned into a precursor to making love. Or did I only think it?

I wouldn't give up. After two tries, I began to improve. "I haven't done this since Georgiana's come-out," he said, referring to his sister. "You are at least *aware* of the moves. If she moved the wrong way once, she did it a thousand times."

"I've never had enough practice really," I said over my shoulder to Freddy. "Wouldn't you like to stop for a while? You've played a long time for us."

"Indeed he has," Richard agreed. "Shall we change places, Freddy? I'll play for a while and then I can watch and see if we can't improve the style."

Freddy willingly rose and took my hand and at once Richard stopped us. "No, Rose. Let your hand droop slightly at the wrist, as though it's an effort to hold it there. There! That's just what I mean." I had to laugh because Freddy demonstrated Richard's instruction, looking every inch the fragile lady of fashion. We stopped while I had a drink and restored my equilibrium and then I tried to do what he said.

I found Richard an exacting instructor, but patient. He made me do certain moves over and over until he got to his feet, saying; "Here, Freddy, can you do the lady's part?"

"I blush to admit that I can," Freddy said. "Unlike you, Richard, I had younger brothers to teach."

I played while they danced. I kept the tune simple, keeping to the basic structure so I could watch them, but I could play no more when I became helpless with laughter. Richard, my delicate, graceful husband, leading the heavier, altogether more masculine Freddy, was funny enough, but the gentleman was a glorious mimic. He simpered, smiled invitingly and tipped his chin up when Richard went too far and winked at him. He borrowed my fan and showed how a lady could use it during the dance to enhance the movements of her arm, bending it "Just so." When they realised my amusement had gone so far I couldn't play any more, they continued, relentless in their mimicry. Richard counted the beats aloud so they could keep their rhythm.

They only stopped when a footman came in to light the candles. Richard sat heavily and looked at me, laughing. Freddy sat too and drank deeply from his glass. I thought they needed a reward and a time to breathe, but I was beyond fine playing. I found a light piece and turned to the keyboard. They listened in companionable silence and when I finished I turned and smiled brightly, bowing my head for their applause.

I complimented Freddy on his mimicry, telling him how much I had enjoyed it and I could see Richard's smile fade and his eyes gaze into the distance. He was plotting.

Then he spoke. "Do you remember our little problem? The impostor?" His eyes gleamed as he turned them back on us. "Rose is right; you're a good mimic, Freddy. Would you like to help us with this little enterprise?"

Freddy didn't hesitate. "Anything I can do."

"You can be rich and stupid. I think we just go along with

them and so long as they haven't seen you, Freddy, we can introduce you as a cony to be skinned."

"Will they skin me?"

"No. You're the bait. Along with us, at least at first."

He went on to explain his plan, less a plan, more a slight manipulation of events. Richard's cleverness was to work with people to let them do what they wanted to do, but to keep control of events and eventually turn them. This time his scheme sounded amusing.

After Freddy had gone back to the arms of his expensive mistress and Richard and I were in bed again, I broached the subject that troubled me. "No one will die this time, will they?" I put my hand flat on his chest, sliding it up to his shoulder. I loved this gentle sensuality.

He shook his head. "There's no reason why anyone should. The man has only damaged my pride, if I have any left." He turned to kiss my hand. "I also find the whole situation quite diverting, don't you?"

I smiled. "I suppose I do."

"If this assassin turns up, then we'll have to think again. But Carier reports no sign of him and we have people watching. No word from Mrs. Thompson yet, either."

"Mrs. Thompson?" I was intrigued.

He smiled, pulled me down to touch my mouth with his. "Mrs. Thompson's main job is to look after the official side of the business, the actual profit making part of it, but she too has a financial stake in it. We try to keep it a rule to take decisions jointly."

"I thought you would make your own decisions."

"It depends which part of my life we're talking about, my love." He kissed me properly.

He tried to swing me on to my back, but I was somewhat emboldened by all the wine I had drunk that evening and I resisted and pulled away. "No. Let me."

He let me. He lay on his back while I tried to show him how much I loved him. He was such a considerate lover, he took such pleasure in giving that I had not yet tried to love him in the way I thought he deserved.

I kissed his mouth and moved down to his throat and his chest. His hands lay quietly unresisting on my body. His chest moved up when I reached his nipples and he gave a sharp gasp of need. I lingered, enjoying his taste. He felt firm and smooth under my hands. I let my breasts caress him as well as my mouth, touching and murmuring as I explored his body.

When I touched him inside his hip, he murmured, "There— oh my God, yes, there." I caressed him and examined his masculinity close up. There were no barriers between us now, nothing I wouldn't do to make him happy. I kissed the tip of his shaft, felt his shudder, loved the taste of him on my tongue, but I didn't linger. I sensed he wouldn't last long if I continued.

I turned him over and kissed and caressed his back in the way I knew he loved and then turned him over again to love him, in the ultimate act of union.

He helped then, but I don't think he could have done otherwise at that point. When I gazed into his face he showed me all his feelings, no mask, nothing. For a moment I felt overwhelmed by his trust, this man who hid so much from the world.

I lowered myself on to him and we watched each other while his body entered mine. He reached up to hold my breasts, pushed against me, made me gasp in delight. Whenever I looked at him, his eyes were open, looking at me, loving me. I tried to tell him in words, but I found nothing to describe adequately the feeling of helpless power, the imperative to drive forward to that shattering climax.

Only when he shuddered with fulfilment did he close his eyes.

When I let myself sink forward, I felt him trembling. His arms went around me and as I slid to one side of him, he turned his head and opened his eyes again.

We looked at each other, until he spoke. "The *coup de grace*. My sweet life, I thought I couldn't love you more. Now I'm not so sure."

I blushed, or perhaps I was already flushed from the act of

love, but I suddenly felt self-conscious about what I had just done. "I'm not sure I'm behaving as a well brought up young lady should."

"You could certainly give a *houri* lessons," he said, more in control of himself, his breathing less ragged. "But never give it up."

"I think it was the wine," I confessed.

"Then we'll order another case." He pulled me close and kissed me, deep and lingering. "You're all there is for me now."

I looked up when the candle flickered. We had only two candles alight, on either side of the bed, just enough to see by. I was surprised to see that the one on his side had almost burnt down. "Has it been so long?"

He looked over at it and turned back to me, smiling. "Time seems to go away for a while, when we make love, doesn't it?"

I smiled in return. "Yes." We let the candles burn out by themselves and lay, entwined, until we fell asleep.

Chapter Ten

The next day the headache I woke up with was not one I would have liked to have carried around with me all day. After he murmured soothing condolences to me, Richard went through to his dressing room and returned with a bottle of lemon-scented liquid that he rubbed gently on my temples. The pain loosened. "Oh thank you, Richard. That feels wonderful."

"Think nothing of it," he said gravely. "I would have done as much for anyone." Considering our positions, the formality of his statement made me laugh, but I was forced to put a hand to my forehead and groan. "Poor love," he murmured. "I'll get you some tea."

He went away and soon Nichols came in, wheeling a trolley. Richard got up and ate, but I could manage nothing, only the tea he made me drink, as much as I could hold. "Now stay there and sleep, you'll be as right as rain soon. Then, if you like, we'll order the gondola round and I'll show you more of Venice."

"But not in that wig," I managed.

He laughed. "No, I think I have to give that up. A shame, I thought it was rather a nice touch. But if you and Freddy insist on bursting into laughter every time you see me in it, then I don't think I have much choice, do I?"

He had made me smile. He leant over and kissed my forehead. "Does it take a pint or two of wine to persuade you to do what you did last night? Should I invest in a few more cases?"

I would have shaken my head, but it hurt too much. "Now I know you don't mind, I might find the courage without the claret."

"Don't mind?" he echoed. "My love, one doesn't look for that in a wife, but when it appears, it makes me sorry we've missed church for so long. I have to give thanks somewhere, you know, for a miracle like that."

"Fool!" I laughed, but soon stopped.

He put his hand to my forehead. "Get some sleep, *mia adorata*. I have some matters to arrange. I'll see you when you feel better."

Remarkably, when I woke up again later in the morning I did feel much better. I sat up in bed and felt my head, which still smelled faintly of citrus, then I realised the headache had completely gone. I hadn't realised such a sick feeling could be over so quickly, treated in the right way.

Nichols looked in on me after about ten minutes and I smiled and asked her if she would find me something to eat. So when Richard came in to see me, I was sitting in my dressing gown by the fireplace, making a hearty, if belated, breakfast.

He examined my face and smiled at what he saw. "I thought you'd feel better when you woke. I suppose we did drink rather more than is usual for a lady last night."

I applied myself to my final slice of toast. "Not all ladies. Even in our local gatherings in Devonshire I've seen some ladies regularly the worse for drink."

"Some prefer laudanum." He dropped lightly into the chair opposite me. "And if you combine laudanum and alcohol the result can be quite devastating."

"Have you tried it?"

He nodded. "It brings blessed oblivion for a time, but the results afterwards can be—distressing. I spent the whole of one season in a haze of laudanum, until Carier contrived to shut off my supply."

"You must have found it difficult." I picked up another slice of toast. "I've noticed, my love, once you're set on something it can be very difficult to divert you."

"Perceptive woman! I seem to be surrounded by interfering people and I don't suppose you'll be any different." He mitigated the comment by smiling into my eyes, forcing me to smile back.

"When Gervase first left, I tried several ways of self destruction, but none of them worked." I found his matter-of-fact tones chilling. "I've never been completely grateful until now."

"I was going to suggest a siesta, like yesterday's," he continued then. "But you've only just got up and you're probably bored with this room and this bed by now."

"Bored?"

He put his hand to his chin, smiling at my vehement response. "You're supposed to be reluctant."

"Why?" I'd never had any patience with hypocrisy. "I love you and you give me the greatest joy I have ever felt in my life. I love being with you, lying with you and loving you. It could be any bed, anywhere, but only one man."

His expression softened. "You should be careful." He came over to take my hand and take it to his lips. "When you say things like that it increases my confidence and gives me all the encouragement I need."

I stood up, put my arms around him. "Why not? You know everything about me."

"Oh not everything, not yet." He bent his head to kiss me.

We went back to bed for an hour or two, as, he informed me, the Italians generally did. I liked the idea. We could rest quietly, doze, make love and chat in peace and quiet, with only the sound of the water and the boatmen outside to keep us company. It was true; the sounds outside were much quieter at this time of day. The whole place took on a timeless quality. Only the buildings bore silent witness to the beauty of the place.

It was getting much warmer now and we lay on the covers, naked as babes, totally at ease. "What did you do this morning?" I asked him.

"Carier and I interviewed cardsharps."

"What?" I sat up, startled, thinking I had misheard him.

"We need someone on our side, if we're to go into the lion's den, and Venice has plenty of tricksters in it, even at this time of year." He pressed me back down on to the bed, into the shelter of his arms. "So we're giving one of them the opportunity to earn some honest money."

I was fascinated. "Did you find one? Can I meet him?"

"Yes and yes. Tomorrow, instead of going to church as we should, we'll learn how to cheat at cards." He laughed at my surprise. "I'll send a note to Freddy and he can come too. After all, it's a skill every gentleman should know."

"I thought honour was all."

"Sweet innocent! When men are wagering their estates on the turn of a card, do you really think they're depending solely on skill and chance?" He drew a hand gently over my stomach.

"I thought they were." I stretched in response to his caress.

"Some of them are but others use tricks they've learned. I've never been very interested in cards, although it amused me for a time to let my parents think I was." I was reminded again of his careless attitude to Lord and Lady Southwood. "I find life more interesting than pasteboard." He looked at me and his hold tightened. He brought me close for a kiss.

"So," I said, when I could, "you're teaching me to cheat at cards and you've shown me a killing. Are you corrupting me, my lord?"

He looked at me gravely. "Do you think so?"

"No. You're opening my eyes to things I've never known, but that's not surprising since I was brought up in one place, knowing the same people. But you're also protecting me, although your touch is very light."

He touched me to prove it. "You're the most precious, the most important thing to me now. If you think I should give up Thompson's, or anything else, I will, to make you happy."

I was shocked. "Oh no." I didn't want that kind of sacrifice. "I shouldn't tell you, but you've enlivened my life immeasurably. Before, I thought I would turn to stone, so many people took me for granted or ignored me and now—well, I've never felt so alive." I laughed then, for no particular reason. "And happy," I added.

We got up later and at his suggestion had our gondola brought around so he could take me on a tour—and Carier could go on another of his fishing expeditions, trying to see if anyone followed us or watched us.

I had only to dress as Mrs. Locke, which didn't take very long and meet him in the salon. He was dressed simply, but not, I saw to my relief, in the wig had made him look so different before, instead wearing one in his usual style.

He smiled when he saw me and took my hand, leading me out and down the stairs again. He helped me into the gondola and we set off with Nichols in attendance. This time after travelling some way up the Canal we stopped and moored near the Rialto. It was very lively here, people dressed fashionably and stopped to shop and chat. "We'll leave the beauties of the art and great buildings for another day," Richard said. "You might like it here. And I have an unaccountable urge to buy you something, if you should like it."

In answer, I took his arm and let him help me ashore in the shadow of the lovely bridge. The high white arches entranced me—not grand enough to be beyond human, still communicating to the individual, but perfect in their simplicity. The windows of the great houses nearby and the unending grey-blue water below reflected them.

Richard took me to a busy shopping area, evidently fashionable and I looked about curiously at the fashionable ladies and the differences between their costumes and mine. There were differences, most of them subtle, but since I was dressed as the sensible Mrs. Locke, I attracted little notice. Richard still drew some admiring glances. He couldn't or wouldn't disguise the grace that seemed to come as naturally as breathing. He either ignored or failed to notice the glances he received from one or two of the more grandly dressed ladies who passed us by.

I bought some pretty trinkets that took my fancy, all of them under my assumed name. Carier had warned the shopkeepers of the imitation Strangs, but Mrs. Locke's credit was good. I bought a little box I fell in love with, an automaton of bird that popped out and sang when I pressed a hidden spring.

We were passing the window of a jeweller's shop when I saw a string of coral beads, perfect for Mrs. Locke. We went inside. I enjoyed my small purchase, but then Richard saw something else in a case. He indicated them.

I caught my breath. It was a simple chain of perfectly blue sapphires set off with diamonds, with none of the murkiness associated with stones of lesser quality. So Richard, so perfect. The price was breathtaking too. I didn't argue, I loved them too much, but Richard, speaking remarkably rapid Italian, persuaded the man to bring the price to a more reasonable level. He ordered them sent around.

We went out into blazing sunshine. "It's growing late in the season. People will leave soon to avoid the unhealthy hot weather that sets in during July and August," Richard commented. "In the season this square is thronged with people.

"I love the soft, warm colours of this place. They contrast so well with the canals, reflecting the bluer sky above." The acid bite of white stone punctuated the blue, preventing the subtleties from becoming too bland I laid my other hand on his arm. "May we come back one day?"

"They say it's a mistake to return but, in our case, we may use this as a refuge and a place of privacy." His eyes reflected all we had come to mean to each other. "If I ever lose you, I will burn the apartment."

The bitterness in his tone reminded me of the constant stresses he was subject to, even here, where we were so happy together. I dearly wished I could help him to forget whatever had been done to him and what he had done to himself, to face the future tranquilly, by my side.

We spent about two hours there, walking, looking about and occasionally laughing at some of the more extremes of fashion we saw, until it was time to return. It was a golden, leisurely two hours for us both. We saw no one we knew and no one seemed to recognise us.

When we arrived at the Opera that evening, it was still light outside but the lights were on inside the great building. We dressed simply, but more formally. I certainly felt shy enough, as I always did when I was going somewhere new and this time I let it show, thinking it would suit Mrs. Locke better than it would Lady Strang.

We asked for Lord Strang's box and a man in our livery took us upstairs. From Richard's increased rigidity and the set line of his mouth I saw this part of the deception wasn't pleasing to him, but we could do little about it yet. As usual, I had Nichols in attendance and I carried the little pistol in my pocket.

We were relieved to find only the Ravens waiting for us, having half expected a large party from their bombastic talk. We always ran the risk of discovery, so bringing our charade to a premature end. They had, of course, hired one of the best boxes in the house and had the management of the place at their disposal. English lords were very profitable for business in Italy. Our hosts were dressed grandly, but I guessed the diamonds Mr. Ravens wore were paste, as were her rubies. I didn't know if rubies that fine existed, apart from the one I had removed from my finger earlier that day, and certainly not in such profusion.

That was where the false Strangs made their mistakes; everything was too grand, too lavish, the jewels and the clothes too elaborate. Instead of concentrating on quality, they equated style with abundance. I couldn't see myself wearing Mrs. Ravens' clothes. They were too bright, designed too much towards excess for my taste and every colour clashed with every other.

"It is indeed kind of you to attend," said Mrs. Ravens, seemingly born to it, as I wasn't. We replied obsequiously and they smiled and bade us sit.

I had attended the theatre before, but never the opera. The great and the good filled the gold and crimson boxes. Richard scanned each one intently then he sighed and returned his gaze to within the box, shaking his head slightly to Nichols and myself. He had seen no one he knew, or who was likely to recognise him on sight.

Light and glitter filled the building, smothered with figured brocade and velvet, silk and satin of every fashionable colour and style. Gentlemen attended their ladies and well-dressed young men filled the pit, all blatantly ogling the boxes for the sights. I loved it. I would find it intimidating without Richard, but I was conservatively dressed and I could enjoy the spectacle without being part of the show. My sister Lizzie would love it here and would flaunt herself shamelessly.

"Do you know Venice well, my lady?" Richard enquired courteously.

"Not as well as you do, I'll wager, sir," Mrs. Ravens replied.

"I have been here for some years, it's true, my lady, though my wife doesn't always join me when I'm here." He smiled carelessly at me, his expression wary, almost asking permission before I realised what he was silently asking me. He was going to flirt with her, I realised with a flash of excitement.

I accepted a glass of wine from Mr. Ravens, sat back and watched, sipping my drink cautiously after the excesses of the previous night.

Richard gave Mrs. Ravens delicate and polite treatment, but left his message unmistakeable. He helped her to stand when she left the box and held her chair for her when she sat down again. Once, forgetting the staid Mr. Locke, he flicked her fan open for her with a careless snap and twist of his wrist. I don't think she noticed the casual elegance of the gesture, but her husband spotted the trick and just for a second his eyes narrowed. Fortunately at that moment the performance began and all eyes turned to the stage.

The bright lights drew my attention. I hadn't expected much of the performance, but I had forgotten two things; Venice is the home of Italian opera and I loved music.

The libretto of the opera featured something mythological with gods and goddesses, but the story was a mere excuse, a chance for the composer and the performers to draw their collective breaths and let go. I loved every overblown moment. I tried not to let it affect me, but at one point the tears pricked the back of my eyes and I had to swallow hard to get rid of them.

All through this most of the audience was lost in its own concerns. Many flirted, waved their hands at their friends or used their opera glasses to scan the rest of the audience, turning afterwards to chat to their companions. The performers played through it all and after a while I forgot everything else.

I tried to analyse some of the music, but I gave up after a while and let it flow through me, take me where it would. I tried to remember some of it, so I could write it down later, but when I got home I found I couldn't; it was the whole experience that remained with me, not the sum of its parts.

After the first act, I blinked and slowly brought myself back down to reality. Richard wasn't looking at me, but at Mrs. Ravens. Although I knew this was only playacting I still felt bereft. I chided myself for being foolish and got on with being Mrs. Locke.

"Would your ladyship care for another glass of wine?"

"That would be most acceptable."

Richard made great play of helping her to another glass and then put the bottle down, seeming to forget me. I sighed and let him get on with it.

Mr. Ravens took it all in his stride, beaming unctuously, watching them both. His wife obviously took pleasure in Richard's attention and I pretended indifference. I tried to take my part seriously, a married lady not particularly close to her husband.

"Do you like Venice, Mrs. Locke?" Ravens offered me a plate loaded with sticky somethings that I refused unhesitatingly.

I lowered my eyes. "It is certainly different. I haven't seen much of it yet—I have been recovering from the journey, but I hope to see more next week."

"You have a house on the Grand Canal, I believe?"

He was so very patronising that I had a strong desire to give him a set-down. I resisted. "Only an apartment, my lord, but the views are very fine."

"Our palazzo has a wonderful view of the Lagoon." He refilled my glass. "We would be charmed if you could find the time to visit us again one day."

"That would be most pleasant."

The occupants of a box opposite to ours were only just arriving. To my horror, I spied Freddy, who accompanied a lady of certain years, so not the beauteous Miss Outridge. They couldn't possibly fail to notice us. I assumed if the lady knew Freddy, then she probably knew Richard.

Sure enough, the lady lifted her opera glasses and scanned the audience. Freddy had seen us and Richard had seen him, but we were as helpless as butterflies on pins as we waited on events. The lady spoke to Freddy who left the box, so Richard, evidently preferring to anticipate the inevitable, got to his feet and excused us both. "I see a client of mine wishes to make herself known to us. Would you excuse us for a few moments? I have no wish to impose her presence on this company and I fear she won't rest until she has spoken to us."

The Ravens nodded graciously and we left, only to meet Freddy with his hand on the door of the box. "She's summoned you."

Richard took my hand. "My great aunt. Freddy's great aunt too. She lives in Italy, though I'd hoped she wouldn't be in Venice."

We had reached the box. A footman opened the door for us and showed us to the front of the box, where the lady was waiting. "Lady Thurl, may I have the honour to present my wife, Lady Strang?" I curtseyed.

The lady looked me up and down with her quizzing glass and then she chuckled. "So you've been netted at last, Strang! I congratulate you. Even in those clothes the girl has style."

I didn't like being talked about quite so personally, or inspected so closely, but I knew many old ladies were deliberately rude. "Now." Lady Thurl leaned forward and used her fan to trap Richard's hand. "You're up to something, aren't you? I've never seen you looking quite so dowdy and I'm sure your wife has better taste."

Richard sighed. "You won't let me lie to you, will you, Aunt Augusta?"

"Not a hope!"

He took a breath and stared across to the box we had just left. "Those people over there," he said, bowing as they caught his attention, "Are Lord and Lady Strang, on their bride-trip."

"The devil they are!" The old lady lifted her fan from Richard's hand and snapped it open.

Richard smiled at her. "And we are humble wine merchants, plying our trade as best we can."

"Ha! You don't even look like a wine merchant. Not oily enough."

Richard smiled. "I've done my best, Aunt. We've found out what they're up to and we've decided to amuse ourselves for a while, to let them take us where they will for a day or two."

The lady studied the false Strangs through narrowed eyes. "They want to fleece you, don't they? I've not reached my time of life without spotting tricksters when I see them."

"I rather believe they do," Richard replied. "So please, Aunt Augusta, if you see any of our friends, ask them not to acknowledge us until we acknowledge them."

The lady fanned herself vigorously. "And who am I?"

My love smiled coolly down at her. "Lady Thurl, a valued customer. And Freddy is someone else, too. He's volunteered to help us in this enterprise."

"There's something else, isn't there?" she demanded. "It's all very diverting, but you wouldn't bother if there wasn't something under it all. Why didn't you come to Venice as Lord Strang, eh?"

Richard face took on a mask-like quality, no trace of a smile now. "When it's over, I promise to come and tell you the whole. Will that suffice?"

"I suppose it will have to." She turned and put a hand on mine. "And I want to talk to your wife, get to know her. Would you object to giving up an afternoon of your bride-trip to gossip with an old woman, my dear?"

Her expression was suddenly frail and fragile. Richard let out a crack of laughter. "You want to know it all, don't you, Aunt? Well, my wife is the sister of Lord Hareton and you know there was an understanding between the Haretons and the Southwoods, don't you?"

It was the lady's turn to laugh. "That will do for society, but I saw you look at her just now and the way she looks at you isn't what one would normally expect in such arrangements. Very convenient she should be who she is, but I heard about it all from my friends at home and I knew there was more to it than they were saying."

Richard looked at her coldly. She was delving too far now.

She saw it. "Very well. You shall have my help, on those conditions. But don't let the deception go on too long. I've a reception in two week's time and I fancy your presence will be looked upon with favour." That was tantamount to a summons.

Richard glanced at me, so I stood up and took his arm. "It's a bargain," he said to her. We left the box, leaving the hapless Freddy to entertain the formidable old lady for the rest of the evening.

When he went with us to the back of the box, Richard asked him to call on us in the morning, which he promised to do. "And don't give anyone else our direction," warned Richard, glancing back at where her ladyship sat vigorously fanning herself. "We don't need social calls at this stage." Freddy smiled and undertook to keep our secret.

We returned to the box in time for the next act and didn't leave it again until the end. I loved the evening, would have loved it under any circumstances, but I knew Richard felt the lack of his consequence, although he would never have admitted it. He said it didn't matter to him, he could manage perfectly well without it, but some of the privileges usually accorded to him weren't there and I think he missed them. I'd never had them in the first place, so I was perfectly happy.

The performance didn't engross the Ravens, who scanned the audience eagerly. During the next interval, they asked Richard about the lady he had visited and he answered them readily enough. "Lady Thurl lives in Italy for her health and she has done me the honour of purchasing her wine from me for the last several years, my lord," he said. He seemed eager to pass on what information he could about his noble acquaintances. "The gentleman is also known to me, her son, Lord Thurl of Thurl in Kent." He used the formal appellation, only usually used on Parliamentary or other business, adding just the right air of pomposity to the information he was passing on. I wondered where Lord Thurl was. Richard told me later the present Lord Thurl was in the army and had only met him briefly, so it was a good alias for Freddy.

I looked up while he talked and saw the three great chandeliers that adorned the elaborate roof of the Opera. I wondered aloud where they found men strong enough to lower them every day for the sconces to be refilled. "Why, they're ten a penny in the country," Mr. Ravens answered me, smiling indulgently, "though it is indeed a great undertaking to run an establishment such as this."

I looked up to the gods, seeing the people up there wreathed in the smoke which had risen from all the candles alight that evening, trapped, unable to go any further. "You'd need good lungs," I remarked idly and saw Richard smile.

"You should hear them when they dislike the performance, you can tell how the evening is going in Switzerland." He caught my attention and we smiled at each other.

Mr. Ravens broke it. "You appear to have some noble acquaintances, sir. It is surprising we have never met before."

Richard turned the smile on to our host, but it became blandly polite as he turned his head. "Yes, my lord, isn't it strange? Perhaps you don't come to Venice much?"

"No, but this is a special occasion and my wife particularly requested it." He patted his wife's hand fondly.

Richard's gaze travelled down to the gesture, but he made no comment. Instead, he said, "I have the honour of supplying several of the English, especially when they visit Italy. The young gentlemen on the Grand Tour particularly."

I watched the gleam in Mr. Ravens' eye grow to something like hunger. If Richard was pulling him in, it was working. If he could attract some of these young bloods to his house, Ravens would be rich.

He drew out his snuffbox. "Perhaps. Would you care to come to our palazzo on Monday night? I have planned a small soirée, nothing grand, just supper and cards, with some music for the ladies, but we would welcome your presence."

He opened the box two-handed again, taking no chances this time and offered it to Richard. He remembered not to be quite so graceful in his acceptance, though I saw he had to stop himself, the habit was so natural. Mr. Ravens had evidently been practising, as he remembered to flick back his lace cuffs before he took a pinch, although it was nowhere near the work of art my husband made it.

Richard turned to me, with the pretext of consulting with me and nodded infinitesimally. "Are you sure we won't be in the way?" I asked Ravens.

"Can you play piquet, ma'am?"

I dropped my lashes over my eyes in a shy gesture. "Barely."

"Then you would be very welcome, my dear." He smiled in an avuncular way.

"It would be a great honour, my lord." I lifted my head and met his gaze. The grey eyes were friendly and I hoped mine looked trusting.

"We would be delighted, sir," Richard said, bowing his head slightly.

We settled down for the final act.

When the opera had finished, I sat for a few minutes in silence, while I let the music circle inside my head, trying to remember the themes for later. I looked up to see Richard watching me, amused. "It was lovely," I whispered. He took my hand and kissed it. The gesture, so public, startled me, but I supposed he felt freer in disguise as Mr. Locke, who presumably hadn't married to please his family, since we had ruthlessly extinguished them all.

I mentioned it to him later, in the safety of our own room and he sighed and smiled. "If Aunt Augusta, who hasn't seen me for two years, can spot the way I feel about you across the opera house, what chance do I have of concealing it in London, where people watch me like hawks at a rabbit?"

"When we met you had no emotions at all, you were so frozen and hidden."

He slipped an arm around my waist. "You, my love, have changed all that. I daresay I'd have more success if I went back to the heavy maquillage I used to wear, but I've lost the desire to use it. I can't kiss you in all that face paint." He bent his head to demonstrate.

"So you're resigned to Society knowing our secret?" I said when I could.

"It seems I can't prevent it knowing." After that we lost interest in the subject.

Chapter Eleven

The following day the sound of bells woke me, myriad bells, commanding the faithful to attend church. If we had joined the British community here, no doubt they would have expected us to attend, but we had protected our privacy too well to let it slip now.

I turned my head to look at my husband, but he was still asleep. I watched him, so vulnerable in sleep I could almost see the boy he had been, before his nightmares had begun.

I slipped out of bed and went to the chair where I had thrown my dressing gown the night before. I threw it around my shoulders, thrust my arms into the sleeves and then went to the two long windows, withdrawing the bolts holding the shutters closed on the first one. I didn't open the other window, because its light would have fallen directly on the bed and woken him.

I stood by the window, looked out at the glow of Venice and listened to that glorious sound, from the deepest boom to the brightest, highest chime.

How could I have got this far? Last year, a forgotten old maid, preparing to dwindle into a dependant spinster, this year the cherished wife of the man I was meant for. How close we came to not meeting at all! Or, if we had met and it had been in company, I doubt he would have noticed me. I never showed well in company. He might even have been married already to Julia Cartwright. I might have married Tom, spent all my life in Devonshire, the wife of a country squire. Once I would have been happy with that but not after I'd met Richard.

If Richard was a country squire, it was enough, more than enough. That he was not sometimes left me feeling inadequate, not up to the position I must now learn to take. I hadn't been brought up to it, as the girls he'd been presented to year after year had—to be the eventual mistress of a great estate and a member of one of the first families in the country. It filled me with dread but I would do it for his sake. Here, in this paradise, I'd start to learn.

The rustle of the sheet behind me told me he had woken, but I didn't turn round. I heard him cross to the chair in his turn and fling on his gown and then felt him slip his arms around my waist and rest his cheek on my hair. We didn't speak, but I put my hand over his and we stood, listening to the Sunday greetings outside.

"I'm so afraid I'll let you down when we go home."

"You won't," he assured me calmly. "If you're reserved, everyone will assume you're proud. Stand tall and always make sure they look away first."

His warm breath tickled my neck. "I love you very much," I said.

"I know. It's all that matters. We'll buy you some fine clothes, the sort that stand alone and you can inhabit them while they speak for you. Shall we buy an estate in Devonshire and go and live there, in seclusion?"

I turned away from the window into his arms. He could have been reading my mind. If I had accepted his offer he would have gone through with it, but it wouldn't make him happy. "No. You are what you are and as long as you're here with me, I'll do whatever's required of me gladly. Will you come to my presentation at court?"

"Of course. My mother will present you. It's soon over and a dead bore. I don't move in any royal set, so be assured that won't come into our lives to any great extent. For the rest, we'll please ourselves and if you're not happy, you must promise to tell me."

"I promise." We kissed to seal the bargain.

I slipped out of his arms and went to open the shutters on the other window. Light streamed across the unmade bed. I turned to see him watching me from the middle of the room, golden hair lit by the sun, tousled from sleep, making him look like a knowing *putto*. I went back to him.

"I said something once about these bells," he reminded me, mischief in his voice. "Do you remember?"

Of course I remembered. It had been in the humble nursemaid's room at Hareton Abbey. "That you'd like to make love to me in the Venice sun, with the sound of the water outside and the bells. You made me blush."

"So I did. Do you think I could make you blush now?" He undid the frogged fastenings at the front of my dressing gown.

"Without a doubt." He slipped his hands inside the gown and I let it slide down my arms to the floor.

He loved me, just as he'd once promised. He kissed my mouth, my throat and went down on one knee to take a nipple into his mouth, running his tongue around the very tip, then the other and then lower still, making me sigh in pleasure. My knees grew weak from his caresses. I gripped his shoulders to keep from falling to the floor and he delved between my legs, kissing and tasting until I thought I might die. But he didn't let me climax, he withdrew when he had me shivering with need.

He stood, slid off his robe and lifted me into his arms. He carried me to the bed and lay me down, leaving my legs to hang over the edge before he entered me, fitting as perfectly as a hand fits into a tailored glove, never taking his intent blue gaze from my face. I cried out in joy, at this promise finally fulfilled and I heard his answering groan as I lifted my legs to wrap them around his waist and pull him deeper into me.

Richard stopped moving and gazed at me, his expression brimful of love. "I wanted to look at you, to remember this moment always, never to forget what we are now, what we feel now. I love you, Rose, I can't think of anywhere I'd rather be, anything I'd rather be doing. I'll never stop loving you, never stop wanting you."

I could think of nothing adequate to say, nothing could express how I felt at that moment. I reached up a hand to place it on his heart. He caught it and brought it to his mouth, placing tiny kisses on the palm, his eyes never leaving mine. He kissed each fingertip, taking each tip into his mouth to caress it lightly with his tongue. My eyes drifted shut, savouring the moment.

When I opened them again I said, "I can't imagine anything I want more than to open my eyes and see you there." At that moment we were everything to each other, nothing else seemed to exist, only this heat, fading into loving warmth.

Richard fell to the bed beside me, pulled me to him and held tight. I kissed his mouth, told him I loved him, felt him move, straighten his legs, take me into his arms. I reached up to kiss his neck, felt his answering kiss on my hair and I sighed, feeling drowsy and blissful.

The knock on the door came as a shocking intrusion, but Richard didn't let me go, only pulled the sheet up over us and called out, "Yes?"

The door opened but no one came in, only Carier's voice, saying, tonelessly, "The gentlemen are here, my lord. Lord Thwaite and the other."

Richard grimaced. "Have breakfast served in the dining room. We'll be there in about half an hour. And her ladyship will require Nichols in attendance."

"Yes, my lord." The door closed on the invisible manservant.

We turned to each other and then Richard kissed my lips repeatedly. "I forgot completely. You have more powers than the river Lethe, my love. Such sweet oblivion!"

"Do you think they heard us?"

He smiled, his lips still next to mine, the touch caressing me. "The people upstairs must have heard us, *ma chérie.*" He laughed softly. "You see, I told you I could make you blush." My face burned. He drew me close, while my blushes subsided. "Would you prefer to wait here for me, or come to us in a while?"

"No. That might make it worse, make it seem as though I was ashamed. Which I'm not," I added, putting up my face so he could see my blushes had gone. His smile and the look in his eyes almost made them return, but I kissed him and then sat up. "We must get up."

He sighed, reaching up a hand to caress me. "Later," he promised.

He brought my robe over to me. I put it on and went through to my dressing room, where Nichols waited for me. I could choose what I wanted to wear today, no disguise needed. While I washed, I decided to wear a white silk gown sprigged with tiny flowers. Together with a quilted petticoat and my pearls, that seemed to echo my festive mood. I was glad to think Mrs. Locke wouldn't have approved. The stomacher was a froth of ribbon bows and lace, all white, very frivolous and when I finally went into the dining room, I was pleased to see the reaction I received. All three men stood and bowed and suddenly I didn't feel quite so shy, even though I knew they must have heard something of our connubial bliss earlier. Richard was right when he said clothes could make a difference.

The man I didn't know was introduced to me as Signor Verdi, but his English was so perfect I suspected him of starting life as Mr. Green. It proved to be so when I asked him where he had learned his English.

"At home in Kent. I'm a clergyman's son, my lady, well educated but with nothing to support it. Since I find it difficult to apply myself to study, I was left with two choices; highwayman or to make my living more or less honestly on the tables." He smiled and took up his coffee cup. "For many years I travelled Europe, playing the tables and I learned many tricks on the way. I'll teach you some of them today. When I made money, I put half of it away and reinvested the other half in my own skill and so you see me as I am now. I no longer have any need of the tricks I learned. I gave up playing two years ago to play for fatter game on the stock exchanges. The memory of me has been lost and I am now generally regarded as respectable." He sipped at his coffee.

I regarded him thoughtfully as I ate. He was a slender man, average height and dark eyes in a thin, clever face that seemed keen to smile. I noticed an air of nervousness about him, perhaps he was highly strung, or perhaps from some underlying health concern. Whatever it was it made for a slight feeling of uneasiness in his presence.

Richard chatted affably to Freddy, letting me get to know our tutor, but occasionally he would glance in my direction and smile and I would smile back.

"Do you know this man, Ravens?" I asked.

"Oh yes, my lady," said Signor Verdi. "He's been around for some time now, but I've never known him take on this much of a deception. Fortunately, he doesn't know me, so I may take part in your scheme if my lord should wish it. He has always played the tables and I have set forward enquiries to see if he has made a great deal of money from somewhere recently. I would guess he has had a windfall and he's decided to reinvest in a larger scheme."

"I wouldn't have thought the expenditure to be worth the returns."

Signor Verdi smiled. "This is only the beginning, my lady. If my reasoning is right, he plans to draw you into his scheme and use you for some time to come. Your husband, in his persona as a wine merchant, will meet several illustrious people in the course of his work and he could draw quite a few people into the Ravens' orbit. The man may even be thinking of setting up a respectable gaming house with fair play, but once a cheat always a cheat."

"Even you?" I said, smiling.

"Yes indeed, even me. But in the markets I play, it's not considered cheating until it crosses the line into fraud. I can satisfy my wish to have an unfair advantage over my opponent without breaking the law."

"But Ravens can't call himself Lord Strang forever, can he? We may go to London in the autumn and then the world will know our whereabouts."

The man nodded, spearing a piece of bacon from his plate and chewing thoughtfully before he replied. "He'll quietly let it drop over the summer, my lady. Your livery will be modified to become the livery of the house and he'll be well established to take advantage of the fresh marks coming his way in the autumn."

"Marks?"

"Another word for cony, my lady. Cony, mark, pigeon, they

all mean the same thing."

I smiled over my coffee cup. "A fool?"

His answer surprised me. "Oh no, my lady, not a fool. That's a mistake many people make. The best marks are people who think they're up to all the games, but who are consumed by greed and superiority. They think they can get the better of their opponent right up to the last minute, but their greed blinds them to the truth."

I bit my lip in thought and decided that what he said made sense. Many things can blind people. I was blinded by love when I first met Richard, but I went ahead anyway, so if it had been greed and not love that had consumed me, I might well have taken that risk. "So you want someone rich and greedy?"

He smiled and his eyes glazed over, as though he was thinking of triumphs in his past. "Or influential. I think Ravens is looking to your husband less for money than for the custom he will bring. He will try to break him first and then try to draw him in."

"But instead, we'll draw him in?"

Richard broke in. "Something like that. I want to punish him a little for what he has done and what he tried to do. If I hadn't seen to it, he would be running up bills all over Venice in my name—our name," he corrected himself with a smile.

I smiled back and returned to my breakfast.

After the meal, we went to the music room where several small tables had been set out and Signor Verdi began to teach us how to cheat.

"He asked us if we played piquet," Richard said.

The Signor brightened. "Then he wishes to demonstrate a skill. Since all thirty-two used are visible by the end of the game, cards cannot be introduced to the hand from elsewhere." Without appearing to move his hand, suddenly there was a card in it, the Queen of Diamonds. He bowed his head, accepting our applause, then pushed back the lace at the wrist and showed us a device hidden there. By manipulating a small muscle in his wrist, a spring was activated, which pushed a card up into his hand to use in the pack.

"How do you lose the extra card?" Freddy asked, leaning

forward to examine the device. Signor Verdi obligingly untied the tapes and handed the device over for him to look at more closely.

"I could find a use for that," said Richard thoughtfully. I couldn't imagine what he would want it for.

"I can show you how it is made, my lord, then you can get your own done. Meantime, please accept this one as a gift." Richard thanked him. Signor Verdi continued to show us how he could slip unwanted cards in a pocket, a coat cuff or a secret compartment stitched into the seam of a coat or waistcoat. "In the lady's case the same principle applies, but the folds of the skirt can prove very useful."

"There are lady card sharps?" I said, surprised and then caught myself up. "Of course there must be, how stupid of me!"

Richard, glanced up from the device in his hand. "Not stupid, merely innocent. I feel we are corrupting you, my love, but you must say if you don't want this to go any further."

I laughed. "Oh no, do you think provincial life is so sinless? We have our share of rogues, you may be sure. Just not the *best* rogues, that's all." They laughed too and I went on, "To be honest, I haven't enjoyed myself so much for a long time. I would really like to be a part of this, as much as I can."

Freddy pursed his lips before saying, "'Fore God, Richard, if you hadn't discovered her first, I might well have made a push for your wife myself."

"She has a great deal of spirit," he agreed, smiling.

I laughed to receive such foolish compliments and we turned back to attend to Signor Verdi.

"In piquet, the deal is all," he said, "but there is some skill involved. A good player can win a *partie* with a poor set of cards, if the *talon* is good and a skilled card sharp can give an opponent hope, only to take it away again."

He picked up one of several packs of cards that lay on a table and broke the seal. We watched him sort the cards for piquet, the sevens up and discard the lower numbers, leaving a pack of thirty-eight and then we watched him shuffle them. I tried to see if he was cheating, but I could see nothing amiss.

Signor Verdi gave it to me to cut. Then he proceeded to

deal, face up, two hands of twelve and the *talon,* the central reserve both players use in the initial part of the game to replace part of their hands. He exchanged five from the dealer's hand, three to the other and sat back while we looked at the result.

It was obvious the dealer won. The dealer usually had the advantage, but since the dealer alternated over a *partie* of six hands, the advantage usually evened out.

"Pique and repique," breathed Freddy, enthralled. One hand was replete with court cards and hearts to give long points, sequences and sets, all high scoring and the other had one court card to avoid the *carte blanche* and very little else.

"Shuffling is a more difficult trick than palming," Signor Verdi warned us. "You must work very hard to achieve it. Were you hoping to learn it for tomorrow?"

Richard shook his head. "No. Tomorrow we're being set up. We will win, I'm sure."

The Signor beamed. "*Bene.* Then we have more time."

Freddy looked up from the cards. "But you can only win three times in a *partie* with this and it's damned suspicious."

Signor Verdi beamed, picked up the cards, riffled through them quickly and gave them to Freddy. "If you would care to deal, my lord?"

Freddy shuffled and then, after letting the Signor cut, dealt face up again. The results were similar, but this time the best cards were with the person dealt to. Freddy and I clapped our hands in delight. It was thrilling to see a skill well executed, however nefarious. Richard studied the cards, his hand to his chin.

"It is more difficult," the Signor said, "but it can be done. I shuffled before I gave you the cards and I cut them. I can either substitute them for a deck of my own, or practise the greater skill of pre-shuffling."

"With the second method, you're far less likely to be caught," Richard said.

"Precisely," the man replied. "Shall we begin? I should like to see you all play a few hands, if you please, to see how you handle the cards. If the methods here are to work, they must look as natural as possible."

We obliged him, taking turns to play a single *partie*. Our teacher watched intently, the way we sat, the way we held the cards, how we sorted them. I had to sort and resort my cards, Freddy did it once and Richard never sorted at all, leaning back, legs crossed, long fingers playing negligently over the backs of the cards. The signor insisted we keep score and I was delighted when I beat both the gentlemen, although the luck was with me rather than the skill.

"You play well," Signor Verdi told me with inclination of his head.

I smiled in return. "An unmis-spent youth. Spent with the old tabbies in the card rooms rather than in the ballroom."

Signor Verdi threw up his hands. "The worst of opponents! You think you are safe with them, but they have probably learned more tricks in a lifetime than you have in a few years. I have been fleeced myself by such a one, who had been skinning conies all her life, almost gaining respectability in the process. I didn't expect it, you see."

He proceeded to teach us how to shuffle to our advantage. We had to learn the fundamentals first and then try to conceal what we were doing after we had mastered the skill. To my chagrin, I couldn't master it, however hard I tried. At one point, Signor Verdi took my hand and examined it.

"A small palm and long fingers," he said thoughtfully. "It may be, my lady, the cards are too large for your hands. A pity. But keep trying."

I looked ruefully at my hands, good for music, but not for cheating. Richard had long fingers too, but his palms were larger and after a while he achieved some success.

Freddy could have been born to it. He only had to be showed the trick it seemed, to master it. "Oh, marvellous!" he exclaimed after a while. "Something I'm good at, at last. Such a shame I can't show it off!"

"It would amuse the ladies," Richard said, concentrating on clandestinely sliding one card behind another.

"And who would play cards with me after that?" demanded his lordship.

Signor Verdi sighed. "I'm afraid, my lord, there is always someone who thinks they can outdo you."

I gave up after a while, my fingers aching with effort and went to arrange some refreshment instead.

It occurred to me that I hadn't yet taken up any of the duties expected of a wife—except one—and I called Carier to attend me in the salon. Together we arranged a suitable dinner and I asked him to send the cook to me to arrange it every day, but I found since we shared the kitchens with the other occupants of the building, we had no cook. "I think we should find one, don't you? I should like my husband to have what he wishes for in the way of food."

Carier seemed to concur and promised to find a cook the next day. "It will have to be a Thompson's cook my lady. We have very special people here."

"You mean all the staff here are from the Box?" I referred to the special box Carier or Richard always carried with them, which held the names of the staff with particular skills who could be relied upon to fulfil special duties.

Carier said it was true. "His lordship won't take any risks where you're concerned, my lady. This place is as secure as the Tower of London."

I went back to the music room, a little awed by the ruthless way I was being looked after. I wasn't used to being thought of as quite so precious.

We spent the rest of the day in practice, at least Richard and Freddy did. I couldn't do it unobtrusively, I wouldn't have deceived a child. I gave up after a while and played the harpsichord for them. I tried to keep it light, but the usual thing happened and in my concentration, I forgot there was anyone else there. Richard had provided a great deal of sheet music for me to work from and I found a piece by Vivaldi I had never seen before. I began to work on it while they practised and by the time dinner was announced, I had fairly mastered it and I played it through once for them, while they sat back and listened.

The state of the room made me laugh when I finally turned to face them. Discarded cards lay everywhere, on the floor

147

where they had fallen from fumbling fingers, thrown carelessly over tables and a large heap of discarded deuces to sixes on one table.

I stood up and curtseyed when they applauded me and then sat down. "What if it's not piquet? What if it's loo, or whist, or something else?"

"Oh Lord!" said Freddy. "Her ladyship's right, you know."

Signor Verdi clicked his tongue in irritation. "The shuffling method will help in most games. However, the palming should be learnt, if you gentlemen think you would like to try."

Richard looked at Freddy, who nodded eagerly. "I've finally found something I'm good at. It's a relief to find out I'm good for something."

Richard stretched his arms above his head and flexed his fingers. "Apart from fencing and shooting?"

Freddy shrugged. "Yes, but I'm not one for duelling, either. I like life too much, I suppose, to want to risk it any more. But I don't dance with any real distinction, my mind's not anything above the average and repartee leaves me gasping with admiration but dumb."

I laughed, recognising some of those traits in myself. "I can't do those things either. But I can shoot straight."

Richard stood, came over to take my hand and drew me to my feet. "You have a lively mind and a great heart, *mia adorata* and you play like an angel." I smiled and bowed my head, accepting his words.

We didn't linger over dinner and after I left them alone over their port, they were back very quickly, this time to practise palming cards. They each tried to use the little device and practised losing discarded cards about their persons. Signor Verdi gave them a stern warning. "I would not recommend using this unless you have to. If you are searched and the cards and devices are found on your person, it is proof of cheating and then Ravens will have a real cause for blackmail."

This made Richard think hard. He dropped his cards and sat back in the chair, frowning. "You're right. We can't use this. It would be playing into his hands."

"We may not need any of it," I pointed out.

"True," Richard admitted. "I hope we don't, but I wanted to know what they did and if they cheated, which they undoubtedly will. We need to draw them in first. Let them gull us. We'll go on our own, just Rose and me and leave you as our secret weapons. You can come later, when we're well and truly embroiled in their plot."

Freddy looked up with glowing eyes, smiling hugely as he gathered up his cards for another try. "I haven't had this much fun for a long time. I wouldn't have missed today's entertainment for anything."

We both smiled as we studied him, an immensely attractive man, glowing with satisfaction. "I think it's time to call a halt," Richard said. "We should thank Signor Verdi for a most interesting day and send him home. And you, Freddy, have someone waiting for you."

"Good God, I'd forgotten! So that shows you how much I've enjoyed myself." He stood hastily and sent a shower of cards over the floor.

Signor Verdi rose smoothly and bowed, first to me, then to the gentlemen. "It has been an honour. I shall wait for your word, my lord." He left the room, closely followed by Freddy, hastening back to his expensive mistress.

"I wish I could meet her," I told Richard.

"Why?"

"So she can teach me some new tricks?" I laughed at the appalled response in his eyes. "No, no, it's just I've never met someone like her before and I'm curious. Oh, I know she won't have two heads, or horns or something, but I've been almost nowhere before this, seen very little. Will you promise to point her out to me if we see her somewhere, if I promise not to introduce myself?"

"Very well." He wasn't best pleased, but he flashed a sudden smile at me. "Life won't be simple with you, will it?"

I shook my head. "I never used to be like this, before I met you. You give me a confidence I didn't know I had."

"I rather suspect it was there all the time. I meant what I said—you have a great heart. Courage is only part of it."

I turned away so he shouldn't see my sudden tears,

blinking them back. "Shall I play for you?"

"Haven't you played enough? Aren't you tired?"

"No." I sat at the harpsichord and picked up some music, then put it down again. "But you looked tired and you might like it."

"If you feel you can," he replied, "I'd love you to."

I played for him while he sat back with his eyes closed, at ease with himself for once.

Chapter Twelve

We got up late the next day and spent the day in *déshabillé*. I read or played while Richard practised his new skills and one other, which worried me somewhat. He used the new device Signor Verdi had given him and one of his wicked little knives. Eventually he mastered it and time after time he could project the knife into his hand or towards a target without hurting himself. He had to hold his hand back until the razor sharp blade had passed it and grasp the handle as it hurtled past the palm, just at the right moment. After an hour or two he could do it every time. I found it frightening. We might find the skill useful and that meant we would be in danger.

After dinner we dressed as Mr. and Mrs. Locke to go to the Palazzo Barbarossa. I was using some of the clothes I used to wear habitually as Miss Golightly of Darkwater, Devonshire, clothes I was perfectly happy with when I was Miss Golightly, but I was beginning to be dissatisfied with now. I'd begun to appreciate the qualities of fine clothes, the way they flattered, the way a well-fitted gown felt on the body. Lizzie would never believe it. I had never set store by my appearance before, I had aimed for respectability and conventionality rather than the elegance I wanted to achieve now. Lizzie had always been the one concerned with her appearance before, being the family beauty and I had given up after her come-out. I had thought I was done for on the marriage market and tried to accept my lot with equanimity, without self-pity.

Now, looking at the plain blue silk gown with its modest robings I could see what was wrong with it. It didn't fit precisely at the waist, or perhaps my stays were laced tighter these days and the skirt should have been made fuller. The silk wasn't of the best quality and had been washed too much and not starched enough, so it hung limply where it should have held its folds. I would get rid of the gown as soon as I was done with silly Mrs. Locke. Nichols fixed a lace cap over my severely dressed hair and I was ready.

I had to wait for Richard in the salon and when he came in, I saw he was as plainly dressed as I was, but with that air he carried that he could never hide. I wondered if he'd been born with that way of carrying himself, the instinct to stand and sit in the most pleasing way, but I said nothing.

He took both of my hands, smiling. "You look just as you did when I first met you. On the whole, I prefer you as you were yesterday, but needs must, I suppose. How many seasons did you make that gown do for?" He looked me up and down.

"Three. I had it remade a couple of times, but I couldn't see the point of throwing good money away on something else. I would rather have spent it on a good riding habit. At least I was happier in those."

"And now?"

I smiled. "Now I'm happier wearing nothing at all."

He laughed. "Cutting the ground from under my feet. Come, we're expected."

We went down to the gondola, where Carier and Nichols waited for us and the boatmen poled us away from our plain, unobtrusive building and towards the magnificent Palazzo Barbarossa.

"I confidently expect us to be richer by the end of the evening," Richard commented.

"Yes, my lord," Carier replied dourly.

"Have you had the information delivered to the Ravens?"

"Yes, my lord."

I turned to Richard, surprised. "Oh, didn't I tell you? I'm sorry, my sweet, I must have had something else on my mind." He smiled briefly at me and I saw his loving expression by the light of the flaring torch on the front of our gondola. I smiled back.

Carier sighed and brought us both back to reality. "I had

some information made available to the Ravens," Richard said. "The Lockes aren't as well off as they might at first appear. Free trading has hit the business badly in England and their credit is fully extended, but this is seen as a temporary setback, as Mr. Locke looks to the rest of Europe for his profit."

"Why did you do that?"

Richard took my hand. "Because then he will know we are vulnerable, easily bent to his will and the game will be shorter. We've found no trace of an assassin here in Venice and the real reason for all this exercise seems to have evaporated. I don't think he's been drawn here and we only wait for word from England before we resume our identities in public."

"So I can throw this gown away?"

He smiled. "Very soon, unless you want to keep it for future use. And you may loosen your hairstyle, wear proper lace and jewellery and go to Aunt Augusta's reception."

We had arrived at the palazzo. Dark was creeping down on us, but all the torches outside the great buildings made it as bright as day. Finely dressed people climbed out of gilded barges at a house next to the one where we were going. The building blazed with light inside and out, sending flaming, flickering shadows over the rippling water and for some strange reason I suddenly felt bereft, left out of something I had a right to. I tried to hide the longing in my expression and I turned away from the light to see his face.

He frowned, watching the people alighting from the gondolas with narrowed eyes. "We're not as alone as we thought. Do you see, Carier?"

"Yes, my lord."

He turned to me. "I'm known to several of those people. The sooner this game is over the better. But let's enjoy it while we can." He stood to help me out of the boat.

The Palazzo Barbarossa was quieter, but we discovered we were not the only guests. Six other people waited there, all unknown to us, thank goodness, all not of the first rank, all flattered to be invited to such a grand house. There were four other ladies, all British. The Ravens had obviously decided where to target their efforts. I suspected one couple, who seemed to be more at home than the others, of being planted there by the Ravens.

They greeted us graciously, gave us refreshment and took us into a large, impressive salon where card tables were set out. The salon was too grand for such an intimate gathering but everyone seemed impressed by the white and gold prettiness of the decoration. Richard sat at a table near me and I saw his seemingly negligent disposal of his coat skirts, achieving an effect others might dream of. The movements came so naturally to him he didn't realise he was doing it.

I first played a game with one of the suspicious couple, introduced to us as Mr. and Mrs. Squires, from Shropshire.

"I'm so foolish," I told Mrs. Squires, "I'm afraid you might have to remind me of the rules from time to time." She smiled at me in a motherly way.

Mr. Ravens suggested we play for a shilling a point initially, since this was a friendly game and he sat opposite Richard, smiling affably. Perhaps he found his resources stretched, since we had put a stop to his credit in Venice. He was dressed as finely as ever, but I was sure his jewels were paste. I saw Richard glance at him once and smile slightly and I knew he thought the same.

I picked up my cards. Mrs. Locke would be a shockingly bad card player. Accordingly I fumbled my hand of twelve and dropped one or two, although I found I didn't feel nervous at all, now the time had come for our first real outing with these people. I had been dealt a fair hand and proceeded to play it as I should, but with a great deal of hesitation. Mrs. Squires kept score and she waited patiently as I sorted and resorted the cards in my hand into points, sequences and sets. I let a low heart go into the *talon* that I should really have kept, as hearts were my leading sequence and picked up a club instead. I did score some points from that hand, mainly from three kings but Mrs. Squires had a strong advantage when it came to my deal.

The hand I dealt seemed to be fair, but I had shuffled the cards thoroughly, as Signor Verdi had taught us to do. I won it, although my margin of victory was not as great as Mrs. Squires' had been. I would make her work for my triumph.

From time to time I glanced at Richard, playing as Mr.

Locke. He was deliberately trying to suppress his natural instincts to sit elegantly and hold the cards in a certain way, but he forgot to let his finger drop when he drank from his glass. He held it up instead to curl it around the bowl and show off its length and slenderness. I smiled as I looked back down at my cards.

"You have been married long?" Mrs. Squires enquired, seeing my look and smile.

I must be more careful. "We've been married for five years but I was ill for some of that time and my husband has to travel for his business, so we haven't been together as much as we might have been."

"I'm sorry." The lady led with an ace. "Are you quite well now?"

"Yes, thank you." I gave her a king for the trick. "Venice suits me."

"It will get very hot soon," Mrs. Squires commented. "Venice gets very unhealthy then."

"We thought we might go to Paris." That at least was true.

Mrs. Squires smiled unpleasantly. "And do you go to Versailles?"

"Yes," I said without thinking and had to amend the statement. "At least, my husband has clients there, so I hope to see it when I go there with him."

She frowned over her cards before selecting one. "Such a great palace! Such a shame our royal family doesn't have that sense of style."

"Have you been presented, Mrs. Squires?" I suspected not.

She sighed. "In my youth. But we live quietly these days. The court of St. James's was not a patch on Versailles." I wondered if they had fallen on hard times and into the clutches of the Ravens. It seemed likely.

As the evening progressed and we played more *parties,* Richard and I slowly began to win more hands and the scores crept up in our favour. I was fascinated to see how cleverly the tide turned, how suddenly I was winning and Richard too. I let my delight show, though not the reason for it and I saw the lady I was playing with visibly relax, as she did her job well.

The salon seemed so empty, even though the Ravens had hired a quartet to play. They played indifferently, all Italian music, filling the room with thready music, which didn't cover the conversation. The wins excited some of the other people. I guessed they were not accustomed to their surroundings or their purported company. Or perhaps the wine was strong. I took care over that. I didn't trust myself to drink too much in case I gave anything away, but most of the others drank freely. Faces grew flushed and voices louder. The guests became garrulous and talked about their lives and their reasons for being in Venice.

We changed partners after we had reckoned the points and, not to my surprise, I found myself several guineas to the good.

My new partner was a red-faced English gentleman, the husband of the motherly lady I had just left. He looked every inch a squire, bluff and hearty. He seemed determined to spice up his card game with some crude flirting. I beat him too, and I watched him overcome his chagrin by increasing the flirtation.

"Your beauty has enlivened this dreary city," was one of his first comments.

I was surprised. He must have that the wrong way round, so I ventured a mild, "You don't approve of Venice, sir?"

He looked indignant I should even ask. "No indeed!" His voice could have carried across a hunting field. "My wife said she wanted to visit it and I am an indulgent husband, so I accompanied her here." He paused to sort his cards and then looked up again. "It's too wet and too gloomy. No horses, either, except stone ones." I dutifully laughed at his mild joke and he roared for a while, thus obviating the need for any more perceptive comments. He continued, when he had wiped his eyes and recovered some equilibrium. "It's too expensive. And the churches are Popish, full of statues and finery, not at all like a proper church. Blasphemous, I call it."

"They call our ways blasphemous," I ventured.

He snorted. "Impudence!"

We played the hand and then it was his deal. While he shuffled the cards he concentrated on me. At first I was relieved, but then I began to feel uncomfortable, especially as his wife was only at the next table. "Wonderful to see an Englishwoman in this God-forsaken place," he said, looking at me rather than the cards in his hands. "You exude the fresh air of England, my dear. Whereabouts do you come from?"

"Dorsetshire," I didn't want to mention my real home county. "I live in London with my husband now, when we aren't travelling."

"A beautiful county. And if it produces women as beautiful as you, I regret never having visited it." He dealt the cards and I could busy myself with my hand. As I picked up my cards my hand brushed his and I knew he'd done it on purpose. His smile seemed more like a leer. "I would very much like to see you again," he roared and then leaned over the table confidentially. I smelled the wine on his breath. He didn't lower his voice. "Without your husband." I was glad my gown wasn't as low-cut as some I possessed.

I wasn't used to this kind of attention but I determined not to let my co-conspirators down. I hoped Squires didn't come here again, but I feared he might be another mark and so would be present until the game was played out.

Squires seemed to enjoy my discomfiture and I had to move his hand from mine once or twice when they met on the table. He tried to pay me compliments that I acknowledged with a small smile and I knew by the time we had to move on again he thought he had made a conquest. I won again, but not by so much.

My third and last partner was "Lady Strang". I studied this impostor, the showy gown, the false sapphires at her neck and I sighed. I thought of my sapphires resting in their case at the apartment and the fine gowns I hadn't yet worn and then chided myself for being so vain.

We set to playing and I could again admire the skill of the professional card sharper, this time used in my favour. I did my best to lose, by putting cards into the *talon* I should have kept and failing to see sets of four, but she kindly corrected me when she could and seemed to have very bad luck. If a player has no court cards, they can claim a *carte blanche* and increase their score, but strangely, she seemed to avoid that, always having at least one in her hand, not usually any good to her. At one point

I was forced to claim pique and repique, the best score possible. When it was over I found myself a heavy winner.

I smiled with delight as we all rose for supper and I found myself claimed by the blustering Mr. Squires, red-faced from drink and crowing with triumph. Richard led in Mrs. Squires, smiling politely as she told him about her children. She commiserated with him at his lack of offspring.

"My wife's been ill recently," he told her, "I can only be thankful she been spared the travails of childbirth."

The lady frowned in sympathy and leaned towards him, patting his hand in consolation, her approach as obvious as her husband's had been to me.

Mr. Squires gave me a cup of punch, letting his fat hand rest on mine again. "I hope you're in the best of health now, Mrs. Locke?"

I assured him I was and sipped the punch cautiously. With some relief I saw Richard coming over to me. His companion held on to his arm with quite a grip so she left a mark on the dark red cloth of his coat. "Sadly, we have to take leave of our hosts. We have to be about our business in the morning and I don't want you overtired."

I played my part and took his arm when he shook off his new friend. We went to see our hosts and made our excuses. They expressed regret, but said they perfectly understood and went to the door of the salon with us. "A perfectly charming evening," Richard told them. "I can understand why you should abjure the reception next door."

Mrs. Ravens' look went to her husband as he said smoothly, "Quite. We find we much prefer quiet evenings with a few acquaintances to such affairs. Besides, it would not be the thing on a bride-trip."

His sense of the proprieties was either unusual or he was using it as an excuse. To my surprise, Richard gave him our card, the wrong name but the right address. I hadn't known he would do that. I asked him about it when we had reached the safety of our gondola. "We'd better do some reeling in of our own. They'll want to invite us for a rematch and they'll need somewhere to send the invitation. Also, although the address is good, it's only an apartment and it might serve to confirm their suspicions about us."

The gondolier pushed us off the side of the building and passed to the next, where the reception was still in full swing, when we heard something we would rather have not. "Strang!"

Chapter Thirteen

Richard turned his head. A young man was waving from the quay. A beautifully dressed young man, either just emerging from the house, or going into it. He paused when he saw me, but Richard ordered the gondolier to pull in. "The game is up, I'm afraid, my love."

"Strang!" said the youth. "I heard you were in Venice! Oh, Lord, have I committed a *faux pas*?" He paused and looked anxiously at me. I thought with some amusement that he must have taken me for a lady of the night.

"Not at all, Wrisley," said Richard, "but you'll do me the honour of not crying my name out like a watchman calling the hours." The youth coloured up. "My dear, this is Lord Wrisley. Wrisley, this is my wife, Lady Strang."

"Oh!" The young man bowed hastily, but elegantly. "Beg pardon. I didn't know you were married, Strang."

"How long have you been abroad now, Wrisley?"

"Just over a year, why?"

Richard glanced anxiously at the Palazzo Barbarossa, but there was no sign of anyone except the footmen outside the door. "I wondered why I didn't see you at the wedding. On the Tour?"

"Yes. Haven't had such a good time in my whole life before! I must say," he added, looking doubtfully at us, "you've changed since I saw you last. Are you coming in? You must have been sent an invitation."

Richard looked down at himself, then at me. "Like this?"

"Well you only live next door, don't you?" said Lord Wrisley.

"Go and change."

"Well, no, we don't live next door," Richard admitted. "I'll tell you about it, if you like, but not here." He turned to me. "It's barely ten. Should you like to change and come back here? I'd love to show you off as you should be." He turned back to Wrisley. "Whose reception is it?"

Wrisley was carrying a black mask on a stick, which he waved in the vague direction of the house. "Contessa Marini's. She's bound to have sent you an invitation."

Richard shrugged. "It probably went to the wrong address." Wrisley drifted off into the house. "Would you like to go, my love?"

I didn't stop to think properly. "Yes. I can wear my new sapphires."

We waved goodbye to Lord Wrisley and promised to return. "My lord," Nichols said from behind us, "this may not be wise."

Richard waved her concerns away. "I'm tired of hiding my bride away. No one from the gathering tonight will be at the contessa's, and our assassin is notable by his absence."

The boatman pushed away from the quay. Richard leaned back once more. "I didn't know the contessa was in residence. She's an old friend of my mother's and if we don't go, she'll probably pay us a call at the palazzo. Then the fat would be in the fire." He turned his head and regarded me, his gaze soft in the gentle light of the lamp set in the front of the boat. "In any case, I want to see you shine."

I turned my head towards where Nichols sat in the rear of the gondola. "Can you dress me in half an hour?"

"If we don't powder, it should be possible, my lady."

"Very well. The dark blue."

We returned to the apartment and I went to my dressing room, as excited as a girl at her first assembly. The suddenness of it and the prospect of dressing as I should, lifted my spirits and the thought of going with Richard made me feel even better.

Nichols was as good as her word. In barely half an hour she had dressed my hair in a more flattering style, taken off the offending gown and dressed me in one of my new ones. I chose a dark blue brocade embroidered over in pink, with its matching petticoat. Then she changed my lace to fine Brussels point and arrayed me in the sapphires. When I opened the box, I found Richard had added a pair of earrings to match, heavy three pendanted girandoles, just right for the gown. I went to the music room, where he waited for me. When he saw me, he bowed, before coming forward to take both my hands. "Now that is more like Lady Strang should look."

He had chosen pink, a deep pink that complimented my gown perfectly. I'm sure no accident was involved in his choice. His waistcoat was of the palest shell pink, seemingly embroidered by mice, with glittering buttons that didn't look like paste to me. The diamond pin was back at his throat and the wig was a perfection of powdered curls, ending in a queue fastened by a black ribbon. How a man in pink could look so blatantly masculine passed my understanding, but he managed it, the tight cut of the sleeves displaying the muscles of his arm when he bent them. When he moved the muscles in his thigh was outlined by the fine fabric, the lace showering over his hands only emphasised their firm structure.

We were poled up the Grand Canal to the house. One or two people were still arriving, so we followed them in through the doors.

Richard didn't need to tell the servants who he was. We were announced and went through.

Unlike the grand rooms next door, this one was thronged with people, all begowned and bejewelled, obviously the cream of Venice society. They all turned to look, every one.

"You're new," Richard murmured to me as we descended the stairs. "They're wondering about us. Stare them out."

A large lady of a certain age surged through the crowds to greet us, the crowd parting before her. I curtseyed low while Richard made the introductions to our hostess, the Contessa Marini.

"Richard! And your new lady wife. Lady Southwood wrote and told me you had finally married and I didn't believe it, but now I see her I can believe it only too well." The contessa beamed and to my surprise took me by the hand. "*Plus bella!* I always knew Richard as a connoisseur and I see he waited for the best he could find."

"I'm glad you can see that, Contessa," Richard murmured, smiling when he saw my blushes.

"To tell the truth," the contessa continued, "your mama wrote to me, telling me you were marrying a little brunette sparrow of a girl and she was very surprised, knowing your preference for blondes, but this is surely not the lady she was describing."

I tired of being talked about. "I've always thought of myself in those terms. Only Richard thought of me differently."

The contessa spread her fan and waved it vigorously, nearly taking out the eye of a nearby guest. "I see no little sparrow here." Her dark eyes flashed. "You are a *coup* for me, my dear. Invitation after invitation has been sent to you and you have accepted none. All Venice been agog to see you!" By her standards, "all Venice" was her particular confined circle, most of who must be present here tonight. "Richard has been courted by the most beautiful girls for years and he has never even turned his head." He turned plenty of other things though, but for their older, married sisters. The reminders were constantly about and it would be foolish of me to ignore them. But he was mine now and I intended to keep him.

"If the invitations are sent to the Palazzo Barbarossa, they won't find us there," Richard explained.

Several heads nearby discreetly turned. Richard moved and led the contessa and me further into the room. He spoke as we walked, so no one could overhear the whole. "We discovered impostors living there. It's their misfortune that we chose Venice as our destination, but I owe them a small service for helping my wife on the road, so I don't wish to condemn them publicly."

The contessa gave him a shrewd glance. "You're up to something."

"Not at all, Contessa," Richard replied smoothly.

At that moment, someone I knew came up to us and bowed. "Richard! I thought you weren't showing your face yet."

"We had little choice, Freddy," Richard said. "Wrisley saw us outside and immediately called out at the full stretch of his lungs. We changed in the greatest haste and returned. I fear I'll have to tell everyone not to use the palazzo next door for us, so I wonder if you would do me a favour and take care of my wife for a while? Once you've heard the same story more than once, it tends to bore and I particularly wish Rose to enjoy herself tonight."

"The greatest pleasure imaginable," said Freddy gallantly, offering his arm. I curtseyed to the contessa and left them. Freddy took me to find a glass of wine and then to a corner filled with some of the younger people.

"Here is the new Lady Strang!" he declared, thus doing away with formal introductions. Then he rattled off the names of the people there, explaining, "You won't remember all the names, but I daresay enough will come back to you to be useful."

Miss Crich, a blonde and pretty young lady, eyed me curiously. "So you're the one. I'd love to know how you did it. I tried for him myself a year or two ago, but apart from a delightful flirtation, I didn't get very far. Some people call him the Iceberg, you know and they've been taking bets for years on who and when Strang would marry." She patted the seat beside her. "Come and sit with me and tell me all about it."

I had little choice. Only then I realised I didn't know how much of Richard's privacy he wanted me to keep. I decided to err on the side of caution. "Well, my cousin—the last Lord Hareton—and Strang's sister, Maria, had an agreement but that fell through."

She flicked her fan in a gesture of dismissal. "An arrangement? Surely not! I would never have supposed Lord Strang would marry to please his parents."

"He was supposed to marry Miss Julia Cartwright, to please them," I reminded her.

"Yes," she agreed doubtfully. Young ladies surrounded our sofa and they leaned forward in a scented wave at the mention of Julia's name. Obviously some of the scandal had leaked out. We had not been anxious to conceal it, but neither had we spread any gossip. There would always be plenty of people for that. "Lady Strang," murmured Miss Crich. "You were there, weren't you, at Hareton? Have you any idea what *really* went on?"

I marshalled my thoughts. "I know some of it. I met the man I wanted, by some miracle he wanted me and Julia got in the way. Meantime, Miss Cartwright preferred my brother's curate to Lord Strang."

"So it's true! Did they really run off together? Is he as poor as they say?" Fans were vigorously plied and the heat increased as half a dozen young ladies moved closer. I unfurled my own fan, lifted it over my mouth and decided I might as well sow some mischief. "Yes, they ran off together. Overnight!" There followed a collective indrawn breath of delicious satisfaction. "And yes, he is poor. Or he was, because I suppose he has the disposal of her fortune now."

"I saw them," someone said and thankfully attention turned away from me. "Mr. Drury is very handsome, isn't he, Lady Strang?"

"Very. He was curate of our parish in Devonshire and he only came to Yorkshire as our escort on the road. He determined to make the most of his good luck. Every young lady in Devonshire was at his feet, but not seriously, you know, because of his lack of personal fortune." They nodded wisely. I omitted any mention of my foolish infatuation with him. It seemed so long ago now and completely irrelevant. "Miss Cartwright decided she wanted him, despite her formal betrothal to Lord Strang. She neglected Strang disgracefully after his accident, intent on seducing Drury." I sighed theatrically and looked around at the sea of rapt faces around me. "She succeeded."

"Accident?" someone said. It seemed they hadn't heard that part.

"Richard was in the coach accident that killed the last two Earls of Hareton," I explained. "He cut his arm badly and his man had to stitch it up for him. Miss Cartwright didn't think her place was by his side."

"I knew it!" Miss Crich sat back and clapped her hands. "You nursed him when he was ill and you brought yourself to his notice. How clever of you!"

I didn't want the conversation to turn to me. "No, it wasn't like that."

"Not quite," he agreed. I glanced up to where he leaned on the back of my sofa, his attention only on me. To my relief I saw his smile, not a frown of disapproval. I looked away hastily, still not sure how much he wanted people to know about us.

Miss Crich continued. "The Drurys went to London, you know, after they married and they're saying the most scurrilous things to anyone who will listen."

Richard leant his elbow negligently on the back of our sofa. "How do you know, Miss Crich? I seem to remember you being sent away in disgrace some time before."

To my surprise she laughed. "Oh that! My mother was convinced I was going to run away with Lord Trente, but I never meant to. I left him waiting at the rendezvous and sent someone to tell him."

"He turned up?" said my husband in some surprise. "But he's a convicted Jacobite!"

"Yes, but I didn't tell anyone about it until I was sure he'd gone. Fair's fair, after all." The laughter was general, but I was just a little shocked at the behaviour of a young, unmarried lady. It would have ruined anyone of my circle, but it seemed here it was more permissible.

Another lady entered the fray, a dark, pretty girl, who stood on the other side of the sofa. "I've heard some of the things Mrs. Drury said. Of course, I never believed a word of them."

"Of course," I agreed, too quickly.

She looked down at me, her finely plucked brows arched in surprise. Her fan flicked shut. "She said Lord Strang had thrown himself away on a little brown thing, not at all his style." She stared at me. I didn't need to look at Richard to know the frozen look he assumed, his eyelids drooping over those cold blue orbs. "She said some dreadful things as well, some things I don't care to repeat." She looked as though she would love to repeat them and probably would have done, had we not been there.

He touched my shoulder. "Julia was always spiteful. What do you think? Have I married a little brown thing?"

They all stared at me, assessing. I badly wanted to drop my head and retreat into the background, but I put up my chin and stared back at them. I caught Freddy's glance and he smiled, so I smiled too.

Miss Crich sighed. "Sadly, no. Lady Strang can give me half a head, so takes care of the 'little' part. And she's not at all brown, apart from her hair. In any case, Julia Drury was always a spiteful package. I never liked her."

Richard leaned forward and lowered his voice. "What will you tell her?"

Miss Crich lifted her chin so her face was close to his and smiled, brilliantly. "I don't speak to her. Ask her yourself."

"We're hardly on speaking terms ourselves." He straightened up. "I wish her joy."

"Really?" Miss Crich turned her head to stare at him.

"She released me from a contract that was particularly irksome to me and left me free to follow my true destiny." He touched my shoulder again.

Miss Crich clapped her hands in triumph. "So I was right. I *said* it was more than dynastic. I knew you wouldn't marry merely to please your parents, any more than I would. Didn't I say?" She turned to her friends, who all agreed that she had said. "And he swept you off your feet, didn't he, Lady Strang? He's very good at that. I've seen him do it any number of times."

Not as he did it with me. "It happened very quickly, but I wasn't against it."

Miss Crich smiled wistfully. "Sometimes I think I'll never marry. Now the best prospect is off the market, I don't fancy any of them any more."

Richard moved around to the front of the sofa. "Somehow, Miss Crich, I don't think you're destined for old maidenhood. You'll make some man's life a delight and a misery and I'll dance at your wedding."

He held out his hand to me. I saw the warm look and felt the light pressure of his fingers. "Some people wish to meet you, my love." I stood to join him, hardly noticing the brief silence as his use of the endearment sank in with the people within earshot. "I told you our privacy wouldn't last long. Now the contessa knows our direction, the world will be at our door."

"I thought you were at the Palazzo Barbarossa!" said the

dark girl.

"Then you thought wrong," he said. "They're impostors. We'll let them play their game, but they'll be gone shortly. Don't you think that's rather an ostentatious place for my taste?"

"I wondered why no one could get in to see you," said Miss Crich. "Are you going to punish them?"

His eyes gleamed. "A little. But I promised Rose I wouldn't be too severe. She has a kind heart." He lifted my hand to his lips and kissed the tips of my fingers before he led me away. I didn't look back.

He introduced me to several other people on the other side of the room who made kind comments and congratulated us, some in English, some in Italian, which, because of my music studies, I could understand tolerably well. I felt much happier here than I did at the Palazzo Barbarossa. I was beautifully gowned and surprised to find the confidence it gave to me. I had the full attention of the most desirable man in the room and people seemed genuinely pleased to see us, although I was not foolish enough to take them all at face value. Some stared after us as we left them, some smiled reminiscently and some must have forgotten us as soon as we left them.

Having done our duty, we returned to the younger set, where they still sat and gossiped. Richard found a chair for me before he went to find a drink for us. Freddy came and sat down by me. "Sensation." he murmured. "This society is starved of it—they were looking for something like this."

I spread my fan to hide our quiet conversation. "That we've come out of seclusion?"

He laughed. "That's one thing. Your impostors are another—everybody wants to see them. I predict a very successful opening if they decide to open their house. But the way he looks at you, attends to you, nobody's seen him like that before."

I lowered my fan. "Gervase said something like that, but, you see, I've never known him any different. I wish I'd seen him before, so I could tell."

"He was known as the Iceberg," said Freddy, "and he encouraged it, because it brought them to him. Trying to thaw him out, you see." I smiled, seeing very well. "Now they don't know what to say."

"Good." Richard crossed the room to us. He stopped to talk to people who spoke to him but unerringly headed in our direction. He was completely in control here, in his world, his movements understated and graceful, his confidence ingrained in him.

"How did you get on tonight?" Freddy asked, as Richard came closer.

"We won," I said, accepting the glass of wine my husband brought me with a smile. "Have you been practising?"

"All day," said Freddy proudly.

"*All* day?" I returned archly. "You're neglecting your friend."

He pretended shock. "My lady!" But only succeeded in making me laugh.

Unfortunately Miss Crich, still seated in state on her sofa, overheard my last remark. "You're here with somebody else, Freddy? Why didn't you bring him?"

Richard looked at her, one eyebrow arched. "Her."

Miss Crich flushed. "Oh." She glanced at me. "But Lady Strang is allowed to know. I don't think it's fair. Married ladies know so much more than we spinsters, they have so much more freedom." She pouted prettily.

"You should find a husband, Miss Crich," Richard told her, smiling. "Then you would know all the secrets, too."

"Does marriage suit you, Lady Strang? Is it better than the single state?"

"Vastly." Without thinking I reached up my hand to him and by the time I realised what I had done and begun to withdraw it, he had taken it and softly kissed the palm. I hadn't meant to draw him into intimacy in public. Miss Crich flushed and spread her fan. I was sorry I embarrassed her so I went to sit in the space next to her. "I wish you would show me how to do that," I said, referring to the elegant gesture she had just made with her fan. "It looks very fine."

She eyed me doubtfully but she did it again so I could copy her. I soon coaxed her out of her embarrassment, not least by showing her, as privately as I could, the gesture Richard had taught Miss Terry at Exeter Assembly Rooms. She gasped as I turned my back on the company and showed her. Freddy saw the gesture from where he stood talking to Richard and grinned. He had been there and witnessed the sensation a well brought up lady had caused, by asking him to go to bed with her in the full glare of the public eye.

It seemed the gesture was very well known. "It's the one you're always taught *not* to do," Miss Crich explained. "When your older sister or your governess or whoever teaches you, that's the one you're taught to avoid. There are others, of course, but they're more private. And she didn't know?" She laughed and leaned closer. "You suit him. You make a striking couple, so you should be prepared to be stared at for some time to come."

The orchestra had taken a break, but when they began to tune up again, the floor cleared and the country-dances began. Now the company had enjoyed some supper and liquid refreshment, they were ready for something more boisterous than the formal minuet. I was led out to every dance, first Richard, then Freddy, then one of the older gentlemen I had been introduced to earlier, then another younger man until I saw Richard sitting out this dance, watching me. I excused myself at the end and went over to him.

"What?" I demanded, without preamble.

He stood and gave me his seat. "Where's the lady who sat out every dance at the local assemblies? I said you would do well, didn't I? And you need no help from me."

He handed me his glass and I drank from it gratefully. "I wouldn't be here without you."

"True enough. But you're liked and admired for your own sake, not for mine."

Then, to my great surprise, the orchestra struck up for a minuet. Richard smiled and held his hand out to me. "The contessa is a romantic lady. You know the married couple is supposed to dance a minuet on their own on their wedding day? Well she has asked that we do it here. I promise I won't talk to you. I'll let you mind your steps."

I was trembling as he led me out, but I took a few deep

breaths and steadied myself before we began. I got through it. I remembered the poses Freddy had struck when he had danced with Richard. I imitated some of them and remembered to hold my head correctly and not look at my feet.

We danced alone and I was glad most of the company was at least mellowed by drink, as they seemed indulgent enough. There was hearty applause at the end.

As Richard led me back to my place, I saw the contessa brush away a tear, but then she was Italian and the Italians were said to be a sentimental race.

She came over to us. "You were perfect."

Richard bowed and I inclined my head in thanks. "You have made my evening a great success," she went on. "I shall write to your mother tomorrow, Richard, and say so."

"You're too kind." I spread my fan to cover my blushes.

"Well done." Richard murmured, so only I could hear and then people swamped us with their congratulations.

Freddy came and claimed me for the next country-dance, but as we walked on to the floor, he asked me if I wouldn't rather go and find a drink with him. I found I would far rather do that.

He watched me seriously, a thing I found he rarely did, as he handed me a glass. "You know what he's done, don't you?"

"I can guess some of it. He's not hiding anything, is he?"

Freddy smiled. "More than that." Gently he twirled his glass around in his fingers. "He's nailed his colours to the mast. Quite deliberately. When he danced with you he let them all see how much he cares for you. Oh, not by mooning or staring at you like a lovesick swain, nothing like that. Just by the perfect care he took to show you off to your advantage, not to his, by his tenderness to you and by the lack of any flirting."

To my shame, I hadn't realised just how much Richard had done by demonstrating that our marriage wasn't the convenient arrangement his mother wanted the world to think. "So I have to make sure he is never let down, never made foolish. I can do that. I care too, you know."

His dark eyes were bright. "That, my dear, is obvious to anyone who can see. But you don't sigh over him any more than he does over you, so it's hard to say how."

"Perhaps we really were made for each other. But don't forget, Freddy, we're on our bride-trip and we're allowed a little leeway until we get used to each other. It may not always be like this."

He sighed. "I suppose so. You remind me of all the women I've passed by and all the ones I've missed."

I laughed. "Freddy, you're getting maudlin. You have a perfectly good mistress waiting for you and you might think of home soon. Take me back if you please."

He smiled and offered his arm. He took me to where we had sat before. Richard was dancing with the dark-haired girl, but they soon joined us once more. "I think our work here is done," he commented, smiling.

"Freddy is getting maudlin," I told him. "I've sent him home."

"To his nice warm bed?"

"To his nice warm mistress."

"Freddy always goes through the weeping stage when he drinks enough." We watched the dancers and the company. I tried to remember some of the people, some of the clothes and Richard was content to stand by my side, lost in his own thoughts. Unfortunately, it didn't last long and I was borne off once more, but when I returned, I asked him if it was time to go.

"I think we might take our leave." We went to find our hostess.

Chapter Fourteen

For the first time since my arrival in Venice we went to bed and didn't make love. I was so tired that when I climbed into bed, I fell asleep almost immediately.

When I woke in the morning and turned over, I found the place next to me empty. A moment's panic followed before I realised the indentation on the pillow and the rumpled sheets indicated he'd been there. I lay back, smiling and marvelling that I could feel so lost without my bedfellow of barely a week.

Richard returned from the dressing room and, throwing his robe over a chair, came back to bed and took me in his arms, wishing me good morning.

I returned his kiss. "Good morning. Will you always want to share a bed with me?"

He frowned and drew back, looking down at me. "Why? Would you rather have a room and a bed of your own?"

"No, no, no! If it was my decision, I'd burn every other bed, so you had no choice but to spend every night with me." He smiled delightfully and kissed me again for that. "But when I woke up and you weren't there I felt bereft. I fell asleep last night before you came to bed."

"I know," he said ruefully. "You look adorable when you're asleep, I couldn't have woken you."

I sighed happily. "You see, if I knew you were coming to my bed every night, I would be so happy."

"Why shouldn't I?"

I hesitated. "Well—you know. Illness and pregnancy and that kind of thing."

"If you're ill, I won't leave you. If you're with child, then I'll order a bigger bed. As for 'you know'—I am familiar with women's problems—" he laughed when I blushed, "—and we'll manage. Happy?"

I smiled and snuggled into his warmth. "More than that. Thank you so much for last night, Richard. I know how much it must have cost you."

He kissed my hair gently. "Strangely enough it cost me very little. I thought I could never show my feelings for you in public, but it wasn't difficult at all. Of course," he went on and he caressed me in the most distracting manner, "we can never fall out of love now. Imagine the gossip then."

"There's no danger of that. Not on my part, anyway."

"You're so sure?"

I didn't need to hesitate. "I'm very sure. I love you, Richard. I'll love you to the day I die." That was all I had to tell him and by doing so I'd made myself completely vulnerable to him. I didn't care.

I couldn't talk then, as he kissed me until I was breathless and moved his body over mine to love me. I welcomed him, loved him in return and wondered if I'd ever get used to this, praying that I wouldn't. Every time surprised and shocked me with its intensity, increased my need for him. I touched his back and felt him respond. He lifted his head and laughed lovingly at me, coming back down to kiss me again as we both found ecstasy at the same time, breaking away as breathing suddenly became more difficult.

We lay wrapped up in each other as we regained our breath. Then he moved to take me in his arms again. A knock sounded on the door.

"What is it?" Richard called out, as steadily as he could, but I felt his heart racing.

"A visitor, my lord," Carier called.

"We're not at home."

I was caught in a fit of the giggles then, for whoever the visitor was they must have heard us. He pushed my head down to his shoulder to muffle the sound. "Abominable woman!"

Carier was still there. "I beg your pardon, my lord, but you might want to see this gentleman. It's—"

"Gervase!" Richard sat up and stared at me, wide-eyed with shock. "Tell him we'll be out shortly."

He gazed steadily down at me, bewilderment clouding his clear blue eyes. "How could I not know? I always know when Gervase is near. It's one of the pleasures—or curses—of being a twin. It must be you!"

"What do you mean?"

"You've taken all my thoughts. When we make love, everything else goes away for a while. It means the link I have with you is every bit as strong as the one Gervase and I were born with. It had never occurred to me before; Gervase has never surprised me like that. We always know when the other is in pain, or in need of help, or nearby."

"A strange link."

He smiled wryly. "Not one either of us looks for." He kissed me one more time and then flung the sheets back. "Would you like to stay here, or dress properly?"

I shook my head. "I'd like to meet him with you, unless you'd prefer to see him on your own."

"No. Come with me." We got out of bed and he helped me on with my robe before he donned his own. I tried to smooth my hair with my hands and, laughing at me, he fetched my brush and brushed it for me, pulling it back over my shoulders afterwards. Hand in hand, we made our way to the drawing room, preceded by Carier, who opened the door for us.

As always, a slight shock went through me when confronted by Gervase Kerre. He was so like Richard I had never understood why I didn't feel the same way about him. He differed only in his complexion, darker and rougher from his years in the tropics and his personal style, which was more casual than my husband's. He wore his golden hair long, tied back, instead of cropping it and wearing wigs and his style of dress was less formal, although the quality remained.

He stood by the window staring at the lovely vision of the Grand Canal, but he turned when we came in. His chest moved as he took a deep breath. I hung back to let Richard greet his brother first. They embraced and then I went forward and hugged him too.

"Have you eaten?" I asked.

Gervase shook his head, so I turned and went out to see to it, thinking they might like a moment alone with each other.

When I returned, they were seated, Gervase on one of the chairs and Richard on a sofa, so I went and sat by my husband and took his hand. "Breakfast will be in the dining room as soon as they can arrange it. Have you only just arrived, Gervase?"

He smiled. "I got here last night but it was late, so I put up at an inn."

"You'd better stay here for the time being," Richard told him. "It would ruin our plans if we were to be seen out at the same time."

Gervase stared enquiringly at his brother. "Here? You've found some mischief here?"

Richard laughed. "It found us. Someone rescued Rose on the road when she suffered an accident. They said their name was Ravens and then later told her they were travelling incognito. Guess what name they used?"

Gervase looked at him sharply. "You're not serious!"

"Oh but I am." Richard proceeded to bring his brother up to date.

At the end of his narrative, Gervase whistled. "You have been busy!" He laughed softly, an echo of Richard's rich laugh, but with a quality of his own. "And I thought I'd been industrious."

Richard was at once alert, his face sinking into seriousness. "Have you had any luck? Any news for us?"

"Oh yes." Gervase picked up a slim folder from a table by his side. He opened it, revealing several sheets of closely written paper. "One of Skerrit's gamekeepers saw the man who shot at you and chased him for several miles, but he got away. He recognised him."

"A local man?" I asked. I hated to think anyone who had known me would have undertaken to kill us.

Gervase shook his head. "No. The gamekeeper had worked

elsewhere in the country. He's registered with Thompson's."

Richard held up his hand. "Shawcross, was it?"

Gervase smiled. "It was. Your memory for your employees is phenomenal, Richard. I envy you." He glanced at the paper. "When he was a footman, Shawcross worked in London. Do you remember his situation?"

Richard nodded. "He stole from his employers, but he did us a signal service by doing it, so when he was caught, I looked after him."

"Just so," said Gervase dryly. "He's very grateful. He knows the man because of his days in the Rookery by St. Paul's."

Richard took a breath. This must mean our putative assassin was an established criminal already. Unconsciously, his grip on my hand tightened.

Gervase continued. "The man who tried to shoot you is called Abel Jeffries. Do you know him?" Richard shook his head. "He's a professional killer. That is, he kills for money. Once we had his name, it was easy to discover the rest. I went to London, collected the information from Mrs. Thompson and came here as quickly as I could."

"Why?" Richard demanded sharply. "Is he coming here?"

Gervase shook his head again. "We don't know. We haven't seen or heard of him since your wedding day. The moment he surfaces they'll inform you. Or would you prefer it if I continued to handle matters?"

"Thank you, no," Richard answered him. "I'm very grateful for everything you've done, but I'd feel happier if I was kept informed myself from now on."

Gervase's face relaxed in a smile. "I just didn't want to interrupt what you have here." He took a sharp breath. "Richard, I've not seen you like this for a long time. When I came back from India you were so remote I hardly knew you."

Richard didn't pretend to misunderstand him. "Some things have come back to me this last week. Or rather, Rose has given them back to me." Gervase nodded. "I'll never be eighteen again, but some of the things I'd forgotten since then I'm remembering now." He raised my hand to his lips, showing me all his love in his eyes. I coloured up, not knowing what to say.

He saw my embarrassment and turned back to the subject in hand to give me time to recover. "So the assassin could still be drawn here by the false Strangs?"

"He could," Gervase agreed. "He knows the yacht is out of commission—"

"That reminds me," Richard interrupted him. "Is it irreparably damaged?"

"Completely." Gervase spread his hands in a regretful gesture. "The explosion killed two crewmen. The rest got off safely, but they left the vessel to burn itself out, there being very little else anybody could do."

Richard sighed. "I'd hoped there might be something we could do. And if he killed two of my men, I want him brought to some kind of justice. What are the rumours? I left enough behind to be spread, did any take?"

His brother smiled. "You left plenty. At first, it was thought you were aboard the yacht, but then some people remembered you'd had most of your luggage disembarked. The surviving crewmen said you weren't aboard before we could stop them, so that one fooled nobody. Then you left a rumour you had taken Rose, badly injured, to her brother's house and Lord Hareton has kept that one running quite well. In fact—" He handed us a cutting from a newspaper and we read, fascinated, about my serious injury and Richard's despair that I would never be presentable in public again. The correspondent had obviously made the most of his moment in the sun, because he had embellished the story. He enclosed the engraving of me I had seen before, the one that looked nothing like me. Someone had passed it off as me but was in fact someone else entirely.

"I've never read about myself before," I said. "May I keep this?"

"By all means," said Gervase. I folded it away and put it on the table next to the sofa.

"They also say you've gone away into the country. I've heard Venice mentioned as a possible place of retreat, but it's only one of many places I heard of before I left. Of course," he continued, as the door opened, "I've been on the road for nearly a month."

"Breakfast is served, my lady," came Carier's lugubrious tones.

We went through to the dining room and continued our conversation there while we breakfasted moderately and Gervase tucked into a huge meal. "I hate inn food," he confided. "It's always overcooked and cold, or so hot it's uneatable for ten minutes and then you have to get back on to the coach having eaten hardly anything."

"You did well to get here in a month, travelling by public transport."

Gervase reached for the jug of small beer. "I took a leaf out of your book. I travelled on horseback whenever I could and took a coach when one was available, to get some sleep."

"Aren't you exhausted?" I asked. "I've had a bedroom prepared for you, you can go there straightaway if you want to."

He sighed in contentment, then glanced at Richard, puzzled. "I thought this apartment only had two bedrooms?"

Richard smiled. "We're only using one."

Gervase flushed red, the first time I had seen him at all embarrassed by anyone. "Forgive me, of course. Look, are you sure I'm not imposing on you? I'd far rather find somewhere else and leave you in peace, you know."

"You can't," Richard said. "We can't go out together until this thing is sorted out and I see your presence here as a sort of ace up our sleeves. No one saw you arrive?"

"No, I don't think so and I stayed at an inn off the beaten track, not one of the fashionable ones." Gervase began to attack a fresh plateful.

"And we could still pass for each other, if the viewer doesn't know us very well, so let's keep your presence secret for a while," Richard continued.

I helped both brothers and myself to more coffee. "Society knows we're here now," I reminded Richard.

He pursed his mouth and picked up his fork, idly drawing patterns on the tablecloth. "And some of them know our direction. I had to tell them, but I have asked them to be discreet and I can trust the few people I did tell. Mostly old friends." He turned to his brother. "Freddy Thwaite is here. He's helping us with the false Strangs."

"How?"

"He's a marvel at picking up card tricks although we don't intend to use them against professional sharpers, we just wanted to know the techniques so we could spot them in use. We've won at the palazzo—now we're waiting to be invited back. They'll want to fleece us this time."

Gervase chewed and frowned in thought while he cleared his mouth. "How much did you let slip at the contessa's last night?"

Richard frowned. "More than I should have, maybe. If this man is hunting for us, he knows we're here and he could find this address if he was clever. I'm hoping the Palazzo Barbarossa distracts any enquirers."

"Does he know what you look like?" asked his brother.

"I think so," Richard said. "But he probably knew in any case. It's not difficult to find an engraving. The trouble is, he may now have a good idea of what Rose looks like."

Gervase sighed. "You couldn't hide away here forever." He thoughtfully speared a piece of kidney from his plate. He ate it and, his appetite seemingly satisfied at last, chased the remainder of the kidney around his plate with his fork for a while.

I poured more coffee. "It had to come. And if that's the only result of last night, I'll be content. Are we likely to receive visitors here now?"

Richard grimaced. "I've told Carier to deny most of them, but some would take offence if we didn't see them. In fact, the Ravens have been denying all and sundry. I had to smooth a lot of ruffled feathers last night."

I remembered one or two English peers Richard had introduced to me last night who had seemed a little stiff but might have been insulted by the Ravens. It was probably a good thing that we had gone, after all and I said so.

"I should have sent them notes, explaining our visit here was in the nature of a bride-trip. They would have understood then. The ones who took offence were the older generation, friends of our parents rather than of us. My father will not approve."

"Since when did he ever approve of you?" Gervase demanded. "He's washed his hands of you so many times that he's in danger of skinning himself!"

Richard gave an unholy smile of triumph. "But he can't, can he? He made us what we are—now he must abide by it."

It was as if I was no longer there. They held each other's gaze, blue on blue, for a long time and then looked away.

I stood abruptly. "I must go and dress." They both stood and Richard touched my hand before I left the room.

Gervase retired after he'd eaten and Signor Verdi came with Freddy shortly afterwards. I knew I could never manipulate the cards without anyone observing me, so while they practised and learned the techniques, I caught up with some overdue correspondence in the drawing room.

I wrote to James and Martha, with a separate note under the same cover for Lizzie, probably queening it over Exeter society by now while waiting for her first London season in the autumn. Then I wrote to Lord and Lady Southwood, a letter I showed to Richard later and to which he added his signature but nothing else. I'd hoped he might have added a postscript of his own, but he seemed indifferent to them. I still dared not ask him what could have caused such a deep breach, or perhaps I already knew. The most likely reason would be the way they turned Gervase away from their door when the scandal had broken. He was tainted and furthermore, no use to them to procreate their line. That task now fell to me.

During the day several invitations appeared, amongst them one asking us if we would care to visit the Palazzo Barbarossa the next day. "Striking while the iron is hot," Richard remarked. "It's just as well. This can't go on much longer."

This time they invited us for dinner. When we got there, we found the same people we had met the other night; the odious Squires and his wife, also conies the Ravens were setting up to skin. We bowed and behaved in a disgracefully sycophantic way and all through the meal, Richard tried to interest the Ravens into taking some of his wine. He'd had a case delivered earlier in the day from our cellar, confiding to me at least he would ensure the wine at the dinner was good.

The dinner was perfectly adequate, three courses, deferentially served by several footmen, among them the Thompson's man, all in Kerre livery. Since I wasn't yet used to liveried servants attending me, I didn't care what they wore, but Richard felt some irritation. Once or twice, he had to stop himself relaxing into his usual poses. The stolid Locke wouldn't have leant back in such a way, curled his long fingers around the wine glass to show them off, taken snuff in anything but a mundane way.

It was easier for me to dissimulate. I could just be what I had been before, a provincial lady. I didn't use my fan much, as the putative Lady Strang was very fond of doing, kept my head down for the most part and kept my conversation sensible. I decided that Mrs. Locke only became garrulous under the influence of too much wine.

After dinner, it wasn't long before Lady Strang stood and led Mrs. Squires and me into another room, for tea and conversation. The salon she took us to was much larger than we really needed. It was decorated, like the hall, with mythological figures going about their everyday life, sending thunderbolts down to kill people, lying about so lightly clad that nothing was left to the imagination, or just metamorphosing into trees or animals. There seemed to be no overall theme to the composition and when I asked Mrs. Ravens what it all meant, she waved her fan negligently and said, "I really couldn't say, my dear Mrs. Locke. They are all just decoration to me. When you have lived amongst such things for some time, you get used to them."

I thought of asking her where a provincial lady from Devonshire would have had the opportunity of getting used to living with such magnificence, but I would keep things comfortable for the time being. It was quite difficult trying to work out who was keeping whom happy. They were trying to lead us on, but our double game meant we were also trying to lead them on, the poor Squires caught between us. It could get quite confusing.

I asked our hostess if she would be presented and she held Mrs. Squires and I spellbound, telling us all about the gown she had ordered for the autumn. It would be frilled to within an inch of its life, laced so tightly she couldn't breathe and worn with the inevitable diamonds. With each frill and furbelow she described, my heart sank, as I remembered I must learn to curtsey and walk backward in the largest hooped and trained gown I would probably ever wear in my life. I was not looking forward to it and I heartily wished it was the false Lady Strang who undertook that particular ordeal.

It was some time before the gentlemen joined us, longer than I thought they would be, but my husband explained, smiling widely. "His lordship has kindly done me the honour of ordering several barrels of the wine he was kind enough to accept today, and also to put in my way a most advantageous business matter."

"His lordship is very kind." I looked at Ravens with what I hoped would be taken as gratitude and admiration.

"Indeed," Richard agreed, a little too enthusiastically. "A scheme has come his way to construct a canal, linking Venice with Milan, so reviving its fortunes."

It needed saying. "But Milan is miles away!"

"It is also, dear ma'am, the centre of industry in this part of the world," said Mr. Ravens, looking at me like an indulgent uncle. "To link it so directly with Venice will be to create an indissoluble connection which will revive the fortunes of this queen of cities."

"It would be very expensive." I couldn't be seen to accept this foolish plan without some kind of hesitation.

"There are many backers to the scheme." Mr. Ravens gestured vaguely with his arm. "Much greater than I. I cannot show everyone the other backers, but I have shown the gentlemen and they are content."

"Mr. Squires has invested too?"

"He has done the honour of promising funds for the venture," replied his pretend lordship. "Our profits should be manifold, for not only may we profit in the canal, we may buy some of the property along the route beforehand. It is bound to increase in value once the scheme becomes more widely known."

I smiled trustingly at our host. "I'm sure you know best, my lord."

The avuncular smile I received in return would have melted butter. "Shall we?" he said and ushered us to the other end of the room, where tables were set for cards.

It was piquet again, but there was no need for Richard to use his newfound skills. Our hosts were skilful enough. The stakes were higher tonight—not so high we would get suspicious, but high enough to let our debts begin to mount. We played for longer this evening, too. When we changed partners and I played with Mr. Squires for a time, I won a little, but my luck changed again. I watched my leering opponent more carefully, but he seemed to spend as much time trying to look down the modest *décolleté* of my gown as he did looking at his cards.

"Have you seen any of the art here yet, dear lady?" he asked me.

"Indeed, sir, it's a very beautiful place, but I haven't seen very much of it yet."

He looked at me curiously, head tilted to one side. "My wife is very complimentary towards it." He reached across the table and patted my hand, which lay at rest on top of my fan. "Call me Edward, my dear lady. Point of five."

"Good," I answered, referring to his bid. "The buildings on the Canal are lovely."

He leered. I saw the line his too-tight hat had made and the beads of sweat on the fleshy forehead. "So are the beauties within."

I got his meaning. Venice was famous for its courtesans. "I wouldn't know, sir, I'm a respectable lady and it's not something I have any opinion about at all."

He looked contrite, but in a playful manner that betokened no remorse at all. In one so large, it looked grotesque. "Indeed I beg your pardon, ma'am. Since you have been married for some time I presumed your mind might be a little broader." I couldn't think why he should think so. "I meant no offence. Quart."

"None taken, sir, I'm sure," I said through gritted teeth.
"Good."

We played out the hand and he came out well ahead of me,
increasing his lead to the end of the *partie*. I found I had no
more cash and, as we had arranged, looked at Richard in
distress.

Mr. Ravens joined us before Richard could leave his seat.
"It is of no concern. Merely use notes of hand, ma'am. I trust
that is acceptable to you, sir?" Richard bowed, smiling and they
went back to their game.

We had decided twenty guineas for me and thirty for
Richard would be as much coin as the Lockes could put their
hands on and the notes of hand we signed as well would put us
nicely into Ravens' debt. We proceeded to game away ever larger
amounts of money. It would have taken Mr. Locke a year to pay
back what we owed at the end of the evening's play.

Richard drank heavily and I sipped as much as I dared.
After a while I realised no skill was required of me; I was merely
a pigeon for the plucking. I grew easier in my mind.

I watched Richard slump in his chair and smile more than
he needed to. I had no idea if he were really drunk or if this was
another sham, but if a sham, he played his part very well. He
freely signed any number of notes of hand, laughing and
recounting one or two stories to Mrs. Squires which, from her
reactions, were on the risqué side. She laughed, struck him
playfully with her fan and hid her face several times, as he
leaned forward to tell her the best parts. The lady was of certain
years, but she giggled more than my little sister Ruth, enjoying
the attention my husband lavished on her. She was sorry when
we changed partners again and she found it was her husband.

Richard and I had Mrs. and Mr. Ravens respectively. They
proceeded, smiling and expert, to skin us completely. If we had
been as drunk as they thought, or as indigent as they imagined,
the following morning would be a disaster for us. We gaily
signed away all the cash the Lockes possessed, without
stopping for thought. It was only at the end of the game that
they totalled the points and even then, Richard did not let us
dwell on the enormity of the debt, dismissing the appalling total
with an airy wave of his hand.

The party didn't break up until one, although there was no music tonight and no suggestion of supper. We were kindly and firmly shown the door.

Once back in the gondola, on our way home, I studied Richard carefully. "My lord, how drunk are you?"

He smiled at me, not the unfocussed smile he used earlier, but a proper one. "Tolerably, my love. A gentleman should always be able to hold his drink. I've drunk much more than this and kept upright for a lot longer. However—" He leaned across me then and without warning kissed me deeply. "Never with such a beautiful companion." He leaned back again, his arm around my shoulders and gazed at me, smiling blissfully.

When I gazed closely into his eyes, I saw they were slightly blurred, the sharp, alert look gone, but that was the only way I could tell. That and the fact that he'd kissed me with passion on an open, well-lit gondola on the busiest thoroughfare in Venice. I was still reeling with shock. I dared not turn around to see how Carier and Nichols were taking it, though I could feel their eyes boring into my head from where they sat silently behind us.

I loved my husband drunk or sober, but he might be much more dangerous drunk. I don't know why I should think that, perhaps the reckless air about him.

He kissed me again, only breaking away at the slight bump when we arrived at our destination. Once I had successfully disembarked he seized my hand and ran upstairs with me, nearly tripping me up on the hard stone stairway. When I stumbled, he swung me up into his arms and carried me the rest of the way, but I was laughing by then, not being entirely sober myself.

Gervase was nowhere in sight but we must have made enough noise to wake him. We ran through our dark bedchamber. Richard immediately went to the windows and flung open the shutters, clanging them against the wall as he misjudged the strength needed to open them. Then he turned and held out one arm invitingly so I went and stood within its shelter.

"Venice by night." His breath was hot on my ear. We stood and watched it together.

The water was black glass, gleaming in the sharp lights from the buildings and shipping. The gondolas, large and small, going busily up and down left trails of sparkling light behind them. The sky was such a deep blue, rich and close to black. I vowed to find a velvet just that colour and immediately despaired of it. It didn't exist. The stars were brighter than diamonds could ever be, their sparkling pinpoints reflected in the water below. In the lights in the buildings on the other side of the Canal we could see people moving against the blinds, ignorant of our scrutiny. They didn't care who we were, only concerned with their own lives. The night, brights and darks running over their walls reflected by the movement of the water, shadowed the honey colour of the buildings. Nothing was still, the movement of the water where we were used to seeing a road gave everything mobility, made anything seem possible.

We turned to each other at the same moment. He took my face in both his hands and we kissed hungrily, not caring who might see, lost in passion. His hands moved over me, pushing aside my clothes to get to the naked flesh beneath.

It was the first time we didn't strip completely, only shedding clothes as they got in the way, taking off each other's and our own indiscriminately. Love took a back seat that night, never forgotten but waiting its turn as our bodies demanded attention.

This is what it must have been like to be his mistress in the old days. To liberate so much passion behind Richard's cold exterior must have been immensely exciting and a victory for the woman who could unlock it. This would be how he managed for so many years without a close companion, moving from woman to woman so none should keep a hold on him, so he was still free. This must have been what he meant when he planned to marry Julia Cartwright, a woman who would never mean more to him than the brood mare his family demanded of him. It would have left him free to pursue his instincts as and when he needed.

His hands moved over my bare skin, impatiently moving aside the fine linen to touch me and bring me to readiness for him. His coat was tossed aside, then I went to work on the buttons of his waistcoat, feeling the fabric give when I tore them away in my haste. I needed to touch him, as he touched me.

I wanted him as much as he wanted me, the fire inside me only demanding, giving no quarter. On the floor, in the dark, lit only by the transitory light of the torches on the passing gondolas, he entered my body, only pausing to make sure I was ready with an impatient touch. I arched up to receive him, lifted my legs, shoving away the fabric between us, offering him everything I had. We coupled as violently as I had ever known in my short experience, surrounded by the litter of our cast off clothing.

I cried out over and over as climax after climax hit me with the intensity of instantaneous release, Richard calling encouragement and endearments.

Time ceased to have any meaning. Only this mattered, the fulfilment of burning desire. I couldn't bear it when he left my body but it was only to guide me into new positions. They varied my response, sometimes more intense, sometimes long and drawn out, exquisite for the torture of slowly building to that shattering conclusion.

A week before I was happy to tentatively explore, to try to love him, but now I wanted him with no frontiers to passion. I would have done anything to achieve it, everything he demanded of me I was willing to give, but I demanded as much as I gave, encouraged by his hands, his groans. The throaty chuckle I loved only drove me on to do more, to demand more from him. We found a footstool, used it creatively as I sat astride him, rocking myself to completion, his hand between us, urging me to diamond sharp orgasms, coming so quickly they became one long, agonising fulfilment. We exchanged no words. We didn't need them.

Eventually I fell to the floor exhausted, bathed in sweat and lost in myself, the tumult only slowly subsiding inside me. My heart pounded and my breath was still unsteady. I wasn't sure where he was until I heard him move and curse softly.

"Damned stays! Why do they have to have quite so many bones?"

I saw him then, a moving shadow on the floor, pulling my stays out from under him and casting the offending garment across the room. I laughed weakly. He stood and came over to me, knelt to put his arms around me. "The power of a few bottles of wine." He gave me a soft kiss me. "Did I hurt you?"

"Not a bit. But I think I might have hurt you." I touched his shoulder, where there was a red mark from a bite I couldn't remember giving him.

He turned his head to see it and laughed. "An honourable wound. And if the philosophers are right love is a war to the death." Then he turned back to me.

I could see the sparkling light in his eyes but the lower part of his face lay in shadow. I must have been all shadow to him, lying on the floor in the middle of a tumbled heap of clothing. "Did I fight well?"

He kissed me. "Better than I would ever have hoped for." He shifted then, stood up and held out his hand for me to take. "Come on. Let's get into bed." I took his hand and let him pull me up, and we climbed into bed where we settled happily together. I noticed the mess we'd made on the floor then and I thought I should try to put it to rights, but decided I was much too comfortable to move any more. I turned to him to kiss him goodnight. "I love you."

I fell asleep, only vaguely aware of his murmured, "Sleep now, my only love, my sweet life."

Chapter Fifteen

The next morning it was Richard's turn to feel ill. I woke up first and saw the clothes were still there, tumbled on the floor, so I turned over and went back to sleep. I roused later when Nichols came in and silently picked over the clothes, separating them into his and mine before taking them away. I felt remarkably fresh, considering the late night and I asked her if she had seen Gervase yet.

"Yes, my lady." She spoke quietly, so as not to wake up my lord, breathing heavily by my side, "He's been up for an hour or two."

"What time is it?"

"Just after nine, my lady."

I opened my eyes wide, surprised, then I thought over the previous evening. Not the latter part, but the Lockes' disastrous gaming. I had better tell Gervase. I asked Nichols to sort out some of Mrs. Locke's clothes for me and threw back the covers when she left the room.

Richard's hand gripped my wrist. "Where do you think you're going?" He turned over and pulled me back to him, so I went, smiling my good morning. "It's getting late. And last night you said the Ravens would probably come to see us today, so Gervase needs to know."

"They won't come this early." He pulled me closer for a kiss, then screwed up his face in pain. "Oh, God!"

"Headache?"

"Two, I think." He closed his eyes again. "If they come early, we're not at home. I can't face them like this."

"Oh, my love, I'm so sorry, can I do anything?"

He kept his eyes closed. "Coffee. Lots and lots of coffee." Before I could leave the bed, he held me to him and opened his eyes cautiously. They weren't as clear as I was used to seeing them. "It was worth every pang, my sweet," he murmured and pulled me down for a kiss. I laughed and left him to wash and dress and order his coffee.

Gervase arched his brows in surprise when I appeared at the breakfast table in the plain and dowdy dress of Mrs. Locke, but as I told him about our evening and we thought they would call, his brow cleared. "Then perhaps you should think about the drawing room, if that's where you want to receive them. It's much too fine for the Lockes, small though it is."

My hand flew to my mouth. I sent for Carier who listened and nodded. "I'll see to it right away, my lady." I stopped him before he left the room. "How's his lordship?"

"Sitting up, feeling better, my lady. Still drinking coffee."

He left the room and Gervase turned to me, laughing.

"He sent some of our wine round in his guise as Locke," I said. "We must have drunk most of it last night. He's not feeling too well now."

Gervase laughed again. "But you're as fresh as a daisy, Rose. Didn't you indulge quite so much?"

"No. But I was Mrs. Locke, you see. She wouldn't have the head for it. Richard wanted to give the impression he was out of control."

"Was he?"

I smiled, thinking of something else. "By no means." I coloured up.

The smile left Gervase's face and he took my hand across the table, holding it warmly in his. "Is this too much for you? Shall I find somewhere else to stay?"

I shook my head and released his hand. "No, I don't mind." It wasn't entirely true. After all those years thinking of intimate relations as something for other people, something I wasn't meant for, the recent deluge of it and its relatively public knowledge, was still uncomfortably trying to settle in my mind.

Gervase must have heard us last night and even with the

gauze over the windows and the darkness of the room, someone might have seen us. I wasn't ashamed but I did feel something akin to it. I would have to cope with it myself, so I resolved to ignore it, to give my husband the respect and love he deserved, without stint. He must always come first.

When we were about to finish our meal, the door opened and Mr. Locke came in. He looked better, if not quite himself. Richard met his brother's gaze levelly. Gervase laughed at him. "There has to be a payment."

"Not too severe, though." Richard sat down by me and reached for the coffee-pot.

"You should try drinking too much in a hot country like India," Gervase commented. "The stuff seems to dry the blood. I drink some boiled water before I go to bed. It helps."

"Does it?" Richard asked with some interest. "I might try it, one day. If I can stomach it, or if I haven't anything better to do." He didn't look at me, but I knew what he meant. I was forced to pay my toast more attention than it merited while my palpitating heart settled.

The maid brought more coffee and we sat over the remains of our breakfast while the servants cleared up around us. We discussed the events of the previous evening and our plans for what was to come. Gervase was eager to take a part, but he must stay hidden for the time being. He said he was feeling restless here in the apartment, not used to the confinement.

Richard had an idea. "Why don't you take one of my coats and wigs and go out as me? Freddy and I still have some practising to do and Rose hasn't seen St. Mark's Square yet."

Gervase could hardly believe that. "*What*? All this time and you haven't seen the glories at the end of the Canal?"

Richard shook his head, smiling. "I know that's the first place you would have headed for, but we've only been out once, to the Rialto."

"At least you've seen that, then." Gervase was an art lover and it must be inconceivable to him that we hadn't immediately made a beeline to the beauties of the place, bride-trip or no bride-trip. "I would be honoured to show you, Rose." He frowned. "What if we see someone we know?"

"You always used to be able to pass yourself off as me," Richard said.

Gervase touched his face ruefully. "Not any more, not to anyone who knows us at all well."

Richard smiled. "True enough. Go as yourself, then. If anyone sees you they'll be happy enough. We're only concealing your presence from a very small section of society here and if you're unlucky enough to come across them, you can always bluff it out. They aren't expecting Mr. Locke to have a twin, are they?" He smiled at Gervase, no shadows in his expression. "Brother, I know you well. You won't be able to stay here much longer, if you don't see St. Mark's Square and the Ducal Palace, the Library and the Ca' d'Oro." He was waving the treasures of Venice in front of Gervase's eyes like a worm in front of a fish.

"Stop, stop!" Gervase laughed and held up his hand. "I submit, I'll join your schemes. I'll be delighted to show Rose those things you've shamefully neglected."

"Should you like to go?" asked Richard of me.

"Very much," I replied. "You make them sound irresistible."

He took my hand. "Irresistible lies somewhere else. But you might like it enough to go again with both of us in while. You couldn't wish for a better guide than Gervase. He knows everything there is about these places. You must take Carier and Nichols. I'm safe enough here, but you may need the extra help."

"Do you think there's any danger?" Gervase asked sharply.

Richard met his eyes. "Not really. Carier and Nichols will make sure you're not followed back here. Believe me, Gervase, I wouldn't let Rose go into any kind of danger."

Gervase wouldn't release him from his searching gaze, but after a moment, he relaxed and looked away. "No, I don't think you would. You're probably right. We'll be safer if I go as I am and no one would dare attack us in places as public as that."

"You'll be doing us all a favour," Richard said wryly to me. "If Gervase is cooped up anywhere for very long he starts behaving like a caged tiger." I smiled, glancing at Gervase who nodded in agreement. "I can practise my new skills, love, knowing you're not bored and you will see the glories of Venice with the best guide I can think of."

I looked forward to the excursion, not least because we would go after the visit we expected from the Ravens. We left the dining room to the ministrations of the servants and I went to see what Carier was doing to the drawing room.

He was in the process of directing a footman to roll up the rug, leaving just the polished floor. The ornaments had been removed and some of the silver, together with a fine Venetian mirror that usually hung on the wall opposite the windows and a small portrait of the twins that would have given our game away at once. The bare spaces on the walls had been replaced with unexceptional, dull landscapes. They had removed some of the little tables and masked the finer furniture with covers and drapery. It still looked attractive but some of the more expensive embellishments were gone.

None of the servants wore livery here, so we were as ready as we would ever be for our expected visitors. We were at home to no one else.

I settled in a chair with a book, wondering if Richard and Carier were right, if they would come today, or if we had it all to do again tomorrow. I hoped the Ravens would come today; now the expedition to see the beauties of Venice had been proposed, I was eager to go.

The Ravens were too wily to hurry over; they would want to see us squirm and worry for a while. It would soften us up nicely, but they were not wily enough to give it a day. They arrived mid-afternoon.

Richard came into the music room where I was picking out a new piece and told me he'd just seen their vessel approaching our landing stage. We hurried into the drawing room and turned out poor Gervase, who had settled nicely with a copy of Doria. He took his book out to the balcony just as the knock fell on the outer door and Carier, prompted by Richard's nod, opened it.

It was Mr. Ravens on his own and he looked around as he was shown into the drawing room. He took his time studying the room and asking after our health. He seemed satisfied with what he saw and bowed to us. We bowed back gravely.

A maid brought in a tray, set with tea and the usual little bits of refreshment. She put it down on the only tea table left in the room and left, remembering not to curtsey too low and giving Mr. Ravens a cheeky smile as she made her obeisance to him. I busied myself pouring the tea and Richard and Mr. Ravens politely discussed the weather until we were ready.

We let him open the subject.

He withdrew something from his pocket and let a pile of notes fall on to the table, next to the tea tray. "I am sure, as a gentleman, you would like to know the reckoning."

Richard let his gaze linger on the notes. I let my mouth fall open in horror. "Of course," said Richard. "We don't wish to be in debt to you, my lord, we value your acquaintance too much for that."

"The full value amounts to ten thousand and fifty pounds," said Mr. Ravens. We let the silence fall. I clenched my hand where it lay on the arm of the chair until the knuckles went white.

Richard, sitting in a chair next to me let his features go rigid. "I had no idea it was that much."

Mr. Ravens smiled broadly. "You have had some trouble in the past, I believe, Mr. Locke." He lifted his tea dish and watched Richard over the rim.

"How do you know that?" Richard stood and took a few paces about the room, coming to rest standing behind his chair, gripping the back rail.

"I have my sources." Mr. Ravens tapped the side of his nose in a knowing gesture. "I had enquiries made about you, and your problems are well known to many of the houses in Venice." They should be, we'd paid enough to circulate the rumours.

"You associate with such people, my lord?" I asked, in as cold a manner as I could muster. It wasn't hard to pretend this time. Miss Golightly, the daughter of country squires, was appalled by debts of such magnitude. In the great gaming houses of London, however, the sum would hardly have merited a second glance. Ravens had been clever, keeping the sum just the other side of payable to a man whose money would be tied up in stock.

"Your husband associates with them, Mrs. Locke," Ravens said. "Can it be you are unaware of his visits to the gaming tables?"

"No." I glanced away. "It has come to my notice before."

Mr. Ravens looked through the pile of notes. "Your debts amount to five hundred pounds. Your husband's account for the rest."

I stared at Richard reproachfully, biting my lip and trying to cry, but not quite succeeding. "You promised," I wailed, entreaty colouring my voice.

He hung his head. "I'm sorry." I had never heard him so miserable

How terrible it must be to be married to the kind of person who regularly gambled away his income and possessions. It was a disease among the British. Every day stories circulated about this person or that being ruined and tales were legion over the Continent about the insanity of gambling. One would never know if the roof over one's head would still be there in the morning. How much worse if you loved that person.

Richard raised his head. "It must be obvious to you I can't clear this debt at once."

Mr. Ravens frowned. "Perhaps you should not have gambled so much if you knew you could not honour your debts."

"Oh, I can honour them," Richard assured him quickly, "but I will need time."

Mr. Ravens tutted and shook his head. "I do not know how long my wife and I will choose to stay in Venice. I can only give you a certain amount of time."

I was beginning to wonder. Were they going to force us to give this man his money, or would he take matters further? He might, after all, pursue the quick kill but the false information we fed him about the Lockes indicated they couldn't put their hands on that kind of money for some time. He couldn't, surely, leave it at that and give us the time we asked for?

Mr. Ravens picked up his cup when, trembling, I refilled it for him and sipped at mine, giving us time. I now knew exactly how a fish on a hook felt, not knowing if I was to be reeled in or released. Ravens thought himself completely in control and he would reel us in.

Richard kept his head down as though ashamed. I didn't look at him, only staring at our tormentor.

"There is something," Ravens said reluctantly, after a while.

"Name it." Richard raised his head to meet Mr. Ravens' eyes. "I'll do anything."

Ravens sighed. "It's only a small matter. It might not commute all of the debt."

Richard spread his hands in a gesture of helplessness. "I would be grateful for any small reduction of what I owe you my lord. A debt like this could ruin me. All my capital is in stock or investments which I cannot easily turn into ready money."

"I think your debt may be much more than you suppose, sir. There is the matter," murmured Mr. Ravens, "of the draft you signed last night. I may not have emphasised the time scale of the project enough for you." Ravens fixed Richard with a harsh stare, his fish hooked and wriggling. "It could be ten years before any returns are seen and until then the principal must be paid every year."

Richard blenched. "Ten years! I thought it a single payment! I can't sustain that amount of money over that length of time! "

"Dear me, we are in a pickle, aren't we?" Ravens tapped the side of one thin hand on his leg and then reached into his pocket and produced his snuffbox. "Still, I'm sure we can come to a gentlemanly agreement. Does your wife have to be here while we discuss this?"

Richard shrugged and glanced at me. "She runs the business. Her money started it up and keeps it going when we're—over-stretched. She has to know."

Ravens stared at me, wide-eyed. He hadn't expected that, at least. "You have a personal fortune, ma'am?"

"Had," I said bitterly.

"Ah." He leaned back, sure of us now. A smile spread across his face. "Now I think we might see a way of—losing that document, leaving you only with the original debt. Do I make myself clear?" We nodded miserably. "I have a mind to start a small business of my own in Venice."

I asked, "Surely, my lord, you don't need to do that? You're a peer of the realm, you can't be short of money."

He smiled indulgently. "The title is a courtesy one. A man still has to make a living, my dear. Besides," he added insouciantly, waving his hand in the air, "it amuses me."

I bit my lip. Richard looked away, towards the window where Gervase sat concealed, listening. "What would you have us do?" Richard's face was drawn and serious, unlike the false Lord Strang, who was now smiling in a most unpleasant way.

"I would like to settle a house in Venice. Not the Palazzo Barbarossa, but a smaller establishment, with fewer rooms but still elegant in tone to suit the most exacting—visitor." He tapped the side of his nose again, in a gesture that looked rather unusual for someone trying to pose as my husband. Richard nodded slowly. "The house I can manage for myself, but I know few people in Venice and you seem to be acquainted with many. If you saw your way to introduce some of those people, we could arrange a commission, which would see your contract torn up after a certain amount of money came the way of the house."

I interrupted him. "What if they win?"

His smile changed to one of pity, the eyes open wide and amusement in them. "They won't."

We let this information sink in. "Did you do that to us?" Richard demanded. If this had been real, I would have begun to worry, hearing that steady tone.

"No. With your reputation, I hardly needed to." He assumed we were stupid enough to take him at his word.

I met his gaze stare for stare. "If we do this, I want it in writing."

"Madam!" He seemed shocked by any such proposal, but I was supposed to be a businesswoman. I could hardly let him take us completely without a fight. "And what if any such document should fall into the wrong hands? What then?"

"We will both have a copy. At the appointed time, they can both be torn up."

He pursed his lips. "I don't think that would be advisable. A handshake must suffice." I sighed, giving in. After all, he had all the cards, as usual.

He smiled, knowing we were defeated. "We can, however, agree to a rate. Shall we say, ten percent of the profits of the clients you bring to me will go towards clearing your initial debt?"

"What about the contract?" I said. It seemed Richard was taking the part of the weaker partner, the one who depended on the other. It was up to me to make the deal with Ravens.

"How many people can you bring me?" he demanded.

I gave the matter a moment's thought. "Perhaps twenty,"

He nodded. "That would be sufficient. After twenty profitable clients then, we'll tear up the contract." I sighed in relief. "You never know," he went on, smiling in a more friendly way, "you might get a taste for the gaming business, rather than losing, you could turn hunter instead of cony. There's much more profit on the other side of the table."

I frowned. "I cannot approve of your activities, my lord. You bring disrepute to the peerage of the realm." I sounded like Richard's father. It would not be the peerage my husband concerned himself with but the people.

Mr. Ravens smiled again and I tired of his superior attitude. I could place one needle under his skin. "I heard that Lord and Lady Strang appeared at the reception of the Contessa Marini the other night. It was the same night we first went to your house, wasn't it?"

He cleared his throat. "We decided, the night being young, we would make an appearance. It was a most agreeable evening."

"Then why can't you introduce these people to your house?"

He put up his chin. "I'm hoping that the clients you introduce won't be of that class of society. We do not wish to attract attention to our little enterprise."

I let him go. "Of course. But I was thinking of Lord Thurl."

He put up his brows. "I don't know the gentleman very well, but I understand his fortune is considerable. His presence would be acceptable."

I nodded frostily. Richard lifted his head.

"May we agree to the terms, as gentlemen?"

He stood up and offered his hand to Mr. Ravens who took it. They shook hands solemnly. Now he was on his feet, our visitor thought it incumbent on him to take his leave and he was soon ushered out, Richard seeing him to the door.

He came back in just as Gervase re-entered from the balcony. They looked at each other solemnly and then, somewhat to my surprise, they both burst into laughter. "Insufferable!" cried Richard when he could, wiping his eyes.

"How many people does he think he can fool like that?" Gervase got out his handkerchief.

"Oh, I don't think he'll use my name for much longer. Shall we get out of here and let the servants put the room back the way it should be?" He held the door for me and we went through to the music room. Richard excused himself to go and change his coat and waistcoat.

"He really can't bear those clothes for long," I said to Gervase.

"They're very badly fitted," Gervase remarked. "Probably uncomfortable."

I smiled. "Ah, you see, I'm wearing the clothes I used to wear in the country. So they were at least made for me."

Richard returned, himself again and we discussed the recent meeting. On the whole, it had gone very well. We could introduce our pigeons the day after tomorrow. Ravens now thought we were well and truly under his thumb, so he would be eager and ready to take on all comers, looking forward to a fat profit.

Chapter Sixteen

Nothing occurred to prevent Gervase taking me out the next day, as after the visit from Ravens, it had grown too late to go that day. In the morning, Richard sent word to the Palazzo Barbarossa we would be bringing two gentlemen to the house the following evening and word came back that would be satisfactory. Richard said he was quite happy staying in and after Freddy came to see him and they settled down to cheating at cards, Gervase and I set off.

I wore jonquil silk and pearls, the delicate colour reflecting my sunny mood, very frilly and frivolous. I found a straw bergére hat to set off my unpowdered hair and protect my complexion from the sun, which grew fiercer every day. We settled into the boat and set off down the Grand Canal, towards the Lagoon.

Gervase told me about most of the great buildings we passed; who lived there now, who had lived there in days gone by, what they meant to the history of this great city. I enjoyed myself hugely.

Many other gondolas dotted the Canal, some grand ones, gilded barges with room to seat a small orchestra. These belonged to the great nobility and were the Venetian equivalent of a coach and six, used on the great festival days when all Venice came out to view and be viewed. One or two people bowed to us, or rather, inclined their heads, for to get up and bow in a boat was to invite disaster. We didn't stop, but nodded civilly in return. "Some of these people will think you're Richard," I said to Gervase.

"All of them, I hope," he replied. "If they don't expect to see us together they sometimes do so, despite the differences in our appearance, particularly if they don't know us well. We had to get used to it again when I came back from India. We'd spent ten years apart, never being mistaken for anyone else and then it all started again."

"But you look very different now." Gervase put his hand up to his face ruefully. "No," I went on, "not just that. You dress differently, your style of talking is different, even the way you move."

Gervase glanced at me. "You know one of us very well. You would notice that."

"I suppose so." We were passing the Palazzo Barbarossa. The shutters were still up, but with the traffic on the Canal increasing the nearer we got to the Lagoon, it would have been difficult to pick us and our little gondola out from the crowd. "And I first saw you together," I went on, my eyes on the blind building we were passing. We passed by and on to the Canale di San Marco, further than I had gone before in Venice. I looked around.

There was nothing like this place, nothing anywhere. The wealth of free men built the beauties of Venice. The great men of the Republic, instead of building to their own glory built to the glory of God and their state, spiritual and temporal, macrocosm and microcosm. Across the Canale di San Marco lay an island, holding San Giorgio Maggiore, gleaming like a jewel in the Lagoon, its Campanile a deliberate echo of the one by St. Mark's. I sat in the gondola for some time after we had come to a halt, just looking, while Gervase wisely stayed silent. Eventually I stood and we disembarked, facing the Ducal Palace.

The upper part of the building was pink and the lower comprised two rows of Gothic arches. The tracery was so fine it resembled fine lace. The whole building had an air of feminine frivolity but with a solid inner construction that gave it form and solidity. Gervase told me the history of the Palace while I studied it.

We went inside. When the Council weren't sitting, genteel visitors could view the rooms and as I passed through the richly gilded and decorated building, slowly one thought took possession of my mind. This must be what true colour looks like.

The gilding around the building showed how rich the city was, as it was meant to, but the paintings in between showed the life of the place.

It was the bravery in using the colours, so rich and so close to each other, the careful way they were placed in the paintings, the firm inner structure of the painting keeping everything together, much as the building outside had its feminine elements underpinned by the strength of its basic design.

When I saw the great Council Chamber, I could have wept when Gervase told me that a fire had destroyed the original decoration soon after completion. The existing hall, with huge paintings by Veronese and Tintoretto amongst others, was very fine and showed the colours that held me captive. When I mentioned my reaction to them to Gervase, he told me the Venetian painters were famed for their use of colour. They were one of the earliest users of the new medium of oil paint, which could be made transparent and glazed, layer on layer, to achieve a richness and depth not achievable in fresco or tempera.

"What would they have made of the ladies today?" I wondered, looking at the carefully draped figures in front of me.

"Women don't change very much," Gervase said.

"Then it's a shame we haven't got anyone today who could flatter us like this."

I heard the amusement in Gervase's voice. "You can be sure of one thing. If Richard can find someone like that to paint you, he'll do it."

I laughed and took his arm. "I had a miniature done in Exeter for him. I see I'll have to have something better done." I sighed. "It must have been terribly exciting, living here in those days."

"You don't seem to have done so badly yourselves, since you got here," Gervase commented dryly. "Richard could have had the Ravens quietly removed, you know, but he never resists a challenge."

Someone hailed us and when we turned, we saw Miss Crich with an older lady who she introduced to us as her mother. Mrs. Crich looked at us through narrowed eyes. "It's not *Richard* Kerre at all, is it? It's Gervase."

Miss Crich laughed. "I said it couldn't possibly be, but Mama said she was sure of it."

I glanced at him in alarm, but Gervase's expression remained bland. "Gervase arrived the day before yesterday, late. We would appreciate discretion at his presence here."

Mrs. Crich sniffed. "Up to something are you? If it's anything disreputable I will not countenance it."

"Nothing like that, ma'am. Merely a desire to keep our presence here relatively quiet."

Mrs. Crich eyed him doubtfully. "Very well, but if I hear a breath of scandal, I consider our discretion at an end."

Gervase bowed. "We are very grateful for your help, ma'am. Richard has entrusted me to guide his wife around the beauties of Venice."

"And how do you like the art here?" Mrs. Crich asked me.

"It's very fine," I said cautiously.

"Listen to Lady Strang," Mrs. Crich told her frivolous daughter. "Take your opinions from these people and remember them. Mr. Kerre is a connoisseur and his opinion can be trusted."

Miss Crich put up her chin and spread her fan with a sharp snap. "I can't help it, Mama. I can't like it and I won't. The figures are too distorted, and there are too many of them."

"It's art," Mrs. Crich told her. "Come and see some more." She turned to us and bowed. "No doubt we will see you again. My compliments to your mama, Gervase."

She went off at quite a pace, towing her bored daughter in her wake. When she was out of earshot, I laughed softly.

"She's a very indulgent mama, for all her vaunted strictness," Gervase commented. "Miss Crich is her only daughter and she tends to get her way in most things. I should hate to have the governing of her."

I turned to him. "Will you ever marry, Gervase?"

I knew him well enough by now to be comfortable with who and what he was, a man who preferred his own sex, but would do his best for the house of Kerre if the duty fell on his shoulders. If Richard had never existed, Gervase and I would still have been friends. He didn't take offence at my question and understood my meaning. "I'm hoping you and Richard will produce what the estate requires. That would be the only reason for me to marry."

"Could you do that?"

"For Richard's sake, I might manage it." I didn't ask any more, this hardly being the place, but linked my arm through his and asked me to explain the story of the painting in front of us. It was an enormous work, the "Paradise" by Tintoretto, one of the glories of Venice, or so he told me, but I didn't like it as much as some of the others. Perhaps it was too large, too grandiose. In any case, it didn't take my fancy and we moved on, out of the Palace and into round into St. Mark's Square, followed by the inevitable attendants, Carier and Nichols.

Gervase stopped so I could take in the great space. "It's not as impressive as St. Peter's Square in Rome, but it has its own charm."

I had not yet seen St. Peter's. We had entered the Square at the top end, by the Campanile in front of St. Mark's, so Gervase took me down, so I could see the front of the Basilica. He let me take it in, standing next to me in complete silence.

It was like no other church I had ever seen in my life. As well as the unfamiliar architectural style, mosaics and great round arches embellished it, some tipped with a point, more Moorish than Christian. When I mentioned that to Gervase he, as usual, had the answer. "The Venetians fought the Moors for many years, but such close connections led to the Venetians adopting some of their art and design for themselves."

"Oh, I see." I studied the building again. "So love and war can sometimes be very close."

"It's a constant theme of Classical art. Venus and Mars. Venus usually wins," he concluded dryly. "She lets him make love to her and then he falls asleep, under her governance."

I remembered last night and I wanted to divert the subject

before I blushed. "A shame it doesn't really happen that way. Richard says the peace won't last long, we'll be at war again before too long."

"Bound to be," Gervase agreed. "The peace of Aix-la-Chapelle won't last much longer."

"Will it affect us?" I asked anxiously.

"It might do, but if you're thinking either Richard or I are considering going for soldiers, you can probably discount that."

I laughed. "No, I wasn't thinking that."

We walked towards the Basilica now, following the mass of people inside.

My first impression was of gold. My austere Protestant upbringing hadn't prepared me for the magnificence inside. Everywhere glittered gold and precious stones, the twinkle of the delicately tessellated mosaics and the inset jewels flashed in the light of the many candles as we moved, creating an impression of overabundant excess.

Gervase slowly led me towards the high altar, the staggering Pala d'Oro, a great slab of gold set with innumerable precious stones, surrounding ancient Byzantine enamels, priceless in both its artistic and intrinsic contents. I could say nothing for a time, I just stood in front of it.

Gervase murmured to me, "I've seen it many times and every time it overwhelms me."

I nodded, beyond words. The colours and the magnificence gave some idea of how rich Venice had been in its heyday, but there must have been much more, personal fortunes commuted into goods, paintings, sculptures, buildings.

More people approached the high altar and the crush was growing oppressive, so we moved away.

Gervase showed me the rest of the Basilica, but I'm afraid my mind was wandering by then. There is only so much beauty one person can absorb in the course of one day.

I was relieved to go out into the sunshine again, out of the relative darkness into the light, but I had to stand still, blinking until my eyes got used to the glare again.

"There's a coffee house in the Square," Gervase said. "It's the oldest in the world and quite unexceptional for a lady to go there. I have a feeling you could use the rest."

I thanked him and we strolled down one side of the Square, trailed by our attendants. I wondered what they had made of the great Basilica, so different to our great cathedrals at home. I wondered what the Italians made of our great grey churches, impressive but austere; their great spaces their main beauty. I would have to ask the contessa, who must have seen both.

It must be mid afternoon now, I guessed. I asked Gervase for the time and he drew out his watch. "You have no watch of your own?" he enquired.

"It broke." It was close on three, as it turned out and I looked forward to my coffee with some eagerness.

I was enjoying the day, Gervase's companionship and the beautiful sights he had shown me. The sun shone and I was looking my best, as I stopped to replace my large straw hat, which I had taken off to enter the church. Nichols came forward to help me.

Then we heard it, both of us and our heads jerked round, the hat falling forgotten to the floor. Gervase called "Rose!" and moved towards me, no doubt in an attempt to shield me. Two shots sounded close together, rocketing me back in time to that awful moment in the coach when we left Peacock's.

Chapter Seventeen

Nichols moved first, deliberately stepping in front of me as I cried out in horror. Gervase, who had stood apart from me while I was putting my hat back on, fell to the ground.

Carier passed us in a blur of movement, calling out to Nichols, "Get her back in the boat!"

I shouted back, "No!" and ran to where Gervase lay on the ground.

I wasn't the only person to run to him. Quite a few people ran in his direction, those that weren't screaming or running blindly. I knelt on the flagstones, looking anxiously to Carier for guidance.

It was obvious Gervase was hit—blood seeped through the fabric of his coat on the left side. "You must go back, my lady," said Carier. "Get into the boat, get to safety."

"No," I replied calmly. "I won't leave Gervase. The man has gone now."

Carier was stripping the coat from Gervase with a knife, cutting away the material to get to the wound, but he paused when I said that and stared at me, startled. "You saw him?"

"Nichols and I both did. We saw him going out of the Square. I know him. We'll talk later. They won't catch him now, but he won't get away from us."

The proprietor of the café came to us with some waiters in tow. With Carier's permission, they lifted Gervase and carried him inside to the private part of the establishment at the back of the building. He moaned, but said nothing. I thought of sending for Richard, but there was nothing he could do and it might alert our pursuers to something I didn't want them to know.

They laid Gervase on a large kitchen table, where Carier and I could get to work. I sent Nichols outside, to see what people were saying and to tell them the gentleman was perfectly all right, just shaken. I hoped it would help to disperse the crowd that was gathering outside, to stop rumour and conjecture spreading as it could do so quickly.

It was easier to see to Gervase now they had lifted him up. He stared at me, bewildered as I took his hand, smiling down at him to try to reassure him. He was so like Richard my heart beat a little faster, but I had no time for feminine hysterics now.

"You've been hit. We're trying to find out what damage been done."

I took a kitchen knife to his coat, slicing it away, and Gervase cried out in pain when I tugged his sleeve off.

It looked bad. Blood still poured from the wound but thankfully did not spurt. Carier pressed hard on the area, causing Gervase to bite his lip hard and I cleaned the blood away so we could see the damage better. I let my breath out in relief when I saw the wound wouldn't be immediately fatal. The flow was easing now into a sluggish trail.

Carier looked up at me, his dark eyes sombre but bearing the same relief I was feeling. "We should get him home, my lady. He'll be more comfortable there and we can treat him better. I'll bind this up for the journey."

I nodded, agreeing with him and while Carier bound the wound, I went to see if Nichols had succeeded in her allotted task.

The crowd was indeed dispersing now, only a few people gazing at my bloodstained gown with curiosity and interest when I emerged from the building. Nichols met me at the door. "He'll live," I told her. "The bullet is lodged in the shoulder, or perhaps lower down, but it hasn't reached his heart. We need to get him home and take it out."

She stood with me as the waiters brought Gervase out. He was lying on an improvised stretcher, a door off its hinges by the look of it, his right hand to his forehead, his hat lying next to him on the door. I remembered mine, but it had disappeared from where I had let it fall. I wished the thief joy of it.

My mind went back to the coach accident last October and the loss of blood that had nearly killed Richard. In my mind's eye I saw the blood soaking my riding habit and the dazed look he turned to me when he finally came around. That was the moment I had fallen in love with him, inappropriately but irrevocably. I had touched the scar on Richard's arm only last night, tracing the white line with my finger as we lay drowsily together, drifting into sleep. Now his brother was wounded and despite what I had said to Nichols, was in some danger of losing his life.

The journey back was a nightmare, but probably better than if we'd had to take to the road. I got in first, so I could pillow Gervase's head and shoulders on my lap, thinking wryly if anyone we knew saw us, they would think Richard's standards of behaviour were slipping badly. We laid him down in the small boat as gently as we could. I spoke to him reassuringly, telling him what was happening and where we were going. He was still conscious, but drifting with the shock of the incident. There was blood on his lip where he'd bitten it.

The water made the journey smoother and our gondolier was a skilled operator, poling strongly but gently so it didn't jolt Gervase too much. The gondolier took the middle channel of the Canal, to provide as smooth and as swift a journey as possible.

Nichols and I didn't speak, giving me a chance to think over what had happened. I don't think the assassin realised we had seen him. It had been mere chance that we'd seen the one person who walked quickly in the *opposite* direction, leaving the Square as everyone else ran towards us. We must have been looking in the direction the sound of the shots had come from as she adjusted my hat.

It seemed an age before we got to the apartment. As we poled to a stop on our landing stage, Nichols kilted up her skirts and leapt ashore, returning quickly with two of our footmen. They climbed aboard and carefully lifted Gervase off me and up the stairs. Poor Gervase was still conscious, groaning gently. I followed up the stairs with Nichols and Carier, one in front of me, one behind, not knowing what we would find when we undid the wound upstairs.

Richard met us at the door, and when he saw my bloodstained gown his face grew pale and tense, as did Freddy's. Freddy took one look at Gervase, said briefly, "I'll go and find a physician," and ran out of the apartment, down to the gondola, shouting for the gondolier to pole away again. The footmen took Gervase through to his bedroom and I stayed behind to talk to Richard.

I took his hand, making him look at me and concentrate on what I had to say. "Gervase has been shot. The bullet missed his heart, but is still in him somewhere and we need to dig it out." I saw his dazed look travel down my bloody gown and I added; "I'm not hurt, not in the least."

Then, blood or no, my husband held me to him tightly before we followed the others into Gervase's bedroom.

Carier had laid the wound bare again and we examined it together. The bleeding had almost stopped. "I'm sorry, sir," Carier murmured to Gervase, "I need to roll you to see the other side." He signalled and a footman came forward to help. They rolled Gervase on his side. Gervase cried out once in pain and then was silent. We looked, but we couldn't find an exit wound. They laid him down again.

"There's no doubt," I told Richard. "The bullet's still inside. We'll have to get it out."

Richard winced in sympathy and took his brother's hand. "It's brandy or me, I'm afraid."

Gervase managed a grin, but only with his teeth clenched. They might start to chatter if he ungritted them. I'd no idea what Richard meant until Gervase looked at him and nodded, briefly.

Richard clenched his fist and swung his arm back. Before anyone could intervene, he clipped his brother under the jaw, knocking him unconscious. Without another word he stepped back and let us take over. It wasn't the anaesthetic I would have chosen, but it worked well enough.

I'd had an interest in helping the wounded all my life and Carier had been in the army. He had seen far worse things on the field than he did in civilian life and coped with them as well as he could, which was very well indeed. I checked Gervase was peacefully unconscious, feeling his wrist pulse, which thankfully beat strongly and his breathing, also even.

The bullet had entered Gervase's body at an angle, breaking an upper rib and coming to rest deep inside the fleshy part of his shoulder. If he hadn't moved towards me at the time the assailant had fired, the bullet could well have entered his heart. His arm would have to be immobilised on that side for the messy wound to heal properly. Carier worked methodically and I swabbed away the blood for him so he could see what he was doing, as he slowly cut away to the bullet and extracted it, using the kitchen utensils that were all we had available. Without his considerable skill it would have been butchery, but we had little choice. We worked quickly, for fear of Gervase waking up and were thankful when we saw the bullet was in one piece and the break to the rib was clean and had caused no more damage.

Carier doused the area in neat gin to try to inhibit any infection. That was something he had done before in my presence, when he had stitched Richard's wound after his accident. Then he bound the wound up as tightly as he could, enlisting my help to pull the bandage firm.

"We'll know in the next few days if there's any infection," he said to me. He always seemed to forget who I was when I was assisting him, addressing me directly and giving me orders I was very glad to undertake, if they would help. "If there is, we'll have to cauterise." I nodded.

"Just call for me," I said briefly and I stepped back to Richard, still standing by his brother's side, watching us work.

"It could have been worse. His rib stopped the bullet going any further. The assassin had to fire from quite a distance away and the Square was crowded. I'm afraid the news will get out quickly. We must decide what to do."

Richard passed his hand wearily over his forehead. "Dear God, that I let you go!"

I reached out and took both his hands in mine. "It wasn't me he wanted. I was standing apart from Gervase when it happened, in clear sight. His target must have been you."

Richard met my eyes, the blue gaze turning icy cold. "Who knows it was Gervase?" He had begun to work things out.

I pondered. "Mrs. Crich and her daughter."

"I'll have word sent round for them to keep their peace and to tell them to rest easy, that he's alive," said Richard. "Let our enemies think it was me they shot."

Nichols was waiting. I glanced down ruefully at my pretty jonquil gown, now stained liberally with brownish red. "I'll go and change. Gervase must rest now, we can do no more here for a while. Shall I see you in the drawing room?"

By the time I had changed and returned to the drawing room, Freddy had returned and was sitting with Richard. He'd found a physician, but we dismissed the man for the time being, leaving his address with us in case he we needed him. The less people who knew there were two Kerre brothers in Venice, the better.

I poured us all a glass of wine. I needed something to strengthen me. I was beginning to feel somewhat shaky.

Despite my determination to be strong, I must have given something away, because Richard stood and despite Freddy's presence, put his arms around me. I rested my head on his shoulder thankfully and let it stay there until he moved to take me to the sofa, holding my glass for me.

"Are you sure you're all right?" he said to me. "Wouldn't you prefer to go and rest?"

"No," I said. "That is, I would, but I want to get things settled first. Tell you what I know and find out what we're going to do about it."

"So brave," he murmured against my hair.

I sat up so I could look at him, taking his hand. "It was Squires. The fat man from the Palazzo Barbarossa. Nichols and I both saw him, as clear as day."

Whatever name Richard had expected me to come up with, it wasn't that. "Dear God!" He fell silent, staring into space, thinking.

I explained to Freddy. "Both times we went to the palazzo, Squires and his wife were there. Except, I don't suppose she is his wife, because the man we were looking for is alone. Gervase brought word from England that a man called Abel Jeffries was the assassin who tried to kill us after our wedding. The man I saw who tried to kill Gervase was Squires. I think Jeffries found us and called himself Squires, using the situation at the Palazzo Barbarossa to get close to us. Maybe he thought the false Strangs were real until he saw them." Richard swore, when he, too, realised how far we had let our guard down.

To my horror the tears sprang to my eyes and I trembled uncontrollably. I suppose it must have been the shock, it was certainly nothing I could do anything about.

Richard came out of his reverie immediately. He put his arms around my shoulders and glanced at Freddy. "I'll take her to bed, then I'll be back."

Freddy, his face clouded with concern just said, "Of course. Take your time."

He took me to the bedroom, helped me to take off my gown and stays and put me to bed, rather as if I were a child. He didn't allow me to do a thing for myself. I found his care of me very comforting.

Then he sat on the edge of the bed and took my hand. "I'm not going until you're asleep. Then I'll send someone in to sit with you. I'll be here when you wake up, I promise."

"You won't rush out and kill somebody?"

He lifted my hand to his lips. "No. We'll work something out, Freddy and I, but we'll try not to kill anybody unless we have to." He was smiling and I took comfort from that, trying to smile back.

He leant forward and kissed my forehead. "I'm thankful you're not hurt and Gervase is still alive. Someone will pay, but how we still have to work out. Don't worry, try to sleep. Close your eyes, remember that I love you." I drifted into sleep then, my hand still tucked into his.

Chapter Eighteen

When I awoke, it was dark outside. He was there as he'd promised, sitting by the fire in his shirtsleeves reading by the light of a single branch of candles. I opened my eyes and watched him, bringing to mind all that had happened, remembering how foolish I'd been when I had promised myself I would be strong.

I must have made a move, because he looked up from his book and smiled at me. I sat up in bed and he put down his book and came across to me, sitting on the bed and taking my hand. "How are you feeling?"

"Much better. It was only shock. How's Gervase?"

"Awake. And complaining that his jaw hurts worse than his shoulder and chest do."

"The wound?"

"So far so good. Carier will change the dressing every few hours. He told me what happened, as far as he can remember."

I nodded. "Do you want to hear my account?"

He shook his head. "I don't want to bring it back to you any more than I have to."

"Did you know?" Richard had a link with Gervase and they could often tell when something had happened to the other.

He nodded. "I knew something was wrong. It's a sensation I only associated with Gervase in the past, but this time I wasn't sure which one of you it was."

I squeezed his hand, where it lay over mine. "I only felt so upset when I realised it could have been you and it might have killed you. I couldn't bear that, but it wasn't until the immediate danger to Gervase was over I let myself think it."

He caught my gaze and we looked at each other. "Love makes you very vulnerable, doesn't it? It seemed so straightforward at first. I loved you and that was that, but it's not. I was only truly afraid when I realised I could have lost you."

He met my look frankly. "It's one of the reasons I fought against it for so long." He paused. "If I hadn't fell in love with you so suddenly I would never have allowed it."

"Then I'm glad it happened that way. I wouldn't have missed this last week for anything, not even a lifetime of spinsterhood."

"Too high a price. We'll have to make sure it doesn't happen, won't we?"

Now my shock had subsided, my stomach was reminding me I hadn't eaten since breakfast. "Have you decided what to do?"

"Yes. With the permission of you and Gervase, Freddy and I devised a plan. Would you like to eat? If you feel up to it, I've ordered some supper served in his bedchamber. Gervase wants to eat, too and I can tell both of you over the meal. Freddy has gone home, but we'll see him soon."

"Back to his warm mistress?"

"Back to his warm mistress," he agreed solemnly.

I threw back the covers and got up. I found I was quite well now, if still a little bit shaky, but that was easy to hide. I went into the dressing room where I washed, then Nichols helped me into a light gown that needed no underpinning and fastened at the front. I sat at the dressing table and while she was brushing my hair and pinning it up, I was able to gather my thoughts and talk to her.

I asked her if she had told Richard what she had seen. "I have indeed, my lady," she replied. "And you saw the same thing, I think?"

"Did you recognise him?"

"I did indeed." She lifted a strand of hair to brush it along its length. "It was that man you met at the palazzo, the one whose attentions you didn't quite like, my lady."

I was surprised. "How on earth did you know that, Nichols?"

She thought back. "Just your attitude, my lady, you seemed to be cautious with him."

My maid must be very observant, to notice slight differences like that. "He called himself Squires, but his real name is Abel Jeffries. I wouldn't have believed such a large man could move so quickly without actually running unless I had seen it for myself."

"Yes, my lady." She pinned up the knot she had made at the back of my head and smoothed the curls that would lie over my shoulders. "It helps very much indeed, to know what he looks like."

When I entered Gervase's room, I went immediately to my brother-in-law. He was dressed in a nightshirt and a voluminous robe, sitting up in bed with his arm immobilized in a sling against his body. A substantial tray lay on his lap, and Gervase was instructing a footman what to put on his plate. "How are you?"

"As well as can be expected." He took my hand with his right hand. "I hope you won't let the unfortunate circumstances of the later part of the visit mar your enjoyment of the earlier part." It surprised me that Gervase could think of the earlier part of the day after the shock of the later part. He smiled. "At one point of my life, when I was at my lowest ebb, Italy saved me. Not the Italy of the tourists, but the beauty that was poured out by so many people a few hundred years ago. It gave me something else to think about, something else to look at and every time I see someone's eyes opened to what I saw, as yours were today, it gives me great joy."

Richard, sitting on one of the two chairs drawn up to a table by the empty fire, was watching me, but he said nothing. What could I do but assure Gervase that our visit to the Pala d'Oro was an abiding memory, that I had enjoyed the day completely up to that final point?

Gervase seemed satisfied. I filled my plate and sat before I said anything further. There were two footmen in the room and so I asked if we could speak freely. Richard looked up, as though being reminded of their presence. "Yes, we can say what we need to."

While Gervase and I ate, he told us the plan. "Our original plan, as you recall, was to introduce Freddy and Signor Verdi as fresh conies to be skinned, to let them lose badly and then to return and strip the house clean." He took up a coffee cup and sipped before he continued, even that simple action displaying his essential elegance, his fingers displayed just so, his free hand lying beautifully at rest on the table. "We thought we would omit the early part of the game. We will introduce Freddy and the Signor, then they will win and win and strip the tables. Then we'll have Ravens where we want him." He put down his cup. "Squires is a customer, we're sure of that now. He would have insinuated himself into the house to get to us. When he discovered Ravens was a fraudulent Lord Strang, he must have been chagrined, but when we turned up, I'll wager he couldn't believe his luck." He smiled wryly. "He might have moved on if it wasn't for that. But from the way he plays, I think he has a passion for it. Did you notice anything?"

I shook my head. "He was too busy flirting with me."

Richard grimaced. "I saw that. He probably felt some sort of power, as he knows who you really are and you didn't know him. He'll pay for that."

"You won't kill him?" I asked, more concerned with the way it would affect Richard than the loathsome Squires.

Richard met my eyes as I put down my knife. "I don't know. I don't plan to, but if he's going to be a permanent threat, I may have no choice. I can promise to avoid it if at all possible, but I will not tolerate danger to you when I can prevent it. Will that do?"

"Yes," I answered, trusting his word. "Will you tell us the rest of your plan, please?"

"Yes." He leaned back in his chair. He wasn't eating much, so presumably he'd had some dinner while I was asleep. "We've decided that so long as we are in company, there's little danger. Also, it seems obvious now his prime target is me, so I'm happy for you to stay here. Otherwise, you'd be in Milan by now, my love."

"Not without you." I wasn't leaving him in danger again.

"And we have to face this, we can't run from it."

He smiled at me with real warmth. "I'm glad you see that. Gervase has said much the same thing. Our plan only needed a little alteration. We thought we might enlist Ravens' help to skin Squires-Jeffries, which is why we want to strip the tables."

More elaborate plans often worked least well. The simpler it was, the less would go wrong. If we could put him in our debt, the balance of power would change, especially if he didn't know we were in league with Ravens. "But you must be in company all the time," I said.

"I know. Don't worry, I've no desire to die young. Not any more." He paused, drinking some more coffee that one of the footmen had refilled for him. "The biggest advantage we have is that he doesn't know we're aware of his true identity. He may be hoping to take us off our guard. Now we know him, we can have a watch put on him; Carier's arranging it now. Then we'll be infinitely safer."

Gervase put his knife down with a finality that suggested that he had eaten enough. "So what do I do?"

"You, my dear brother, have done enough. Unwittingly, you flushed our man into the open. Now, Carier tells me, rest and recuperation is the most important thing for you. We must be careful the wound doesn't take infection."

"So I can sit in the sun and dream of glories past? Richard, that would bore me beyond bearing!"

Richard smiled at him. "You have no serenity, my dear brother. Just a few days and then I hope the game will be over. Then we can enjoy Venice and maybe somewhere else when you're feeling better. You can give Rose a cultural tour if you both wish and I'll tag along behind."

I looked at Gervase, who stared at us, appalled. "This is your bride-trip! Are you sure you wouldn't rather be on your own?"

I laughed. "We can hardly abandon you to your fate, after causing you to be so gravely injured." I wasn't sure I wouldn't prefer to have Richard to myself for a while longer. Still, if we were to have a companion, I could only think of one other person other than Gervase I would like to have with me—my sister Lizzie. I knew Gervase wouldn't intrude on our privacy and there was no one else Richard trusted as much as we two, so we could be comfortable.

"Just one thing," Richard added. "We must make sure Jeffries doesn't know our direction here. Carier is doing what he can, but we're doubling the guard in the apartment. There'll be a few more footmen until we know for sure."

"Shouldn't we move?" Gervase said, alarmed.

"No, we thought of that," Richard told him. "We can keep this apartment secure enough, we know it well. A new direction would entail new study, new routines." He turned to speak directly to me. "Would you like to keep this apartment for our own personal use, or would you like to have somewhere else here? Or perhaps," he continued, taking my hand, "you would prefer never to see Venice again?"

"Oh no. I've loved being here. I would like to keep it, please."

He smiled. "I hoped you'd say that. We might buy the rest of the building when it becomes available. It would make a comfortable residence when we felt like coming here and if we owned the whole it would be more secure."

Could we afford it? I hadn't yet accustomed myself to having such wealth at my disposal and I didn't like to spend money too extravagantly. For years I'd dreamed of saving my allowance so I could afford an establishment of my own one day. Just a modest house in Exeter I'd thought, a single lady and a companion living her own life had been my ideal. Now my brother's newfound fortune, my marriage into a family similarly circumstanced, made this so laughably achievable I could look further. Although now all I wanted was a room and one other person.

"If you don't mind, that's enough for me. I'll get some rest," Gervase said.

I saw how pale he was, how shaded his eyes. "You'd be well advised to do that." I went over to the bed, but instead of taking his outstretched hand, I leaned over and hugged him, careful to avoid his injury. "I'm so glad you weren't hurt any worse." He kissed my cheek.

Richard and I left and went through to the drawing room, which I was glad to see returned to its proper appearance. So much had been in my mind earlier I wouldn't have noticed if they had removed all the furniture, but the sight gave me some pleasure now. We sat on the sofa and Richard reached across to the table, picking up a paper. "I have something for you." I stared at him in surprise. Hadn't he given me enough? "It's an old custom in my family for the groom to give the bride a present on their first morning together as a married couple. By tradition, it's usually land, to give her some independence of her own, but my bride-gift is slightly different. I'm sorry it was delayed, but Gervase brought it with him from home."

He gave me the paper, a legal document, signed at the bottom in three different hands, one of them his. "You know," he said, slipping his arm around my shoulders, "that everything you own is in law mine and I hope you know I consider it to be ours, but this is yours alone. We've arranged a legal contrivance, a trust which makes it in effect yours."

I tried to read the document, but legal language is a language of its own, not understandable unless one is taught it as formally as you might learn Latin and Greek. "I don't understand."

"It's a full quarter share in Thompson's. Now there are four principals. It gives you a say in what goes on, a vote on the important matters, a right to be consulted. In monetary terms it's not much, but that's not what I wanted to say to you with my bride-gift."

I understood so well that it took my breath away. I just sat, staring at him, holding the paper, suddenly so valuable. "You can't do this. You don't have to."

"No," he agreed, smiling. "But I want to."

For Thompson's was his own, the thing he and Carier had created independently, with no help or even knowledge from his own family. Everything else was inherited, created by someone else, but Richard had told me once Thompson's was his guarantee of independence. It owed nothing to the existence of the Earl of Southwood or Viscount Strang and everything to the existence of Richard Kerre. He was letting me into every area of his life, letting go of "I" and "me", replacing it with "we" and "us".

I was discovering that this was typical of him, this generosity, but I was also aware he might regret it. Perhaps one day he might want some independence from me, somewhere he could be on his own and I resolved not to get involved unless he asked me to, to appreciate the gesture but not to intrude. I had always been taught the first duty of a wife was to obey. It was something I had never treated completely seriously, seeing how couples I knew managed with that dictum, but Richard was showing me the value of co-operation, something I knew to be very rare, in marriage or out of it. When he gave, he gave completely, without reservation. The gift overwhelmed me.

He was watching me, but I didn't know what to say to him, except to thank him.

"It's your right," he said and drew me to him for a kiss, which effectively stopped any further discussion.

He was very considerate and gentle that night, reassuring me with his love, comforting me out of the remains of my shock, holding me close all night. I fell asleep in his arms and woke up in the morning, seemingly never having moved.

We sent a message to the Palazzo Barbarossa the following day, to inform them we were bringing two illustrious clients to see the "Strangs" and word duly came back they would be welcome at about eight. Freddy joined us for dinner and Signor Verdi arrived shortly after. With some trepidation and a good deal more caution than before, we stepped into the gondola and were poled up the Canal to the palazzo. I took comfort in the thought this was nearly the last time Mrs. Locke would make an appearance, for I had found the pretence was becoming tiresome.

I liked Mrs. Locke, but I wanted some time to get used to being Lady Strang and Mrs. Locke was getting in the way. Richard, though, seemed to be enjoying the masquerade as much as he had when it had first begun. He had sharpened, gained an edge of recklessness and danger.

We introduced Freddy as Lord Thurl and Signor Verdi as Signor Contarini, whereupon his accent became distinct, his command of English much poorer. He confided to us in the gondola he and Freddy had contrived a scheme to pluck one pigeon and fatten the other, should he be there.

"I'm depending on it," Richard said. "We need to reassure him we know nothing, suspect nothing. I shall behave as though my shoulder is stiff, but apart from that, no one is to refer to the incident unless we are asked."

It had taken a long time that morning to persuade him I should go and then he had nearly reneged on our agreement at the last moment, asking me if I wouldn't rather remain at home to care for Gervase. I had strenuously resisted any attempt to leave me behind. I persuaded him I must face Squires-Jeffries again and in any case, it might arouse his suspicions if I didn't make an appearance. He was obviously much wilier than we had previously given him credit for.

Ravens met us at the door to his smaller salon, the one decorated with mythological scenes and bowed to Lord Thurl, expressing surprise he had not met him before. "I've been abroad," Freddy explained and Ravens was all smiles.

"You are welcome here, my lord. I hope we may meet many more times. Shall we go in?"

Squires-Jeffries was already there, with his "wife", smiling as unctuously as ever, but examining Richard and myself closely. His scrutiny naturally made me uncomfortable, but I dared not show him any of my new found aristocratic arrogance. I lowered my head instead, tried to remember who I was supposed to be, but at the same time I realised that if this was a public masquerade, it couldn't have been more false. For no one here was as they seemed, even the servants were Thompson's and watchful. What a tangle!

We sat down at the tables and began to play right away. The stakes were high, but we knew Ravens would not expect the Lockes to honour any notes of hand tonight, so we could play comfortably on their behalf. In any case, we were being allowed to win, although only modestly, perhaps a sign of good faith from our new employer.

This was a new battle of wits I was engaged in, one that required a great deal of concentration.

Freddy was enjoying himself hugely. He had decided to bluster, to be the great lord condescending to spend a night with the hoi polloi. He dropped more names than I knew, though my sister Lizzie could probably keep up with him. He claimed intimate acquaintance with them all.

When I played a *partie* with him, he flirted with me outrageously, so I responded. There was none of the uncomfortable oiliness I had felt before when Squires tried to flirt with me. In any case, such a valued client of the Lockes deserved all the attention I could give him and Ravens might appreciate it too.

"Have you been to the Haymarket, yet, Mrs. Locke?" The Opera House in London was a favourite meeting place of the fashionable world in the Season.

I shook my head, examining my cards closely and sorting them carefully. "I hope my husband will take me when we return to London. Point of five."

"Good. If he does not, you must apply to me," he said, positively winking. "I usually have a box at the beginning of the season."

"You are too kind, my lord."

"Not at all." He patted my hand.

I beamed back at him. "Sequence of six." He had mastered the shuffling technique so well the hand he had dealt me was unbeatable, a dream.

"Good." He gave me the point and I added up all the other sequences I had, three in all. "It would be an honour to entertain such a lovely lady as you in my box."

Ravens sat at the next table, playing Richard. He could easily hear our conversation. I flicked open my fan, inwardly cursing when I heard the sharp click, demonstrating the expertise I had been practising for the last month or two. Mrs. Locke wouldn't be quite so expert. "My husband might remain here, my lord."

"Then you must bring a companion," he said firmly.

I decided Mrs. Locke was tiring of her husband. "Your lordship is most kind. I would love to come, if you send an invitation."

"Count on it, dear lady." I had no doubt he would remember; although the invitation would come from the irrepressible Freddy Thwaite, not Lord Thurl.

We played out the *partie* and then I moved on. This time I was with Mr. Ravens, showing he had let Richard win the set, as it was the victor who changed tables. He beamed at me, showing his pleasure and then I dealt to begin the set of six. He let me win, not as much as I had won from Freddy, but I showed twenty guineas profit from that hand. Perhaps that was how he was allowing us to pay off our debt, or perhaps we were expected to hand it all back at the end of the evening.

While we played, I glanced across at Squires-Jeffries, now playing with the Signor. He was losing. I could see the sweat on his forehead, rolling down his cheeks and beading his nose and his look of concentration. It would be my turn to play him next, if he won. At least he would get a fair hand from me, but I didn't think he would be rising from the table just yet. Then I saw his grip on the cards was slackening, his creased brow clearing, although the distressing rivulets of perspiration remained. He wasn't losing after all; he was winning because the cards he had drawn from the *talon* were excellent. Signor Verdi was teasing him, punishing him, though not as much as Richard might do if provoked into losing his temper.

So he came to the table where I sat, after Ravens had lifted my hand to his lips in an attempt at gallantry and moved on. He sat heavily, smiling in greeting. I wasn't sure yet if he knew who I was, I had to continue to be Mrs. Locke. I dealt the cards.

If he admitted to me that he knew me, then he must also know I had seen him and we knew what he was up to. It would change our game, but we'd agreed on this as part of our plan. I started generally, but I couldn't take too long. I only had six hands of piquet to do it in.

"Do you like Venice, Mr. Squires?"

"It is a very pleasant place with ladies such as you in it." He leered at me. I felt Richard's tension, though I didn't look at him.

I had a more normal hand this time. "Point of four. I have seen the Basilica now, a most impressive building. Of course, my husband has seen it before, he spends much more time in

Venice than I do."

"To?"

"King."

"Good. I myself was in St. Mark's Square today. I hear there was quite a commotion yesterday."

This could be my opening, but I had to be careful. I leaned over the pad to total my score for points. "Oh?"

"A nobleman was hurt," he said, looking at me directly. "They said it was Lord Strang, but here we see him, well and thriving, so it must have been someone else."

I managed a smile. "It must have been, sir." Did he suspect Gervase had arrived? That would be a pity. "My husband, on the other hand, woke up with a very sore shoulder this morning. Little could be done about it and I think it still pains him more than he admits."

He tapped the side of his face, ostensibly studying his cards, but I could see he was intrigued. "I'm sorry to hear that."

"Sequence of four."

"No good. Five." I passed him the paper so he could total his score and watched him note it down carefully. He took his cards seriously, conversation coming to a halt while he studied his hands and worked out his score, his concentration obvious. He looked up and smiled. "Your husband is a signally fortunate man, Mrs. Locke."

"How so?" I said brightly, trying to draw him out. "Fourteen queens."

"No good." He must have four kings or aces. He concentrated on the paper. "To have such a lovely wife, of course." I watched him take a sip of wine, waiting until he had done with his scoring.

Now we came to the second part of the hand. He led and we began to play it out. "I wish he thought so," I said, sighing slightly.

He looked up at me. "I would have thought was evident to all. How long have you been married, ma'am?"

"Five years, sir," Mrs. Locke replied.

He accepted the lie. "Not enough time for a marriage to

become stale, I would have thought."

"I think he admires—other qualities of mine," I said sadly, trying to be pathetic.

It seemed I succeeded, at least in convincing him I didn't know who he was. He accepted my masquerade and began to tease me on it, asking me questions I had to improvise the answers to. It was just as well I was giving up Mrs. Locke. Her life was becoming too complicated for me to cope with.

I sat opposite the man who had tried to murder my husband twice, death in my heart, sure now I would kill for Richard but unable to touch his would-be assassin. Richard wanted to know too much for us to kill him in cold blood, or perhaps at all. I spun stories for him about Mrs. Locke and her sad life—her poor health, her unsatisfactory husband and Squires-Jeffries laughed at me. I was sure he didn't know we had seen him now. He was too arrogant in his teasing, too sure of himself and he was winning at cards.

Unlike our host, whom I saw was now having a very bad time, passing between Freddy and Signor Verdi. Freddy was having the time of his life, losing to someone and then beating Mr. Ravens. Signor Verdi was winning with the detachment of the professional.

Eventually I got to play my husband. We played a desultory *partie*, hardly looking at each other, a couple only together because of the wedding ring, bored and dissatisfied with their lives and each other. Richard won and as he got up to move on I caught a whiff of the perfume he habitually wore. It swept me into a sudden desire for him. It took me completely by surprise. I don't know if he noticed, but he glanced down at me as he passed. I dared not meet his eyes.

At the end of the evening we were sure we could call it a complete success. By the time we broke for supper, Mr. Ravens was looking decidedly black. We didn't know how much he had lost, but it was he who now resorted to notes of hand. Richard and I had to look serious, as our conies had hardly been skinned. It was risky, to let an amateur like Freddy play the game but after this evening I knew that if Freddy had been forced to earn his living he would have done very well indeed.

We left together, Freddy kindly offering us a seat in his

gondola, *our* gondola. We didn't want a post mortem with them tonight, we wanted it on our territory, so we invited the Ravens to visit us the next day, at about midday and they accepted, grim-faced.

We travelled past the palazzo in silence and then, when we were out of earshot, Freddy let out a quiet crow of triumph. "I can't remember when I enjoyed myself so much!" He looked around at Richard and me, sitting behind him and the Signor.

"I told you," said that gentleman, his heavy Italian accent magically dropping away. "Freddy is a natural at this. With practice he could beat anyone!"

"So if your fortune on the tables at home suddenly improves," Richard commented, "I'll get very suspicious and refuse to play with you any more."

Freddy laughed. "Oh, I can promise you now I won't do it there. I always thought excessive play a bore before, but knowing you're going to win somehow puts a gloss on things."

I let my hand trail in the dark water and then looked up to see Richard watching me, smiling. "That's not too clean, you know."

I smiled back, got out my handkerchief and dried my fingers, feeling like a child caught out in mischief. I saw he had stretched his arm along the back of the seat and I leaned against him, resting my head on his shoulder.

Freddy and Signor Verdi were busy discussing their success animatedly, their backs to us, so Richard put his finger under my chin and tilted my face up to his. He wasn't drunk tonight, so he didn't kiss me with quite the abandon he had done the previous time, but it still sent a thrill through me. "Did I imagine it earlier?" he murmured.

There was no point denying it. "No, you didn't." I lowered my voice even more, put my mouth next to his ear. "It was the scent of you as you passed me."

He laughed softly as I withdrew after flicking my tongue around his ear. He mouthed, "Wanton!" and I sat up hurriedly when Freddy turned to talk to us again.

When we got back to the apartment, Gervase was still up, waiting for us. He saw from our faces as we entered the drawing room it had been a success.

We toasted our triumph and I sat down next to Gervase while Freddy and Signor Verdi recounted their adventure. They had given the notes of hand to Richard and he counted them up while they were talking. Eventually, he looked up, something like awe on his face.

"Twenty thousand and some pounds!" he exclaimed softly. "How in God's name did you manage that?"

Signor Verdi grinned. "I doubled up on the last two *parties* I played with the man. The first time, I let him think he was going to win, but the last hand of the *partie* gave me the advantage. But he came so close, poor man!"

"Poor now, certainly," Richard remarked dryly.

"The second time I devastated him. So delicately played! I had to be careful, you understand, because I was playing with a professional, but by the last hand I wanted to give him a remembrance of me. He is good, certainly, but not as good as me. He cannot shuffle a deck so the opponent deals himself a bad hand, as I have tried to teach you. He has not the finesse, only the general understanding, which is well enough for most, but not for me."

"You are superb, Signor Verdi," I said warmly, since it was obviously expected of someone. He stood and bowed. I caught Richard's attention on me and I was lost again.

I wondered if this would ever wear off, if I would ever feel normal when I was with him, or if this was normal from now on. Somehow, sitting across from him, able to look at him but not touch him made matters worse, but this was like the first time I had looked at him and for all I knew, like the last. I felt totally lost in him and helpless and foolish for feeling it.

I looked away, towards Freddy, who was telling Gervase how he had dealt the cards and how much he had won. "He'll come here tomorrow," he said and turned to Richard. "What time did you tell him to come?"

"About twelve," Richard replied. "Would you like to be here when he arrives, or would you like to be announced?"

An unholy gleam lit up Freddy's soft brown eyes. "Oh, I'd like to be announced after you've dropped your bombshell!

Immediately after, I think, don't you?"

The sparkle in Richard's eyes echoed the gleam in his friend's. "An excellent idea. Come just before and go into the music room next door, then Carier will fetch you at the right time. I always find precise timing improves these things enormously."

"Rather like a play," I put in. I didn't meet his eyes.

"Very much," he agreed. "And Gervase, if you could come in at some point, it might persuade the gentleman of our veracity."

"Delighted," Gervase said.

"Signor Verdi?"

Richard turned to the gentleman, silent up until then, but he grimaced and spread his hands in a very Italianate gesture. "I would prefer not to be here at all, if it can be arranged, my lord. I would like to retain the integrity it has taken me so many years to achieve."

"Would you? A pity. I was going to ask if you would like to join a little enterprise of ours. Would you come and discuss it another time?"

"Discussion is one thing," said the gentleman cautiously, "And of course, I am always open to a good business proposition, but I would rather avoid this meeting you plan for tomorrow."

Richard accepted his refusal. "Very well. There's one more act to our play and then we're done. We'll discuss the matter further then, if you wish."

Signor Verdi said he was delighted, bowed to us all and took his leave, wishing us good fortune on the following day.

Freddy and Gervase were still involved in discussing all the affairs of the evening, but Richard stood and held his hand out to me. "I'm sure you'll excuse us. After her recent shock, I'm anxious to make sure Rose gets enough rest." They both stood and bowed to us and we left the room.

We went sedately up to the bedroom door in silence, but as soon as we were inside the room and closed the door behind us, I fell on him as though my life depended on it. Laughing, he swept me up and on to the bed, asking no questions, responding to the fire in me and there, fully dressed, we made love urgently, as though we'd been apart for months. My tension released, like a violin string snapping and I enjoyed the sensations coursing through me, as it became less of a need, more a delight.

I had taken him totally by surprise, but he responded as I wanted him to, recognising and knowing what I wanted without words, without explanation. The only items he'd removed were his coat and wig, which when I was sentient again I was thankful for. The coat was made of inferior material and would have been scratchy against my skin. Although terminally dishevelled, I was still dressed. When he finally gasped in his own moment of ecstasy and took his weight off me, we lay side by side in a confusion of clothes, getting our breath back.

He put his hand to his forehead and laughed. "What brought that on?"

I looked at him, my breath still unsteady, then I sat up and began to unhook my bodice at the front. "I don't know. But when you walked past me this evening, dressed in that dowdy suit, but smelling so deliciously like you, it reminded me at a most inappropriate time what we've done here and what I'd like to do." I smiled and slid the gown off, turning to the tapes at my waist. "You're corrupting me, my lord. I was a well-bred young lady before I met you."

"And now you're a lascivious wanton?" He loosened the laces of my stays at the back for me, so I couldn't see his face. "You've a long way to go before you reach that point, my love. But you are constantly surprising, tremendously exciting, a joy to be with."

I got off the bed, the easier to remove my petticoats, pockets and side hoops. I glanced at him and saw him leaning on one elbow. He watched me by the light of the candles. I caught his gaze and kept it, as I lifted my shift over my head, letting it drop to the floor and then bent to undo my garters and unroll the plain stockings Mrs. Locke wore.

He hadn't moved, but watched me, smiling. I felt totally at ease with him now, dressed or not, as once he had promised me I would. I went back to him without hesitation and began to unfasten the buttons of his waistcoat. He let me, touching and caressing me while I undressed him. He distracted me from a task I had never undertaken before, discovering the intricacies of men's dress at first hand. I hadn't realised the stock at his neck was fastened by little buckles at the back, for instance, or how to divest him of the complicated arrangement of buckles, buttons, breeches and stockings at the knee. It kept me busy for a while and made him laugh again. He didn't offer to help, but watched me struggle until I cursed and tried to pull it all apart by brute force.

Then he pulled me up to him, lay back and had his laugh out, only stopping to say, "These are easy, my sweet! Wait until I'm in full Court rig!"

"I wouldn't dare to approach you then, you'll be far too grand to touch."

"I shall make you." He sat up and began to make some sense of my efforts, kicking the bundled up breeches, stockings and buckles free of the bed. He pulled his shirt off over his head so he was as naked as I, then he turned to hold me again. He told me the most gratifying things—that my skin was satin to his touch, my mouth the softest he had ever kissed, my love the sweetest. He caressed me to demonstrate his words, loved me again. It was a wonder we got any sleep at all that night.

Chapter Nineteen

I waited until after breakfast to dress properly the next morning. I chose the white flowered silk I'd worn before, making sure I looked my best, every inch the aristocrat, then I went into the drawing room and found a book. Usually, I would have some kind of sewing to keep me busy, but I had lost the desire and the time recently, something I would have to rectify if I ever spent enough time out of bed.

Richard had retired to his dressing room to dress and had not yet come out, but Gervase joined me and began to tell me about the joys of Italy.

When we heard the knock on the door, Gervase opened the long windows on to the balcony outside and stepped out. I heard him open the doors to the music room a little further along, so he could get away silently if he needed to. The sounds of Venice came in through the windows, the water lapping against the buildings, the calls of the boatmen. The door opened and a footman announced, "Lord and Lady Strang, my lady."

I stood to greet them and watched their faces closely as they came in. "Tell my husband, if you please," I said to the footman, who bowed and left.

I held out my hand and waited for the gentleman to bow over it. He did so after a mere second's hesitation, enough for a swift glance around the room. The only item absent this time was the portrait of the twins. Either he hadn't heard the footman's announcement, or he chose to ignore it, for he said, "I trust we find you well this morning, Mrs. Locke?"

"Perfectly," I assured him. "Do sit down, I'm sure my

husband will be in directly."

They sat down and looked around, taking in the things we had had removed or covered up the last time they had visited. "Have you undergone a change of fortune we are unaware of, Mrs. Locke?" asked Ravens. "There seems to have been a change in this room since I saw it last."

"It was my brother-in-law's idea. He's staying here for while. You may meet him soon."

"Your brother-in-law," said Ravens. "Is he the instrument of this change?"

I smiled. "Not at all. Quite the reverse, in fact."

"You're looking extremely well this morning, Mrs. Locke." Mrs. Ravens stared patronisingly at me under half lowered lids. Mr. Ravens appeared perturbed, worried, his hands clenched on the arms of the elegant chair he occupied. I was surprised to find I didn't feel at all nervous or concerned. I was here on my own territory, better protected than the king, waiting for my husband, entertaining frauds. I began to relish the situation and enjoy myself.

"You're very kind," I said in reply to her. "I gave orders for tea to be served when you arrived."

She bowed her head in a stately manner in reply, but didn't look as put out as her husband. Such was her supreme air of superiority, I believe it would have carried her anywhere.

I decided to have some fun of my own while we were waiting for Richard. I felt justified, there was only Gervase to hear and they had insulted us enough just by impersonating us.

"Lady Strang, I heard you went to the Contessa Marini's reception the other day, the first night we played cards at your house. Do you know her well?"

The lady spread her fan. "Oh yes, she is an old family friend, you know."

Halfway through this speech her husband cleared his throat repeatedly, but the lady didn't stop in her revelations and I was able to say, seemingly puzzled, "But I read you lived quietly in the country before your marriage. How could you meet the contessa in Devonshire?"

"She's an old friend of the family," Mrs. Ravens repeated with dignity.

"I see. I heard you created a sensation there."

"It is very kind of you to say so," Mr. Ravens said before his wife could make any more *faux pas.* "It was a dazzling assembly. All Venice society was there."

"What did you wear, my lady?" I asked, full of interest. "I have always taken an interest in fashionable dress."

"Green," she said, "with emeralds."

The door opened and a footman brought in the tea tray. He was closely followed by Richard, at his brilliant best, in fine blue broadcloth and a white waistcoat, immaculately and finely embroidered in blue and silver thread. The diamond glittered in the precisely creased folds of his neckcloth, in a negligent style Mr. Ravens could only echo. The Ravens had their backs to the door, so they didn't notice his entrance. He waited behind their sofa as the servant arranged the tea on a table at my elbow. He smiled at me, although I tried to keep my attention on the lady opposite.

Mrs. Ravens, obviously a fashion follower, was describing her gown, her confidence rising with every word. "Pomona green silk, with furbelows and embroidery, with the emeralds I had on my marriage. I received some flattering compliments, but I fancy I looked very well." She preened.

Richard walked around the sofa and took my hand. "Strange. I could have sworn you wore blue, with sapphires." He kissed my hand and turned to bow to the Ravens, taking his time, letting them stare. "Just so," he said gently, breaking into their thoughts.

They came out of their reverie, tearing their gaze away from the vision before them. At least Mr. Ravens did, but his wife watched, fascinated as Richard disposed himself on the sofa next to me, elegance personified.

Mr. Ravens seemed to pull himself together. However Richard was dressed, he was still as far as they knew under their control, their creature, although now surely they must be having doubts. "I cannot imagine what has caused this change in you, sir—"

"My lord," Richard corrected him.

The man stared, but carried on "The fact remains, last night was a disaster for you and for us and we must study to rectify it."

Richard took his tea and I gave the Ravens' tea to the footman, who passed it to them, bowing. Richard looked every inch the arrogant aristocrat, almost as haughty as the first time I had met him. "A disaster for you, perhaps. But then, we intended it to be."

Ravens stared at him, aghast. Richard put his tea dish down on the table by his side and picked up one of the notes of hand with elegant, jewelled fingers. "These are useless, as I'm sure you're aware. So are the ones you hold belonging to us. We could perhaps make an exchange, but these add up to about twenty thousand pounds, so we might add other considerations to make the exchange even."

Mr. Ravens sighed heavily. "So your game was deeper than ours."

Richard allowed a small, frosty smile to cross his face. "If you hadn't afforded my wife some assistance on the road to Venice, I might have made it a lot worse. As it is, there are one or two matters we require your assistance with and then we'll call it even." He leaned back, completely at his ease, one foot stretched out negligently before him, "The first requirement is that you must undertake never to use my—our—name again."

"I beg your pardon!" said Ravens, blustering for all he was worth. I didn't like the expression on his face, angry and determined, as though he was truly in the right. "You may be in the same game as us, but please do not insult me by claiming to be Lord Strang. His lordship is at present by his wife's bedside in Devonshire, waiting for her to recover from an attempt on her life. We ensured that before ever we decided on our course of action here."

Richard sighed. "So that one took, did it? It's true, there was an attempt, but we were very lucky." Only I saw the merest twitch of the finger on the hand that lay apparently at ease on his knee. "We decided to leave several smokescreens behind us."

He looked at them for a few moments in silence, picked up his tea and finished it in his own time, putting it down ever so gently afterwards. "Sometimes I could wish I were in the same game as you. Should you like it, Rose?"

"No," I confessed. "It would be most uncomfortable, not knowing where the next penny was coming from. And I haven't any emeralds."

He regarded me, smiling. "You will have. You'll suit them."

"You said I suited rubies."

"Those as well," he added and turned back to the Ravens. "Whether you believe it or not, I am the man whose name you've been taking in vain."

They looked at him mute, waiting for his next move.

I knew what he meant, so I raised my voice slightly and called, "Gervase, would you like some tea?"

There was a movement from outside the open window. "I thought you'd never ask," said Gervase.

I hadn't seen quite such a look of confounded chagrin as now settled on the faces of our visitors. Gervase stood behind me while I poured his tea for him. This allowed the Ravens to see the twins together. Gervase came to take his tea dish from me with his good hand. He sat down in a chair at my side. His other arm was still in a sling and he was dressed in his own style—simpler, but with that same attention to quality that all the Kerres demonstrated. There was no disguising the similarity between the brothers and no attempt to.

Richard spoke. "Yes, we are identical. Yes, we do think each others' thoughts from time to time and, yes, my shoulder's been stiff for a day or two."

Forgetting everything else, I turned to him. "You didn't tell me!"

He smiled at me and for one moment he let his arrogant expression slip. "There was nothing you could do. I was well aware of the reason."

I recalled the way he'd woken me that morning, concluded there couldn't be anything really wrong with his shoulder and smiled back. "The perils of being a twin."

"Indeed," Gervase added. "When I came off my horse and

broke my leg in India Richard knew at once."

I was surprised at that. "So it works over distances?"

"Over half the globe," my husband replied.

I suddenly thought of something and had to work very hard to prevent myself colouring up. "No," said Richard quietly to me and I knew he was trying to reassure me that what we did together was totally private.

I turned my attention to the Ravens now. They must have believed us finally. "I must beg your pardon, my lord," Mr. Ravens said. He didn't sound very contrite.

Richard inclined his head graciously. "As long as you don't do it again I forgive you."

The doorknocker to the apartment sounded and I heard it opened, then Freddy was announced. "Lord Thwaite, my lady."

Freddy stopped on the threshold and looked around. "Oh Lord, late again! I missed it, didn't I?"

"You did," Richard agreed and made him known to the Ravens.

Mr. Ravens rose and bowed deeply to him. "You, my lord have a true talent. It is a pity you were not born into slightly more indigent circumstances, as it would have been a pleasure to see you at work."

Freddy bowed in return, highly amused. "Thank you. I've only been at it a week, my—" he broke off and looked guiltily at me, "—friends think I've been abandoning them."

"Friend." I corrected him and he bowed to me, smiling charmingly.

Gervase lifted an enquiring eyebrow at Richard who explained; "He has Miss Outridge here."

"Good God!" Gervase flicked an appalled glance at me. "And Rose knows?"

"She takes great amusement from it," his brother told him. "She teased him about it at the contessa's and Miss Crich was completely won over."

"Is the whole of London in Venice?" Gervase demanded, taking the view I had so often noted about these people, that their set constituted the whole.

Richard smiled. "No, but when you set foot outside these doors, London will know as fast as the post will take it."

Gervase sighed. "At least in India that took half a year, if it got there at all." He sipped his tea.

Richard turned back to the Ravens. "By the way, this is how it's done." He drew an enamelled and bejewelled French snuffbox from his pocket, flicked open the top with one hand, all without looking and offered it to Mr. Ravens with negligible grace. Not one lace ruffle was disturbed. Mr. Ravens stared at his hand thoughtfully for one moment before taking some of the proffered snuff. Richard offered it to Freddy, but not to Gervase, who disliked it, then took his usual infinitesimal pinch. He applied it to his nose with one hand, clicking the box shut with a finger on his other hand and returning it to his pocket in one swift movement. He took his seat again.

Mr. Ravens sighed. "I tried. I read as much as I could find and that movement was mentioned of you somewhere, so I did my best."

Richard bowed his head in acknowledgement. "Like your skills, it only requires practice. Now shall we discuss the business of the day?"

"By all means, my lord." The man was all obsequiousness now.

"The man Squires," Richard said then, getting down to business. "How well do you know him?"

Ravens' eyes opened wide and he looked with astonishment at Richard. Whatever he had been expecting from us, it wasn't this. "Squires?"

"Is he one of your creatures?" I asked.

Ravens shook his head. "Certainly not, my lady. I met him here in Venice. He seemed to be the one person I couldn't avoid, so it was a great relief to find he didn't seem to know Lord Strang any better than I did. And then..." his eyes gleamed and he looked up to meet Richard's perceptive gaze, "...I found he was a card player. He couldn't get enough of the tables, kept on asking me when I planned to open my house properly. He didn't seem to be short of cash, but I could find out nothing about him. I'm surprised you're interested in him, my lord, he seems a nonentity, not at all your kind."

Richard smiled grimly. "Not at all my kind, Mr. Ravens." He paused. "This man has tried to kill me twice—no, three times, if you count the yacht."

Gervase interrupted him. "Oh I should count the yacht. I've seen what's left of it."

"And I saw it go up," I added.

He covered my hand with his own. "Three times then. I think he knows me much better than you do, but his addiction to the tables kept him with you. Do you know he cheats?"

Ravens smiled expansively. "I do not flatter when I say he doesn't do it nearly as well as your friends, my lord." Freddy nodded, grinning. "I have been aware of it and while he thinks he has the upper hand I, in fact, have been controlling him. I was planning the final *coup* soon, in fact."

"I would strongly advise against it," Richard told him. "The man is a killer." Ravens blenched, the complete lack of colour making him appear unhealthy. "But I'm glad you're seeing him again."

The dossier on Jeffries was lying on a table by his side. Richard took it up and opened it, although he didn't really need to refer to it. "The man's real name is Jeffries. He is known to the authorities as a hired man, who will kill anyone in cold blood for the right amount of money."

"My God!"

Richard ignored the interruption. "When we turned up at your house, I don't suppose he could believe his luck. He's bided his time since then. Has he asked you for our direction? Have you given it to him?"

Ravens stared in front of him and his wife gripped her hands together, looking at her husband anxiously. Then her attention went to Richard. "He has asked us, yes, my lord, but we haven't told him, not yet. You see, it was obvious he set some store by the information, so we thought we would make him pay for it."

I felt, rather than heard or saw Richard's relief and I heard Gervase's sigh. "So he doesn't know this address through you," Richard said.

"Certainly not, my lord."

Richard bit his lower lip, lost in thought. "Then we can go ahead. There's danger from now on. If you'd rather bail out now, Freddy, we could easily manage without you."

Freddy's heavy brows went up. "If you think I'd leave you alone now, especially with Rose to take care of, you're a madman, Richard Kerre!"

Richard smiled. "Thank you, Freddy." Then he turned to me. "I'd feel happier if you were away from here."

My reaction was as emphatic as Freddy's. "There's no way I'm leaving you now, Richard." I searched frantically in my mind, trying to find a way to persuade him. I was determined I wouldn't leave him now, to sit in some out of the way place and worry myself sick about him. I would stay, one way or the other, but I would prefer it to be with his blessing. I met his eyes, cold and anxious. "I'll never leave you again, I promised that. In any case, I'm safer here. I'm well cared for and we have no guarantee it's only you he wants."

"I want to bring him here," Richard told me.

"I'm not leaving." Then I added, "You gave me a share. I intend to be a full voting member, so you need me here to cast my vote."

His expression changed at that and he smiled grimly. "Is there anything you won't use to stay here?"

I shook my head. "Nothing. And if our bodyguards have two people in two places to look after, it's bound to weaken our defences. You need me here, I need to be here, so I'm staying."

For a long moment he didn't move, looking at me straight in the eyes, then he sighed. "You won't go whatever I say, will you?" I didn't answer, knowing he required none. To my great surprise he leaned forward and kissed me gently on my mouth, his lips just touching mine. "Very well. You stay."

For a brief moment only the two of us were in the room. Then, with a deep breath, he addressed to the others. "As you no doubt heard, my plan is to bring him here."

Freddy shook his head, but Gervase waited for his next words, knowing from experience there would be a good reason. The Ravens sat still, watching him, fascinated. He spoke to them, now. "We will come to your house one more time as the Lockes and we will comprehensively strip him so he needs his kill and the money he can expect to collect afterwards. He won't be pleased, he'll be taken off balance, which is what we want and it will give me great pleasure to see him lose it all. Then, when he asks for our address next time, give it to him and send word by Patchett,"

"My footman?" Mr. Ravens asked, confused.

"*My* footman," Richard corrected him. "He merely works at your palazzo. That's all you have to do. After that, disband the house and come back to me in a few days. Ask for my man, Carier. We may have something for you. More than that you don't need to know."

The Ravens were forced to agree with our plan.

Freddy leant forward in his chair. "Can't we intercept them at the palazzo?"

"It's much more certain here," Richard said. "I have no intention of killing unless it becomes absolutely necessary, but if it does I should like to know my immediate geography very well indeed."

"Do you have to bankrupt him?" Gervase queried. "This man is dangerous, we know that. Angry and desperate, he could be even more dangerous."

Richard smiled sweetly. "Less dangerous to us. When he's angry and desperate he won't behave like a professional and we have much more of a chance of taking him off his guard. What I want to do is disarm him and talk to him. I don't want him so much as the people he's working for. I might be able to buy him off, much more preferable to any other way, don't you think?"

We would all agree with that.

Chapter Twenty

This was now serious, far more serious than the light-hearted adventure we had gone into. Talking it over with Richard later, when we were alone, he pointed out it would have to be faced sooner or later. "I haven't given up persuading you to go away somewhere safe."

"Give it up," I advised him. "I'm not leaving you. Besides, you need Mrs. Locke to stop him suspicioning anything and withdrawing. Then we'd only have to face him somewhere else, another time."

He tilted my chin so he could look me directly in the eyes. "You have a great heart, my love. I'm only just beginning to realise what this marriage will to mean to me. You won't let me do things on my own, will you?"

"No. You can become the kind of autocratic husband so many are, but if you do that, something we have will die." We regarded each other and eventually he nodded briefly. "I want to help you," I continued. "Has anyone else ever seen what killing another person does to you?"

"Carier," he admitted.

"But you can't turn to him for support and love, can you? I can at least be here for you always, to help you when you need it, but if I don't know what you've done, how can I sympathise completely, help you the way I want to?" I knew I was right, but it would be very difficult for him, so long on his own, to depend on anyone else. It would have to come gradually, but I was determined upon it. We let the matter drop there, although I knew he would try again sometime in the future.

When I next dressed as Mrs. Locke, the situation was altogether more serious. I wore two large, double-sewn pockets into which I put the pistols Richard had given me for the journey to Venice, both loaded. Wearing both of them balanced out the weight and made the load more comfortable. As Mrs. Locke, I would wear a substantial hooped skirt, unlike the smaller side hoops I usually used and the guns were well hidden but easily accessible. I also slipped one of Richard's wicked little knives into one of my garters, for extra protection. Then I dressed.

Freddy and Signor Verdi were already at the palazzo when we arrived. We had informed the Signor of the change of plan and given him the opportunity to withdraw, but he chose to accept the hefty bonus Richard was offering, together with the risk. I was glad to see him.

We played piquet again and I tried to concentrate on the matter in hand. The Ravens were good actors, they didn't once betray the revelations of the previous day and accepted our calling them "my lord" and "my lady" with as much equanimity as they had previously done. There was no hand pressing, no knowing nodding, nothing.

The Squires were already there, seemingly keen to continue with their run of good luck. They were allowed to win at first. The rest of us played nondescript, mostly ordinary hands, although when I played Richard, he dealt me outrageously good hands. I came out of that *partie* many guineas to the good. I meant to make him make good his debt, just to teach him not to tease me. He watched my face closely when I picked up my cards, but after a small gasp the first time, I realised what he was doing and positively refused to respond again. Freddy was equally gallant, but not with quite the abandon Richard had shown, dealing me far more believable hands that would beat his, but only if I played well.

When I played with Mrs. Squires, she seemed perfectly at ease, conversing with me about the places she had seen and how much she enjoyed Venice. I didn't know what to make of Mrs. Squires. We knew she must be hired, but we didn't know how much she knew about Jeffries' ultimate goal, or what her instructions were. I didn't think she was cheating tonight and thinking back, I didn't think she had cheated in the past, but she never took unnecessary risks and seemed only to be playing because she had been paid to undertake the part.

Squires-Jeffries, on the other hand, played with total concentration, total involvement. The handful of pasteboard held his life for the few minutes it took to complete it and then he couldn't wait to pick up the next hand. He did his best to conceal his passion, but like most devoted card players from the youngest, freshest convert to the oldest matron in the assembly rooms of England, he had that look of abandonment in his eyes, the gleam of fanaticism that betokened obsession, the look about him that he would play all night and not notice the time. I couldn't be afraid of him while he was so unaware of his partner. He tried some gallantry on me, but I behaved with far more propriety before, although I hoped not enough to give him any cause to suspect me.

He beat me, but not by much, so I was in debt by thirty guineas to him when he rose to move on. All the time I played with him, I had been aware of Richard's close regard, as he sat across from me playing Mrs. Ravens. She kept up a playful flirtation with him, the sort he could respond to in his sleep, so he could watch me without too much distraction, but not be observed to be watching.

I knew Jeffries wouldn't try anything here, he would prefer to do the job cleanly and get away. If he could gain access to our apartment, he would kill us both and leave us there, while he got away. If there were not too many servants, he could kill them too and give himself several clear days, but that would not be possible unless he obtained our direction. He knew who we were, but not, it was to be hoped, of our involvement in Thompson's, or the special nature of most of our attendants here. He tried to get the information out of me, but I was cagey, as I would be expected to be.

"Such a lovely lady deserves to be seen more about the fashionable resorts in Venice," was his opening gambit.

"Lord and Lady Strang were kind enough to offer us a seat in their box at the Opera," I replied. "We had a most enjoyable evening and we were even called across to greet Lady Thurl and her son." Jeffries glanced at Freddy, blithely engaged in a *partie* with Richard. "My husband's customers, you know," I continued. Jeffries smiled grimly. I babbled on. "Indeed it was very kind of them, since we are hardly of their world—"

"I think," he said, leaning forward slightly and lowering his voice, "you would fit in to that world very well, my dear. You must permit my wife and me to take you out one day. Have you seen the shops at the Rialto?" I admitted that I had. "Then, have you been to St. Mark's Square?"

He knew I had. "I have seen it, yes, sir, but I haven't yet seen all the beauties there. We—ran out of time." I hope he took my hesitation as an accidental slip. I couldn't be seen to be too clever.

His smile would have melted butter. "We are planning a small reception next week, I wonder if your husband and you would be available? I can promise you the guests will be quite unexceptionable, beyond reproach."

My blood ran cold. I had never thought that he might try to entice us to his lodgings. That would be even better for him. I murmured I must consult with my husband, which I did as soon as we broke for supper. I could see the news had not surprised Richard. He accepted the invitation without hesitation. "But you must be prepared for a last minute refusal, sir. My wife is frequently ill and I don't like to leave her when she is indisposed."

Jeffries looked disappointed. "It would be a great shame."

"You must come to dinner," I said impulsively and received a quelling look from Mr. Locke in return. "But we cannot offer you anything grand."

"I'm sure anything you offer must be of the most charming," Jeffries said, heavily hinting at a none-too-subtle *double entendre*.

I simpered. "If you give us your direction, we'll make sure you're invited to the very next dinner party we hold," Richard said, thus converting a definite invitation to a more nebulous one. Jeffries smiled unctuously and gave us his card. Richard made a great show of feeling in his pockets for his card-case, only to realise he had left it at home. He promised to send one as we retook our places at the tables. We had his address.

This time Squires' luck changed. Ravens suggested we increase the stakes, to which everyone agreed and from then he could win nothing. His face and hands became sweatier as the evening progressed, the cards dealt him varied from fair to poor, but he didn't win another *partie*, except from me, because I was the only one not cheating at all. Richard's skills had developed enough for him to attempt the shuffle, so he could ensure a good win on his own deal and Freddy, Mr. Ravens and Signor Verdi positively sparkled. It seemed Jeffries' skills in cheating were but modest, basic ones, having not had the benefit of the tuition of an expert.

At the end of the evening, Jeffries was a fleeced lamb, a skinned cony, a target hit. He gave us several notes of hand, promising he had a small enterprise in hand that would pay off handsomely in a day or two, when he would return to repay his debts. We presumed the enterprise was Richard's death.

After Jeffries left, Ravens found a bottle of wine and we solemnly toasted our success. "He's desperate," Ravens told us. "I've seen it before. He needs to play and he needs to pay off his debts so he can do so. I have an appointment to see him in the morning, when I shall refuse him any more credit."

"Don't go alone, and give him our direction. Here." He pulled the missing card-case from his pocket and gave him one of Mr. Locke's cards. "Perhaps you'd like to leave that lying around."

Mr. Ravens took it, looking at it thoughtfully. "Thank you, my lord, I will allow him to persuade me to give it up."

"After you have done that," Richard told him, "you would be well advised to leave the palazzo immediately. Your landlords are now aware you're impostors and Jeffries might well come back."

"We have already packed," Ravens assured him.

We left shortly after that and went to our lodgings, but not before Richard had given Signor Verdi his thanks and a banker's draft to pay for his considerable services.

When we got home, I asked Richard if he was planning to put the Ravens in the box. "What, thoroughgoing villains like them? I should say so! And they have a streak of snobbery that will serve to keep them loyal. I could find work for them."

"They mean no harm," I said and he raised his eyebrows in surprise. "Well, only financially."

"They did try to blackmail us, my love."

"I think they would have dealt fairly. They would have returned our notes of hand, I'm sure of it."

"A kind heart." He took me into his arms. "And a true one."

We were in the bedroom by then, so he began to undress me, letting my gown slide to the floor. "The last time we shall see Mrs. Locke. You can appear as your own beautiful self from now on,"

I laughed at him. "Richard, please! You know I'm not beautiful."

He'd bent his head to kiss my neck in the place he knew had most effect, but he stopped at that and looked at me, his arms loosely about my waist. "You are and you will be to the rest of the world. Everyone will say you are and so it will be accepted. Besides," he added, his eyes gleaming brilliantly, "my taste is known to be impeccable, so you must be beautiful, mustn't you?"

We laughed, but his laughter stopped abruptly when he undid the tapes to my pockets and they fell to the floor with a decided clunk. He swooped down on them and investigated, finding the loaded pistols. He gave a low whistle. "Did you think we'd have to shoot our way out?" He weighed one of them in his hand.

"I didn't want to leave anything to chance."

He pulled back the hammer, enabling the trigger to drop and sighted down the barrel. "Would you have been able to use them?"

I nodded and took the other one from him. "I'm a country girl, my lord. I was taught to shoot in my childhood. James is inordinately fond of field sports, so we were always involved in those kind of activities."

"So you can shoot. I'm not sure I would have liked to have known you were armed tonight."

I frowned at him. "Don't tell me you weren't armed!"

"That's different."

"How so?" I wasn't best pleased by his assumption the guns wouldn't have been much use in my hands. I was considered a very fair shot at home. "Come here."

I seized his hand and pulled him out to the corridor, going down to the front entrance and turning to face the blank wall at the end. This was the longest range we had in this small apartment so I supposed it would have to do. "Is that an outer wall?"

"I think so." Amusement crept into his voice.

I lifted my piece and sighted along it. "You see that picture? Watch the ship in the middle." The picture in question was a seascape, a ship in full sail on the ocean, not a very large one. All the better for my purposes.

I fired without hesitation and the corridor exploded in fire and smoke. As I lifted my weapon, he had lifted its partner and fired at the same place. Two simultaneous explosions, creating an immense sound in such an enclosed space, made my ears ring.

The sound brought me to my senses. I clapped my hand to my mouth and dropped the pistol, appalled by what I had just done. All at once, the doors opened and people erupted into the corridor. Carier and Nichols, both wielding pistols of their own, Gervase, confused by the noise, but with his hand in his dressing gown pocket, no doubt in search of his own weapon. Richard was now helpless with laughter, so he was no support. There I stood, in stays and petticoat, my hands to my mouth in horror.

Eventually Richard straightened up. "There's nothing to worry about." He laughed again and stopped long enough to say, "Her ladyship was merely showing me how well she can shoot." Then he was off again.

After an incredulous stare, Nichols went away, about her duties. Carier said, "The building will have been roused, my lord," in censorious tones and went away to deal with it.

Gervase looked at both of us in astonished amusement. "Well, we might as well see how you've done." He went up to the end of the hall.

As the smoke cleared, Richard's laughter began to subside and we could see again. "You've both gone straight through the picture," Gervase called down to us "Right through the centre, there's no ship left any more. You'll have to redecorate this wall."

"We'll just hang another picture over it for now," Richard said.

We went up to view the damage.

I was still appalled by what I had done. We looked at the black, shattered holes we had made in silence for a few moments. "All right, so you can shoot," Richard said eventually to me. "But I reserve the right to challenge you to a target shoot when we get home,"

"Accepted," I said straightaway. We shook hands on it.

Richard studied the ruined picture again. "I'm rather pleased you can shoot. It makes me easier in my mind about your staying here. Meantime, my lady." He turned to me, making me acutely aware of my appearance. "I can't think your esteemed sister-in-law would think it at all proper for you to appear in public like this. I would urge you to spare my poor brother's blushes at once and come to bed."

I coloured up and lifted my hand to my breast in confusion, which only served to draw attention to my lack of covering. Richard watched me, amused, but Gervase took pity on me. He took my other hand and kissed it lightly. "It's just as well I don't notice such things then." He looked only at my face, something few other men would have done in the circumstances, then nodded to Richard and went back to his own room, leaving us alone in the corridor in front of the shattered remains of the picture.

In a splendidly courtly gesture, Richard offered me his arm. "Shall we?" He led me back into our room, just as if we were entering a ballroom. Once there however, not on the best of terms with him for laughing so much, I insisted on cleaning and reloading both the pistols.

I brought the case into the bedroom from the dressing room and sat by the cold fireplace. I used the table we had used to breakfast from so much in the last week or two. He lay on the bed in his shirtsleeves, his chin propped up on his hand, watching me.

I glanced up at him. "We might need these in the morning."

He sat up and opened the drawer in the nightstand. "Or these." He brought out another pair of pistols, larger than mine but equally ready for use.

I realised the ridiculousness of the situation, as he had meant me to. I laughed and forgave him, but I carried on with my task, determined to be ready for our would-be assassin. Richard replaced his guns in the drawer and I finished my task while he watched me. "I have rarely seen anything more erotic."

"What?" I looked up from my task, startled.

"You. Half-naked, cleaning that gun. You're so absorbed in what you're doing you're not aware of how you look."

I put down the last flintlock. "And how do I look?"

"Delicious." He climbed off the bed and came over to demonstrate

We got up early the next day and breakfasted with Gervase on the broad balcony outside the apartment, Carier in grim attendance. He had warned against our doing so, for fear of being seen, but the weather was becoming much hotter now and the cool breezes outside were preferable to the heat gathering indoors.

"We should move on soon," Richard said. "If we travel north we can avoid the heat."

Gervase picked up his coffee cup. "I'm going south. I can't come this close without going back to Rome. You know my house in Rome, don't you Richard?"

"A positive palace compared to this," Richard commented.

"You're most welcome if you want to come. It will be hot, but not as unhealthy."

Richard leaned back, the breeze ruffling his short hair. "Should you like to do that, sweetheart? We can go to France, make our way home slowly, or spend a month or two here, in Italy. If we're careful, that may give us more time to ourselves, without the need to enter society more than we wish to. If we go to France we may be drawn into Versailles."

Gervase made a face. "I only went there once. In October. It stank then, so Lord knows what it's like in July."

I knew which option I'd prefer. Italy beckoned. "Perhaps we could defer Versailles."

He reached across the table and took my hand. "Italy it is, then. I'm glad you chose that. Despite the heat, I think it's the best choice. We can sail across to France from Naples when we get there and go home that way."

I smiled back at him sunnily. Anything that deferred the inevitable entry into reality was a good thing, but I had fallen in love with Venice and it gave me a desire to see more of Italy. I was pleased we would keep the house here, it meant the door was always open for us to come back. This was where it all began, the greatest love affair I was ever likely to know and the rescue of a human being out of the remains of an exquisite automaton.

A frantic knocking sounded on the door of the apartment and we knew the last act had come. Carier went to the edge of the balcony and looked over, confirming to us a gondola was moored there. "They must have travelled up the very side of the Canal," he commented grimly. "I've been watching but I didn't see their approach."

"Is everybody armed?" Richard asked and we all nodded. Gervase strode through the open doors of the music room and Richard took me to the drawing room. Carier handed him his wig, discarded in the heat and Richard paused to settle it carefully in place before he nodded to Carier who went to give instructions for the door to be opened.

We heard the bolts drawn back and then a crash as it was shoved back on its hinges and the door to the drawing room burst open. First we saw Mr. and Mrs. Ravens, white-faced, entering the room with rather more haste than we were used to. Jeffries followed close behind her, a pistol in each hand and several more stuck into his belt. He shoved them into the room.

"Good morning," said Richard calmly. "Rather an early hour for a visit."

"My lord," Ravens gasped, "he made us! He's held us

captive for an hour now, him and his doxy—"

"Mind your words," Jeffries snapped. "She's nobody's doxy!"

I tried to copy Richard's calm pose. I sat, careful to make sure I didn't block any access to my pockets and asked them if they wouldn't rather do so.

"Yes," said Jeffries. "Everybody sit down." He waited while they did so, but Richard made no move towards a chair. Jeffries motioned with his gun.

Richard met his gaze steadily, but still made no move. "My wife leaves."

Jeffries smiled, not a pleasant sight, since he seemed to have lost a great many teeth since we saw him last. He must have been wearing false ones before. "No. Now, my lord, sit down and before you do, empty your pockets."

Richard obeyed that much, putting the pistols and several trinkets on the small table. He must have expected that, as he put up little resistance. Then, taking his time, he sat, stretching his legs in front of him, watching Jeffries. Waiting for his opening.

"Do you know who I am?" our captor sneered, still looking straight at Richard.

"Tell me," he invited cordially.

"Your nightmares."

Richard laughed. "Hardly. I've killed one or two of those in my time, but you don't qualify. Who paid you?"

"What?" said Jeffries, startled from his villainous pose.

"You could hardly do all this on your own, could you?" Richard continued imperturbably, "Why should you want to? You've tried three times and failed, what drives you to try for a fourth? You must be paid very well to do this, so tell me—who is it?"

Jeffries frowned. "And why bring these people?" Richard continued, indicating the Ravens.

"I want my money back," said Jeffries shortly. "They said the money and the notes of hand were in your safe."

Richard raised a brow at the Ravens and they stared back at him, miserably. "They lied."

"You'll have something worth taking," Jeffries pursued. "Her ladyship here will have jewels. They'll do."

Richard put his hand to his chin thoughtfully. "Why do you think I would consent to that? You are, if I'm not mistaken, planning to kill us, so why should we show you where we keep our valuables?"

Jeffries shrugged. "What makes you think I'm going to kill you?"

"Trying three times was a good indication," Richard replied. "Tell me—did you recognise us immediately when we turned up at the Palazzo Barbarossa?"

Jeffries smiled again. I wished he wouldn't. "The minute I saw you."

Richard smiled at me. "I said I should have worn that wig." I was calm enough to smile in return, but only just.

Jeffries continued. "I'd followed a false trail until then. So I intended to play the tables for a while and move on, but then you walked in. So clever, my lord, so clever you never noticed us. I knew we had you."

"We?"

"The lady outside is my partner. I usually work alone, but my principals insisted," the man explained, not at all loath to talk now he had us under control.

The man had several guns and an accomplice, so disarming him would be difficult. He had a gun in each hand, so if we could make him put one of them down, we might have a better chance. Jeffries was talking now, giving us a chance to work out a plan of action. "I nearly had you the first time. If you hadn't moved at the last moment I would have had you, or if I'd waited I might have had you both with one bullet." He smiled again.

I remembered that at the moment he fired on us in the coach, Richard had moved to kiss me.

"And what about the yacht? Why bother with that if you planned to kill us in the coach?"

Jeffries shrugged. "A special request. I thought of it as insurance, in case I missed you in the coach, but the female half of the couple asked me to set it anyway. She wanted that yacht destroyed. Easy to do. I just helped stow the luggage and left an extra package at the back of the kitchen fire."

Richard's mouth firmed at that evidence of sheer spite from his erstwhile fiancée. "Then the attack here, in the Square."

"I was sure I'd got you then."

"As you see," said my husband, waving his arm about gently so as not to agitate our would-be assassin. "You didn't. However, I do have a score to settle with you about that. You hurt someone dear to me and nearly killed my wife. I find that impossible to forgive."

"I'm not asking you to forgive me," said Jeffries. "Just show me the safe."

Richard nodded and stood, going over to the picture behind which lay the safe in a leisurely fashion. He opened it and then Jeffries ordered him to stand back, so, with a small gesture, he obeyed.

Jeffries thrust his hand into the small aperture in the wall and drew out the black box that contained my diamonds. His eyes widened when he saw them, as did the Ravens', still sitting in silence.

He had put one of the guns back in his belt. He thrust his hand into the safe once more and drew out the sapphires. He would have gone back for more, but then Richard made his move. He dropped to the floor, while at the same time, a shot came from the window and Jeffries dropped his gun.

Richard extended his arm as Jeffries dropped the jewels into his left hand and went for one of the pistols in his belt. He cried out in pain and shock as my husband released one of the knives strapped to his wrist by one of Signor Verdi's little devices. It struck Jeffries' shoulder with a soft thunk.

Richard leaped on top of our recent captor and pinned his arms to the floor behind him, kneeling on his thighs to prevent a kick, as Gervase walked through the open window with the other flintlock. He stood at the head of the man as Richard released his arms and disarmed him, tossing all the weapons on to the table.

Only then did he stand, side by side with Gervase and order Jeffries to his feet. He glared at them from where he lay on the floor and groaned.

When we heard a noise from outside, I moved, realising what might be going on. I hurried across the room, drawing my pistol from my pocket and standing behind the door. Jeffries opened his mouth.

"Be quiet." Gervase drew back the hammer of his pistol with a steady hand. Richard had armed himself from the arsenal on the table and we all stood and waited. My own breathing came unevenly and I tried to steady it, knowing I needed a steady hand. Now the moment had come when I wouldn't be shooting at a target, or a dumb animal, I was nervous, swallowing to keep my fear under control.

The door slowly opened and Carier came in before the woman we knew as Mrs. Squires. Her collaborator wasn't in her sight until she was well into the room and by then I could press my pistol to the side of her head and say, "Drop it."

Chapter Twenty-One

The woman froze, neither dropping the knife she was holding to Carier's neck, nor driving it home. "You wouldn't. You haven't the nerve."

I wasn't sure I wanted to be spoken to like that any longer. "I would," I said, just as calmly. I turned the other gun in my hand, as I had seen Richard do once and swung the butt against the side of her head.

She fell sideways, out cold, leaving nothing but a scratch on Carier's neck. Ignoring my racing heart I bent, picked up her flintlocks and put them on the table to join the others. Since no one made a move, I found her pockets and made sure she had no other weapons hidden there.

I took a deep breath, crossed to where the decanters sat on the sideboard, poured myself a large brandy and drank it down without a choke. Richard watched me appreciatively. Nobody else moved.

I looked down at the man on the floor. "He's bleeding. He'll ruin that carpet."

Then Richard said something I never thought I'd hear him say in front of anyone else. "God, how I love you!" His voice held sheer delight and his eyes glowed. I smiled back.

He glanced down at Jeffries. "Someone get a sheet and put him in a chair. My wife is right—he owes us the price of a carpet."

Carier left the room and returned with a footman bearing a cloth which he laid on a chair. Between them they lifted Jeffries and sat him down. He was in a bad way, with a bullet through one shoulder and a knife in the other. Carier pulled out the knife and made a pad out of a piece of the cloth, which he clamped to the other shoulder to stop it bleeding. "The bullet has gone right through, my lord."

"Pity," Richard commented. "You and Rose might have enjoyed digging that one out."

Jeffries was still conscious, but silent, unlike Mrs. Ravens, who was weeping jaggedly. I was glad to see her husband was soothing her with every appearance of affection. I poured them a glass of brandy each, which he accepted with profuse thanks. While Carier dealt with the injured man, stepping over the sleeping female half of the partnership to get to the door so he could fetch his case, we let Ravens tell his story.

I poured brandy for Richard and Gervase. It was early in the day, but they needed it. Ravens sipped his brandy, his arm around his distressed wife. "There was nothing subtle about it. He came into the palazzo and demanded money, then your address. I don't think he planned to kill you here. From what he and his—" he looked down at the woman on the floor and then deliberately said, "—*doxy* were discussing, they wanted to kidnap you both and dispose of you quietly in the middle of the Lagoon."

Richard thought it over. "A beautiful place to die, but not yet awhile." He sipped from his glass. "I thought they'd do something like that. Carier had orders not to let them out with us under any circumstances. As it was," he continued, leaning forward to meet Jeffries's eyes, "you were too fond of your own voice. Too clever by half, as my old nurse might have said." He paused and finished his drink, pushing aside part of the arsenal on the table to find a place for the empty glass. One of the pistols fell to the floor and Gervase smiled as he saw it. He waved the gun he still held in his hand negligently in Jeffries' direction. "Don't," he advised.

Jeffries stared at them, the two brothers, so alike, especially when seen apart. Gervase smiled. "Quits on the wounds, I think. I happened to be escorting Rose on that day, but you weren't to know that."

Carier returned and silently set to work on Jeffries' wounds, stripping and cutting away his clothes until he sat bare-chested in front of us, still silent. Then he spoke in a low voice. "I knew you were a twin, but not how alike you are."

"We are, aren't we? You have no idea how many people have said that to us over the years." Richard's voice hardened then, giving it a cold incisive edge. "Who paid you?"

"Why should I tell you?"

"Perhaps you haven't been paid yet?" Richard suggested then. "How much?"

Jeffries met his eyes. "Two thousand pounds. A thousand each."

Richard's eyes flew to me in alarm and then back again to his prey. "So it was both of us? You don't have to tell me, in that case."

He waited while Carier stepped in front of him to bandage the knife wound. "I'm sure I know who it was. If you'd said the contract was for me alone, it could have been any number of people. As it is, there's no one who wants my wife dead except the man she rejected."

Jeffries said nothing. Richard waited until the bandages were in place and Carier had put a shirt over them, forcing the man's hands through the sleeves despite his cries of pain. Propriety would be observed in this case.

Then he examined the woman on the floor. He seemed satisfied; she breathed regularly, so he left her there. He crossed the room to stand behind Richard, a principal of Thompson's, ready for the decision we must make.

Richard said one word while we all watched Jeffries closely. "Drury."

The man's eyes opened wide before he could prevent it and then dropped again when he realised he had betrayed himself.

I went to sit by Richard. Gervase made room for me, keeping the pistol trained on Jeffries. "What to do?" mused Richard.

"He's incompetent," I said. "Let him go."

"He would have killed you," said Richard, not looking at me. "No one threatens you. No one."

"Kill him," urged Carier from behind us. "Kill them both."

Mrs. Ravens shuddered, but nobody except her husband took any notice.

"My casting vote," said Richard. He said nothing more for some minutes. He took a deep breath. "I can't let them go unpunished. They wanted to kill us. They won't be paid the balance of their contract, but that's not enough. I want to send the message back to the Drurys that we are not to be treated in that way. We could send them back blind." He was not speaking metaphorically.

Now both Mrs. Ravens and I gasped. I was appalled at the thought, almost worse than a clean death. Gervase cried, "Richard, no!"

"Remember this, Jeffries." The man started at Richard's use of his real name, the first time Richard had used it. "Oh yes, we know you, where you come from and what you're capable of. I have a long arm and if you come near me or mine again, I will have you killed. If we kill you now, you won't be able to report back to your employers, so I'm inclined towards clemency. Have you anything to say?"

For Jeffries had opened his mouth. "My lord, I regret my actions and if you let me go, I promise never to take up a contract against you again."

Richard sighed. "Your word means nothing to me. If only it was that easy." He turned his head to look at Carier. "We did something before that meant the man concerned could never hold a gun again. What was it?"

In reply, Carier stretched out his hand, wide open, palm down, to demonstrate. "A clean cut here, my lord." He indicated the soft part between the thumb and the first finger. "It destroys the grip."

Richard sat quietly next to me, considering the problem, cooler than a judge. This still appalled me, this mutilation, but I could see the sense in it. It would send a message to the Drurys and render the man incapable of firing a weapon again, but was not as severe as blinding. I could live with that. I hoped he could.

He looked at Jeffries, met his eyes. "Then that's what we'll do."

Jeffries gripped the arms of the chair convulsively and his face turned perfectly white.

"You will have that part of your hands cut," Richard told him, "and bound so it will not heal back properly. Then we'll release you and give the wherewithal to return to your employers. You will tell them to leave us alone, if they do so, I'll bear them no ill will. Don't come anywhere near us again."

He signalled to the footman, standing silently waiting for orders. The man stepped over the woman and helped Jeffries to his feet. Just before he left the room, Jeffries, leaning against the footman for support, said; "If I had known you were so dangerous, I would have brought reinforcements and you wouldn't be alive today. Or I would have come to *you* for employment."

Richard looked at him with contempt. "I don't employ men to do my killing for me." He looked away, towards the footman. "Have someone take the woman away, if you please. She's too much in the way where she is and much though I admire my wife's handiwork, I don't need to look at it any longer."

The footman bowed his head and led a trembling Jeffries from the room, presumably to meet his fate. I didn't want to think about it.

Then Richard turned to the Ravens. "If you think this is too rich for your blood, then go your ways." He gestured to the door. "But if you would like to join our enterprise from time to time, that can also be arranged. Think about it, go to Thompson's Registry Office in the London and give them this." He took a card from his waistcoat pocket, one with his real name on it and scrawled his signature on the back.

Mr. Ravens stood, bowed and took the card, reverently putting it away in his pocket. He turned to his wife, still overcome by it all and helped her to her feet. "No," I said, rising to my feet. "Your wife isn't recovered yet. Let her rest for a while."

I went over to where my jewels lay tumbled on the floor and bent to pick them up, also recovering the boxes they should have been stowed away in and came to sit back down again.

"Lady Strang," said Mr. Ravens suddenly. I stopped from

my task of untangling the necklaces that were entwined together and looked at him.

"Pardon me," he continued, "but can they be the diamonds I have heard so much about?"

I lifted the tangled necklaces and watched them untwist in the bright sunlight, sending sparks of fire around the room. "These? Yes, these are the diamonds I was married in."

Not for the first time, I felt a thrill to know I was here, with Richard, legitimately mine.

My hand sought his and we watched together as the jewels slowly untangled themselves, then curled around each other again, seemingly as one.

About the Author

Lynne Connolly has been in love with the Georgian age since the age of nine, when she did a project about coffee and tea at school. One look at the engraving of the Georgian coffeehouse, and she was a goner. It's the longest love affair of her life.

She stopped looking around old houses and visiting museums long enough to go to work, fall in love for a second time, marry and have a family, but they have to share her with her obsession, which they do with good grace and much humor.

To learn more about Lynne Connolly, please visit www.lynneconnolly.com. Send an email to lynneconnollyuk@yahoo.co.uk or join her Yahoo! group to join in the fun with other readers! http://groups.yahoo.com/group/lynneconnolly. She can also be found at MySpace, Facebook and the Samhain Café.

GREAT
cheap
fun

Discover eBooks!
THE FASTEST WAY TO GET THE HOTTEST NAMES

Get your favorite authors on your favorite reader, long before they're out in print! Ebooks from Samhain go wherever you go, and work with whatever you carry—Palm, PDF, Mobi, and more.

Samhain
Publishing Ltd

LaVergne, TN USA
01 March 2010
174550LV00004B/2/P